PILLOW MAN

William has a good, steady job in retail. He works in the bedlinen department of an Oxford Street store. He knows everything there is to know about comfy. Lucy has a portfolio career which, in her view, is no kind of career at all. Her life is in a mess; her love life even more unsatisfactory than that. She wouldn't be comfortable if she sat on a sofa in Heal's. Unable to sleep, she thinks a new pillow might be the answer. William and Lucy are not connected. Yet the pair of them share a terrible memory from the past — the sort of joint recollection that changes with the light, depending on who you were and where you were standing at the time. The question is: what to do with it?

NICK COLEMAN

PILLOW MAN

Complete and Unabridged

CHARNWOOD
Leicester

First published in Great Britain in 2015 by
Jonathan Cape
an imprint of Vintage
London

First Charnwood Edition
published 2017
by arrangement with
Vintage
Penguin Random House
London

A catalogue record for this book is available
from the British Library.

ISBN 978–1–4448–3351–5

Published by
F. A. Thorpe (Publishing)
Anstey, Leicestershire

Set by Words & Graphics Ltd.
Anstey, Leicestershire
Printed and bound in Great Britain by
T. J. International Ltd., Padstow, Cornwall

This book is printed on acid-free paper

For Jane

Take it from me, Nat: the best head-piece ain't a hat.

Louis Jordan

PART ONE

1

Siberian Duck

I try to imagine her not sleeping — and I wonder whether her not-sleeping is the same as mine. There is no comparison, of course, even in my imagination.

Her insomnia is an animate thing. It is alive with movement: a low-level, full-body wriggle right on the edge of sleep. I can see her marking all those wakeful seconds and minutes into the small hours with irritated dabs of her fingers all over her body, dabs and scratches chasing the strange little tickles which torture her like midges. They are not predictable, you see. The tickles appear randomly all over her skin, and without warning. Under the duvet, on top of the duvet, legs crossed, legs akimbo, arms in, arms out . . . it doesn't seem to matter how her body is positioned. And it's definitely not the duvet's fault. She's washed it over and over again with non-bio and super-bio and just plain water, and even bought a new one. But on it goes. Chin, nape, hip, ribcage, nape again but a little further to the left, middle of scalp, side of ankle, cheek, an endless tattoo of tiny sensory welts. On and on. Tickle tickle tickle. Little soft sensations all over. Downy kisses.

But not nice.

I imagine her wondering about it. I suspect

she may worry about whether she's ill, or going to be. How does multiple sclerosis start? With random tickles all over the body? Or what about the other one, the even scarier one: motor neurone disease? How does that kick off?

Or Parkinson's?

Stop. STOP! Shut up.

Get up.

I can see her getting up and going downstairs, enjoying the cooler air and the sensation of kitchen floor tiles under her feet, tickles in abeyance now she's vertical and padding about. Toes flexing up and down against the grippy rubber. Leaning against the kitchen sink to drink down a full glass of water (perhaps it's a hydration issue?) and wiping her mouth with the cuff of the long-sleeved T-shirt she puts on to go downstairs; then just leaning there, jaw slightly slack, staring out of the kitchen window into the hole made in the dark blue night by her reflected silhouette, waiting for the tickles to begin again.

But they don't begin again, because she's no longer trying to sleep. She's making calculations . . . What would be the least disturbing, most comforting thing to do in the circumstances? Should she go to the doctor? Should she look up tickles on the Net? Should she take more baths? Or fewer? Is it happening to the surface of her skin, tickling from the outside, like kisses? Or is it coming up from under the skin, tickling from the inside, like worms? Should she move house — uproot everything and start again elsewhere in a new city with a new job and new people to get involved with? Or maybe just move rooms?

Should she sleep with him or would that ruin everything?

Maybe that's what's going on. She longs for him too much. He is kissing her in his absence, psychically . . .

Maybe she should just go back to bed.

She feels the ache of sleeplessness seize her body and then her mind. She trudges upstairs again and dumps herself back onto the mattress. It no longer feels quite as sticky, she'll give it that. But she knows what's going to happen any second now, and sure enough it does.

★　★　★

Her name is Lucy. I found that out quite quickly, not because she told me but because, after only a few seconds' discussion, her mobile rang and she answered it with a graciously mouthed apology to me — smiling too, which was nice. Not everyone bothers; some people just hold a hand up to silence me, like I'm staff, and that really pisses me off.

Not that I show it.

'Lucy Taplow,' she said into the phone. 'No, no . . . No, I'm sorry. I'm shopping at the moment, in the middle of something. Can we speak later? . . . OK. Let's do that . . . Yup. Later. Bye then.'

She has a lovely manner, Lucy Taplow.

When she finished her call she apologised again and said, 'Where were we?', as if we already had something going. She looked me in the eye, eyebrows raised, not sizing me up at all but just looking. She has a really interesting face:

5

what they call 'sculpted', which I always take to mean 'carved with a sharpish tool' rather than 'built up with small gobs of clay'. In Lucy's case the tool was very sharp. She has the sort of cheekbones on which you might crack an egg and a mouth as straight as a ruler. You don't see many genuinely straight mouths but Lucy has one. She also has wide-open blue-grey eyes and a mop of hair the colour of damp straw that looks hard to do anything with. She has a look of being slightly surprised. It's not a conventionally beautiful face by any means but it is beautiful. I like to think that this is because Lucy is a beautiful person. She is in her thirties.

'I'm after a really comfy pillow,' she said. 'One that'll last a long time and stay comfy.'

I nodded, returning her gaze, taking her seriously. Waited for more information.

'I've made do with whatever I've always had thus far,' she went on. 'Whatever's in the linen cupboard, you know. Any old thing. But I don't think it'll do any more. The time has come to take my pillowing seriously.'

I could see this was meant as a sort of mild jest, but not the sort you laugh at — not in my job. I nodded again and began to speak, but Lucy hadn't finished. I shut my trap.

She said, 'Where *do* they come from, pillows?' Smiled some more. 'I mean, I must have half a dozen at least but I have absolutely no idea where I got them or how old they are or even whether they're doing anything like a reasonable job. I have a favourite one of course, but I never think about whether it's . . . well, whether it's suitable

6

or not. I just put my head on it at the end of the day and try to go to sleep.' She paused, just enough for me to notice it was a pause. 'And that's just it: I can't. Sleep. Not at the moment.'

I had a feeling about Lucy, you see. Just had the feeling that she wasn't a sleeper. You get a sense of these things when you've been in the job as long as I have. And I had a very strong feeling about her. She's what I call a 'non-dorm'.

Behind the friendly, open, slightly red-rimmed smile I could see she was serious about her insomnia, and worried. We discussed her situation in practical terms. And once we'd established that she'd already availed herself of the best mattress she could afford — it's an essential thing to do, as buying the best food you can afford is — I introduced her to her options, starting from the pure Hungarian duck down at the top of the own-brand range — rather pricey — through the more affordable down/feather mixes in the middle, to the synthetic foundation pillows at the bottom which hold up the entire squashy edifice of the Palace of Pillows, and which in fairness I wouldn't recommend to a dosser, even for six quid. Their main virtue is that you can wash them a lot, but you get no loft worth having with a synthetic, and the right kind of loft is what brings joy to the resting head; joy through the sensation that something is working quietly, diligently, resourcefully, *softly* to support you and your very best interests even while you sleep. It's a lovely reassuring feeling. Goes straight to the heart of what it is to be alive.

And as I expected, mere mention of the

Hungarian down caused Lucy to react, hitching one end of her mouth up, so that the straight horizontal became a jointed diagonal. She didn't say a word, which was encouraging, but even so . . . Seventy, eighty pounds for a pillow? A hundred and fifty for snow goose? It seems a lot, I know. But no pressure: we must let the lady come to her own decision without pressure but with a full awareness of the facts, such as they are. And the salient fact, in pillow world, as in so many worlds, is that you pay for what you get, and a good night's sleep is an investment in itself. Well, that's what I always say.

She shifted her weight from one leg to another, changing her angle.

'The thing is, though,' she said, 'how am I going to be able to make a proper decision? You don't know about a pillow until you've tried it — and I certainly don't want to fork out fifty quid on a whim and a prayer.'

I couldn't tell whether 'whim' was another joke or a mistake, although I liked to think it was a mistake. But never mind. Whatever. Lucy was presenting me with the opportunity we all look for in this business. The opportunity to demonstrate. I seized it with both hands.

I smiled.

'You are absolutely right, madam. No one knows about a pillow until they've tried it. How can they? And while we don't offer an overnight trial service, we do suggest that you take full advantage of our demo bed, which is located over there, behind that screen. That's it. Just there. Let's grab a couple of examples and see how you get on with them, shall we . . . ?'

I gave her my best twinkle and a streamer of anxiety passed across the wide blue-grey screen of her eyes. That's normal. People have a natural resistance to getting into bed in front of relative strangers. I understand that. It's an associative thing. We are at our most vulnerable in bed. After all, when we lie down on a mattress we are normally supine or curled up or spreadeagled, not to mention passive, unclothed, unsighted, slack, ready for darkness . . . The list of vulnerabilities can be as long as you want. In bed, we are like sacrifices. But I'm glad to say that the streamer evaporated soon enough from her eyes and I turned to the perspex stacks we use for display and dispensing purposes and drafted two pairs of pillows to the cause. By the time we'd reached the demo space, Lucy was smiling again, making a joke of it. I do think it's sweet how nervous people get.

'So, what next?' she said, after I'd pulled the screen to behind us. 'I lie down and you give me the pillows one after another?'

'We can do it that way if you like,' I said. 'You'll see there's a mattress topper on the mattress too, but we can take that away if you prefer. The important thing is that you make yourself as comfortable as you would in your own bed. There's no point in you lying there stiff as a board. I don't care how much of an insomniac you are: if there's one thing all sleepers share it's a need to feel secure and comfortable and *like themselves* when they're lying down. There you go. How's that feel?'

9

Lucy had kicked off her shoes and was now lying on the bed on her side, slightly curled up, one foot hanging clear of the mattress, with the first down/feather mix under her head. A rather nice Siberian duck. She looked tense, almost coiled, her streaky hair spreading over the pillow behind her head like a spray of fluid. I squatted down so that my head was level with hers, my eyes matching her eyeline. I tipped my head on my shoulders so that I shared her angle too, as close as makes no difference to lying next to her without actually getting onto the bed, like in the morning when you wake up together.

'How's that?'

She blinked slowly.

'Oh, well, I . . . er. It's very nice. Supportive but soft.'

'Yes, it has decent loft, that one. But we can turn the wick up in either direction, if you like. We can go firmer or softer, with equal loft. Which do you think?'

'I think I'd like to try something less firm, just to see what less firm means — this seems really nice and soft as it is.'

I handed her a pure-down alternative — our most competitively priced one — and then she turned over and presented me with her back, her face to the screen wall.

This turning-away sometimes happens and I'm not entirely sure why, although I imagine it's to do with that feeling of vulnerability again — and perhaps the need to clear the mind of all extraneous material, the better to concentrate on the primal experience of lying down. I looked at

Lucy's hair, now on my side of the pillow, and thought it looked less like a spray of fluid than what it actually was: a spray of hair. Slightly wiry hair actually. Looked like tricky stuff. How old was she? Thirty-seven? Thirty-eight? Thirty-nine? Something like that. That would make her fifteen, fourteen, thirteen years younger than me. When she turned to face me and raised herself up on one elbow, her hair followed the back of her head without a ripple or even a shiver.

'Well . . . yes, amazing,' she said. 'I think that one was even better than the first one. Gorgeous. I see what you mean about loft, I really do. It's like a cloud. A supportive cloud.'

I smiled, I hoped confidently rather than unctuously.

'In fact,' she continued, 'that one's so great I don't think I'll even bother with the other two you brought.' She looked at her watch, stood up abruptly. 'And I'm going to need to get my skates on. I'll take the Siberian down. How much is it? Forty-five? Crumbs.'

I accompanied her to the payment station with an unsullied pillow of Lucy's choice sealed in its polyurethane case, straight from the dispenser stack. She thanked me for my help as we went and remarked that my job must be nice, looking after people's comfort and well-being. 'Doing the soft sell,' she said. This was another of her jokes and I could see it was kindly meant. She's obviously a really nice, open-hearted woman with a bit of a playful streak, which is something I appreciate.

★   ★   ★

I watch her descend the down escalator until the top of her head is lost to sight.

I imagine her getting home with her new pillow and taking it straight up to her bedroom to put it in place on her bed. Will she tear open the packaging or carefully cut it with scissors? I suspect, from what I've seen, that she's a bit of a tearer who feels guilty about the tearing and thinks she really ought to go downstairs into the kitchen and get the scissors, but what the hell, she's here now and the plastic's only going to be recycled anyway . . .

I wonder how I'd react to that, if I was there, living with Lucy in a small house in north London, blending our lives together like feather and down.

. . . And then she'll come upstairs again at the end of the evening, at bedtime, and see the new pillow, chubby at the head of her mattress, and decide that this magnificent artefact warrants not only a clean pillowcase — well, obviously! — but the best and softest one she has in the airing cupboard, the superworn white cotton percale one she was given by her mum twenty years ago when she left home to go to university. And out it comes and on it goes — and then into bed and have a really good read before drowsiness begins to take her and the book drops, which is the signal to reach out blindly to switch off the bedside lamp, eject her cushion and sink sink sink her head into the Siberian duck and wait luxuriantly for the lofty rush of oblivion . . .

Then . . .

Tickle.

2

Bats

Lucy Taplow was pretty firm in her convictions about baking and this was good because her convictions, in her opinion, weren't always firm enough. But she was certainly clear in her mind that well-made bread was a good thing, and that to do baking was to do good. She felt all joined up by the activity, as if her mind and her fingers and her baking heart were all of a piece; a piece that might be mixed and remixed and rolled out and stretched and pummelled and folded in on itself and, at last, put to the fire, all without losing its essential coherence. This feeling never left her. She loved to hear dough sigh under her fists and then to watch it rise and fill itself out in its own defiant way. She took delight in the swollen, bursting glands of a loaf, and in the way you could never predict precisely how one was going to come out, but that if it came out all right on the tongue, it really didn't matter one way or the other whether the loaf was a gargoyle. In point of fact, there was no such thing as an ugly loaf.

She also liked getting sticky.

So the morning after her visit to the bedlinen department was not entirely filled with despair. Today was a baking day, or was going to be. And there would shortly come a point in it when things began to look up, most likely at that moment when Lucy first dipped the webbing of her surgical-gloved fingers into a bowl of warm water to sloosh off the first new skin of dough . . .

But that would have to wait. For now she had to find some way to get out of bed, this bed of surpassing woe in which she had endured yet another sleepless night. Well, virtually. The new pillow had been a tremendous success in the sense that it was comfortable, its qualities of softness and loft providing night-long succour and support to her weary head. But that was all it had done. It hadn't sent Lucy's head to sleep. It had not come close to doing that, except in the first few minutes after putting the bedside light out, when the luxuriance of the pillow had contrived to douse Lucy's cerebral light for a gorgeous forty minutes or so. But after that . . . Purgatory. Neither sleep nor full waking, just grey-blue twists of endless night. Torture. Torture.

She lay and scowled at the fissure of dim early-morning light showing at the base of her bedroom blind, where the fabric had fallen askew the evening before. This wasn't funny. Lucy ached all over and her thoughts barely merited the name. She felt empty, brittle, a vessel so void of content that it must be a vessel in pieces. What was the better word? 'Shards'. In shards. But why use the word 'shards'? That's what poets say when they mean 'pieces' but want to sound like poets, so they say 'shards' instead . . . Oh, for crying out loud. Lucy shuddered.

She loathed the way her mind worked sometimes, as if it had an autopilot — a default setting, even — which in times of high stress and often in times of no stress at all would allow her brain to freewheel undirected and without effort down irrelevant paths instead of getting to grips with reality.

She must get out of bed. Go to work. Get on her bike, inhale deep draughts of dawn air and get down to it at the bakery. That'll pull her together. Yeast and flour and salt and water and oil and elbow grease.

Lucy heaved her head off the pillow. She sat up and looked back at where her head had been and was cheered a little to watch the new pillow plump itself up in a series of barely perceptible stop-time expansions. She imagined a tiny *pluff* sound to accompany them. And while she gazed she found herself thinking yet again about the guy in the bedlinen department who'd worked so hard to sell her the pillow; the guy who had littered her wakeful mind all night and now threatened to colonise her morning. What was that all about?

Christ, all the more reason to get going.

But what *was* that all about?

The guy — his name tag had said 'William' — was not the sort who colonised her mind as a rule. In fact it was hard to imagine him colonising anyone's mind, such was his dullness of feature and efficiency of manner, and his use of the old-fashioned 'madam'. He was, now she came to think about it with her just-out-of-bed mind, a kind of Essence of Old-World

15

Department Store, being a figure composed almost entirely of deferential clichés and emotional disengagement, his face stapled by heavy spectacles, his body clad in a synthetic uniform blazer of the most unbecoming kind. He was a person all right, a person of flesh and blood and unfulfilled passions, no doubt, and probably a perfectly nice one beneath the polyester; yet he had allowed himself to fuse with his bedlinen department to such a degree that it was hard to tell quite where the valanced mattress toppers ended and the man began. And yet . . . *something* about him clung on determinedly in the roof of her mind like a tiny bat. Perhaps it was the surprisingly pointy shoes he wore to ferrule his perma-creased trouser legs. Bat shoes.

Quite nice shoes, actually. But it wasn't the shoes.

She dragged herself into the bathroom and through the first rituals of the day; decided not to eat breakfast until she got to the Jones; gulped a mug of tea, dropped a couple of ibuprofens — she allowed herself the conviction that an anti-inflammatory painkiller would at least take the edges off her shards — and scrunched her bike over the litter of circulars and unopened envelopes in the hallway. First light was bright and fresh enough to stall a truckload of the blues and as Lucy pedalled through the empty streets of what she liked to think of as her patch of residential Edwardian north-east London, she teased at the bat in the roof of her mind, offering it all kinds of inducements to loosen its grip on

16

the rafters and drop into her waiting hands like a harmless ball of fluff and leather. Over and over she tried to make the case. But it wouldn't let go. 'William' was not for dislodging.

And so when she arrived at the Jones, only seven minutes late for her shift in the bakery, Lucy was at least awake.

3

Toads

I am not always charming and forbearing. That's for work. Take me out of the store and I no longer feel quite so obliged to maintain the act.

I say 'act' and of course I mean it. It is an act. But it's an act I believe in. I take a certain pride in what I do, not because of the job's status — let's face it, no one works in the bedlinen department of a department store for the social status, whether it's in Oxford Street, as ours is, or in High Street, Middle England; nor do I take pride because I am one of those drudges who thinks that 'taking pride in what I do' is the secret to getting ahead, like 'really wanting it' and 'really believing in myself' are for young people. I might be well mannered but I am not stupid. No, I take pride in what I do because I like what I do. I actually like it.

I used to beat myself up about this. About liking it and why I shouldn't like it and what it means that I do. It still sometimes seems strange to me that I do like it, as if by enjoying the life of the department-store retail executive I am somehow bypassing my real self and thereby wasting him, rather like a small town that clamoured for decades for relief from the unendurable traffic generated by everyday life and then found, once the bypass had been built,

18

that it became a ghost town, unvisited and invisible: not really there any more.

I was once a musician, you see, a proper one; one who could play and had a vision about what being a musician might do not only for me personally but for the rest of the world too. And for years and years after I stopped being a musician I felt quantifiably disturbed about what I might have lost as a consequence of my — and I laugh out loud to write this down (in fact I'm going to use italics) — *radical lifestyle downshift.* The switch from VineHeart to duvets was not an easy one. To travel that road, as the idiom has it, is to lose one's sense of directional control and to be subject to strange, unfamiliar forces. It's a skid, really, followed by a sickening roll and then silence and inertia, followed after a pause by ominous dripping sounds.

Crash bang wallop.

Plink.

It was all over in as many minutes as it took for me to jump down off a low stage beneath a low ceiling, slam my guitar into its case, shove my way past a tech guy doing something techy to do with that afternoon's soundcheck, stomp down the 'backstage' passage, open a door, ascend a wrought-iron staircase, make a circuitous journey home, then get the application for summer cover work at the store into the post. But it took me years to accomplish as an emotional journey (and I snicker to write that as well).

Years. It was like being seasick for years. Some days I'd be all right, if a little numb. And that was all right too: numb can be a friend, if experienced on the right furniture and with the right lighting. But on other days I'd be visited by a physical sensation in every part of my body that would stop me dead in my tracks no matter what I was doing: a plunging, unstable, all-suffusing nausea, gassing me from the inside; I'd have to steady myself with my fingertips against something solid and wait for the gas to dissipate, which it would do surprisingly slowly. And I'd get this horrible, paralysing feeling for no apparent reason other than that I was standing stock-still on a promontory of carpet in a department store, plumping a pillow. Some nights I would go home and cry.

That's what you get for thinking life can be simplified. But then again sometimes life has to be simplified. You have no choice.

I regret the circumstances of that simplification, of course, but the change those events brought about was a necessary one. I mean, look at me now. I'm all right. I've got a nice enough flat in uber-trendy Dalston. It wasn't uber-anything when I bought it in the early Nineties for next to nothing, but what can I say? I am a man of foresight. My mortgage is derisory and my grooviness inestimable. If passers-by want to clock the guy in pointy shoes emerging onto the street from my front door and think, well, there's one fashionable fucker with his digit on the pulse — there's a dude who's got life *right* — then that's fine by me: I'll sell a pillow to anyone. But I do have to wear a long trench coat over my department-store crimplene if I am to sustain the mystique, especially to myself. The crimplene was once hard to put on in the morning, especially the tie. But bodies and minds can get used to anything — and now I quite like the disconnect the crimplene implies. I like the disguise. What can I say? I wear a sleeve on my heart.

I am also fifty-three years old, so who am I kidding anyway? My finger may or may not be on the pulse but the skin on my knuckles is increasingly flaccid and I'm not entirely convinced that the purple thing on the back of my left hand isn't a liver spot. Great hands, mine, but they've been around for more than half a century and are feeling it a bit. It brings me a shiver I can't give a name to to say this, but they now properly belong, my marvellous hands, among folds of Egyptian cotton and envelopes of duck down, not braced against wire and maple in a torrent of sweat. Or clamped around the throats of toads.

They were what did for me as a pro musician, really, the toads. The toads on the road. And not only on the road but in the lay-bys and bus stops and on the pavements that run alongside the road. And in the phone boxes and in shop doorways and lurking under drain covers and behind gateposts. They were absolutely every-where, on every surface and in every recess, anywhere you might blindly put your hands without looking first — cold and clammy and twitchily responsive to the accidental touch, like some biblical plague but worse because they weren't always recognisable as toads. In fact some of them came off on first contact like reasonable, attractive people in good clothes. People who wanted me or liked what I did. Who occasionally gave me money. Expressed a desire to have sex with me, occasionally.

But it's an unavoidable fact that toads litter the road to success and after a while you just get sick of squishing them; get sick of the road too, which gets stickier and stickier the further you proceed along it and the more toads you squish. And the closer you get to the horizon, the less attractive the prospect of arrival seems, for the simple reason that you begin to see the details of what awaits you there. What once looked like a golden place — a destination straight out of the classiest brochures, hazed with sunny welcome, a place that will insulate you for ever against clamminess — on closer inspection looks like a cramped, tubelit office space populated on every surface with toads: toads glaring at you with their empty reptile eyes, spitting and hissing at each other, standing on each other's backs and shitting in each other's greedy mouths. A horrid spectacle.

VineHeart were a good band but they weren't worth the wholesale toadification of life. Yes, we'd have gone on a while longer if it hadn't been for the accident — I reckon we might have got another couple of years out of it, enjoying our modest but just about profitable levels of hipness and popularity in the post-Eighties music-world scramble for ownership of 'what happens next'.

But actually, looking back, the accident was a blessing in disguise. It happened just as I started to really lose the plot with the toads, and it stopped me from going back to the band; from saying, 'Sorry, guys, too much stress for a while but I'm over it now' and holding my hand up as I had learned to do, humbly, any time the toads had got inside my underwear and the old panic and revulsion had taken over. It got me out of the story before everything became so toaded up that I became a toad too. By then, I could taste toad spit in my own mouth and it was perhaps no coincidence that the accident happened just as I began to register the fact that the toad spit I could taste was the product of my own salivary glands.

So I took off. Laid the Telecaster down and turned off the road. VineHeart immediately ceased to exist too, which was as it should have been. When it started in 1986, the band had been my idea — my little life project, to be fair — and even if the name was a bit dodgy, the concept was good. Not so much original as well conceived. A bit challenging but not so challenging as to be pretentious or excessively retro or offputting to anyone who'd ever got the right ideas about both *Marquee Moon* and the Hot Club de Paris. Twang. Shimmer. Swing. Edge. Mesh. I loved it. Some other people clearly did too, although not the significant handful of music journalists who seemed to admire the concept and the effort but roundly despised the musicianliness of the operation and conse-quently saddled VineHeart with the label 'muso band' — and once that kind of opinion starts to solidify into a consensus, then you're stuck with it for ever. 'VineHeart? Wishbone Ash for French hipsters' was one inaccurate zinger, for which I never forgave the gentleman who coined it so self-satisfiedly.

It was inaccurate on every count. Only one of the four of us was even slightly French, and I'm only half French. We had no interest in being 'hip' or otherwise, and certainly not in terms that would appeal to the kind of people who wear sunglasses indoors at night. As for Wishbone Ash . . . Where to begin? Perhaps best not to. Not least because I have actually got nothing against Wishbone Ash, even if their music is dreary and preposterous.

So in all the nineteen years since my self-exfenestration as a musician, I have never been bitter. Not full-blown bitter, anyway. Only cross — and the crossness was instantly modified by the accident. Smithereened, really. Atomised. The accident changed my crossness into something altogether different and much more socially acceptable; and it affected everything else too, to the extent that I even considered going to live in my mother's homeland where accidents do happen of course, but not to the man known to all who knew me then as Guillaume Carberry.

Not any more. After the accident, that would, *finalement*, be that. No more accidents for Gil. Never again would Grumpy Guillaume make the mistake of rising to the bait. Over. *Terminé*. This would be because the afternoon and evening of 18 April 1993 would actually constitute Guillaume Carberry's last hours. Ever after that day, Guillaume would be William Carberry and he would see the world afresh, as if with new, rather less artistic eyes.

Never liked the name Guillaume anyway. And certainly not for someone who's only *half* French. If you sound French you need to be all French or not at all.

★　★　★

I wonder how Lucy Taplow got on with that pillow?

I have suggested to management in the past that we institute a simple, no-commitment after-sales service, to follow up in cases like Lucy's where the potential exists for a material benefit to everyone involved. The customer would benefit from the kind of bespoke follow-up attention that shades the retail experience into the realm of therapy; the store would benefit from the boost to our reputation for treating our customers as valued clients rather than as cash dispensers. 'Added value' and all that. Relational, not merely transactional. But management rejected the proposal out of hand — on legal grounds, they said. They thanked me for my initiative and proactive thinking and said they'd given my idea some serious thought, but that to offer such a service would inevitably lead to grey areas in which the company might be seen to be making promises it couldn't keep. Retail is retail, they implied, therapy is therapy — and although the twain do meet sometimes, it isn't advisable to blur the line between the two in this particular sector. Sleep is tricky, they said, from the legal perspective.

I suppose they had a point. I have to confess I felt a bit embarrassed about it all after thinking it through.

Still, I'd like to know how Lucy got on. As non-dorms go, she was bright and breezy beyond the call, neither self-pitying nor passive-aggressive. She had the eyes of an insomniac but not the heart, I felt. And plenty of soul, albeit a troubled soul. I liked her a lot.

I wonder if the tickles really do afflict her sleep, as much as they do mine. They are certainly appalling, like some sort of medieval torture devised by a toothless pervert in a dungeon in Aquitaine for ladies who flirt too much, or children who laugh at their elders' farting. Tied down in the dark and tickled with feathers.

I really should go and see a doctor about it.

4

Dough

The Jones bakery was bedlam, despite the hour, a bracing assault to the senses. Every clank of the mixer, sloosh of water, flump of dough and peep of Europop from the iPod mini-speakers on the shelf by the door was amplified then pinged around the room by walls surfaced with ceramic tiles and sheets of stainless steel. It was Lucy's favourite bedlam.

The Jones was a lively independent bakery supplying bread and cakes both to the local populace and to its own cafe and sandwich bar over the road. It did all right. It had been there — what? — a dozen years now? — financed by an early killing in the dotcoms boom and sustained with some enthusiasm by a middle-class clientele which preferred its bread grainy and its cakes robust.

Lucy's co-workers in the bakery spoke barely a word of inessential English but they seemed prepared to embrace the ideological niceties of the Jones as readily and as unexpressively as they hefted flour sacks over duckboards to the large Escher mixer tubs — not with enthusiasm, exactly, but with the kind of tenacious commitment to the moment that Lucy had learned long ago was the trademark of the immigrant worker who has no alternative. She

27

was awed by the ability of Tomas, Oleg and Nelson simply to keep going through the kind of long shift that would leave her hollowed out with exhaustion. She felt guilty that she had been given permission, lately, to start her early shift two full hours after the boys had started theirs — a reward for six years' loyal service in the engine room and a recognition by management that if you want the best possible results you have to cut your mixture to fit your tin. Nevertheless, the guilt was tempered by the sure knowledge that hers was not a commitment to the moment but to the life. Lucy's transcendent baking was done at home, but the stuff she did at the Jones still carried weight for her, and she barely felt the weight at all. It was the stuff of real life.

She'd drifted into the baking as she'd drifted into so many of the other activities which had filled up her 'work portfolio', as she called it never less than jovially. For the past six years or so she'd confined herself to labouring at the Jones and, for a shorter stretch, to a tiny vintage clothing stall on Camden Market, which did passable business for her and her dismal partner, Steve. But to examine the full historical inventory of the portfolio was to reveal a chronic inability to settle to anything. She'd taught English as a foreign language, she'd taught drama, she'd gardened, she'd cooked on a yacht, she'd been a legal clerk; for a number of months she'd worked in the 'communications section' of a major overseas-aid charity (which had been altogether a strain). Almost the most work-fun she'd had was over one surprisingly profitable summer and autumn after university, sewing sequins thickly onto cheap bras and then flogging them to clubbers from pitches on Portobello and Greenwich markets. She'd certainly never cracked it as an actor, despite her decent drama degree and a number of promising connections in the profession — but that was because she hadn't really wanted to crack it anyway. Not really. She quite liked doing the acting but she couldn't stand the acting life and, in lots of cases, she couldn't stand the other actors either.

She had got through men with the same random profligacy, drifting along with the current, bobbing on the surface, finding herself attached to lovers as flotsam attaches itself to other flotsam in open sea. She thought of lifelong love as a myth, so the drifting was all right. What wasn't all right was the way this randomness registered in Lucy's gut as a symptom of a deeper failing, one she'd always known about but never been able satisfactorily to identify or fix. And this is where the baking came in. Baking grounded her. It earthed her. At the very least it tethered her.

This morning she joined Nelson and Oleg in the warmth of the kitchen, slightly late as usual. Oleg was where he always was, at the cake counter, already finishing up his first batch of the day's lemon tarts, his lick of concrete-coloured hair standing up almost vertically above his pudding face like an aerial. Lucy had amused herself for a while by wondering whether Oleg's unvarying facial blankness resulted from the concentration required to tune in to signals from outer space — she even alluded to his antenna out loud on one occasion but quickly regretted it and spent the rest of the week having to be super-emollient just to break up the tide of hurt resentment that pulsated back at her from Oleg's impossibly tiny colourless eyes.

Nelson, on the other hand, was both redoubtable and a sweetie. Lucy was very fond of him. She enjoyed his instinctual kindness, his reserve, his matted forearms, his unflappability and his determination to maintain an Argentine perspective on all eventualities, despite the fact that he'd lived in north London for the best part of two decades, waiting tables, playing football and baking with a slow, methodical perfection-ism which never failed to impress the sloven in Lucy. He was in his mid-forties now, but Nelson still looked firm in limb and clear of eye, a short, even bandy, figure of immense tensile strength and no gift whatsoever for conversation. And so when the three of them worked together, no vocal sounds intruded upon the mechanical hubbub. Lucy liked it like that. Instead of chat she indulged in what she liked to think of as mental yoga. Stretches. Bends. Even though she also knew that this was not proper, programmed exercise for the brain, but idiot dancing. The real benefit — idiotic or not — was that it amounted in Lucy to a true abandonment to the moment.

'Hi, guys,' she breezed effortfully, slinging her coat on the hook behind the street door and glancing at the whiteboard on which important instructions were felt-tipped every day (this morning it bore only the inscription 'Branston Pickle'). 'Sorry I'm late.'

Oleg ignored her completely while Nelson paused with his tray of tins to shoot her a sympathetic look. Something effervescent was playing on the iPod. It zizzed non-specifically.

'Sleep?' he said.

'Nah. Another bad one. I bought a new pillow and everything but I still lay there wide awake most of the night.' She walked into the fridge-larder and yelled over her shoulder, 'It's really weird. I lie there completely still with my eyes shut, unable to move, like some paralysed slug, and listen to my body just refusing to go to sleep. I have no idea what it thinks it's doing. It mutters to itself. Keeps up some sort of weird commentary. You'd think it would say stuff like 'Sorry, love, not tonight' but it doesn't — it talks to itself, not to me. I have no idea what it's going on about.'

She emerged from the fridge with a tray and went to put on her bonnet and wash her hands — she was supposed to have done that first, but well, never mind. Oleg raised his head slightly as she greeted him by name.

'The thing is,' she said to the room as a whole, 'I have no reason not to sleep. I'm not unhappy. I don't drink coffee. I don't have a bad conscience about anything. I like my fellow workers — including you, Oleg, even if you won't say hello. I have no *reason* not to sleep . . . ' She looked up and saw that both heads were down over their work. She sighed

31

mock-theatrically. 'And now I'll shut up and get on with it.'

The morning passed at its usual pace but with rather less of the habitual freewheeling going on in her head. Her insomniac mind would not flow. It kept settling heavily on the same subject like an exhausted body onto an old sofa, unable to motivate itself to get up and go elsewhere. And the more she tried *not* to think about William, the harder it became to ignore the feeling that she knew him from somewhere. The feeling hung in her like old curtains.

Halfway through the shift she dropped a tin and the mixture it contained bellied over the rim sufficiently to make contact with a duck-board, which necessitated binning the lot. Then, as she sheared away the excess dough from the blades of the Escher, she let the entire apparatus slip back into its tub with a shattering crash, which caused even Oleg to look up from his glazing. Lucy felt tears surface and quickly sucked them back inside.

'You need sleep,' said Nelson, quadrupling his verbal output for the morning. Oleg sighed audibly above the zizz of the iPod.

And so it went on into the afternoon, when at last, her shift complete, her exhaustion comprehensive, Lucy Taplow clambered onto her bike and toiled back home, shoe soles slipping off the pedals, eyes torn by a negligible headwind.

'This has got to stop,' she muttered to herself out loud at the kitchen table and then fell asleep, her head in the basket of her arms.

She awoke to dimming light, the muscles of her neck screaming. She swore repeatedly and extravagantly, which was unlike her. But then what were the chances of her getting to sleep tonight if she'd spent the afternoon comatose on the kitchen table? Still, she knew one thing now. It was decided. She was going back to see William. Her mind had made itself up. She'd rather liked the feeling the mattress topper in the store had given her — the sense of a shallow but conscientious cradling, the feeling of being lightly held. She was going to ask William's advice.

The evening passed reluctantly, as if it didn't want to face its conclusion. Lucy certainly didn't want to face it. She dreaded the drawn-out, torturous process of failing to go to sleep in the proper location, on her bed. She spoke to her mother on the phone and then Steve rang irritably to find out whether she'd made the time to do the stitching on the sleeve of the Fifties bolero jacket she'd bought for the stall nearly a month before. He was irritable most of the time these days and Lucy was beginning to take it personally. She watched the news and then the beginning of *Newsnight* without engagement and wished she had a good book on the go rather than the self-consciously literary historical novel she'd been given by her mother for Christmas. 'It's both historically accurate and beautifully written,' her mum had said assertively after presenting her with it, 'and it's quite unusual to get both at the same time. Such an unpleasant, *complicated* century, the fifteenth' — as if unpleasantness and complication constituted the ultimate mark of distinction. The word Lucy now wanted to add to the canon of the book's controversial virtues was 'tedious'. She just didn't care about anyone in the story and she couldn't remember who was who — Bedford? Somerset? Warwick? These are counties, not people — and who had done what to whom and for what reason. She retired to bed and stared, unseeing, at the patch of wall between the wardrobe and the window, before eventually conceding that this was just silly and laid her head down upon her cloudy new pillow — mmm — and put her light out.

William, William, William.

And in the end sleep came, quite some time after she concluded that William must be a type. He must represent something or someone to her fugitive mind. But what kind of type? Who or what did he remind her of? Was there some left-field sexual thing going on here? Perhaps it was the name: William Holden? Willem Dafoe? William . . . the Conqueror? Prince William? No. None of the above. Lucy prided herself on taking people as they came and not concerning herself with social status and not judging and *never* taking first impressions as ineradicable. But this first impression had left her with both too little to go on and too much. She felt haunted by the pillow man. And, oddly, it was after thinking for a while about all the people she'd ever known who were now dead that she slid into a deep and dreamless sleep and did not wake again until morning.

5

Geese

My mum is very ill. As in seriously ill. Cancer.

She went back to the family farm in the Haute-Vienne after my dad died, when I was in my mid-twenties, and farmed geese there to no great profit, as was the family tradition. She's been retired for some years now. But the Haute-Vienne was where she came from and that's what counted, she said, when she lost my dad to the disease which is now colonising her own body. Despite what she used to say to us, I don't think she was ever very happy living here in England anyway — not many French people are, let alone French people of peasanty background. But there it is.

She's had a decent innings, as they don't say in France, but I can't pretend I'm not finding it difficult. My sister Bérengère lives and works in Paris and is making the four- to five-hour journey to St Mathieu every weekend she can, but it isn't really enough either for her or for Maman.

Maman's closest neighbour, Mme Jacquet, takes up the slack, and there's plenty of that. Meanwhile, Maman's own sister is nowhere to be seen. She's not even making excuses; she's just clapping her hands over her ears in Clermont and going 'ooh la-la-la-la-la' as loudly

36

as she can. Bére's children are big enough now not to be disturbed too much by their own maman disappearing for days at a stretch but I'm not sure I can say the same for their dad, who tries to be tolerant but succeeds only in being childishly martyred by the whole process. Bérengère is in bits. I don't feel so good about it myself. She's truculent and evasive, our peasant mum, but we seem to love her.

I get over when I can, but it isn't enough. I last saw her a couple of months ago and, as is *obligatoire*, I was shocked. The less said the better. But I get twice-weekly bulletins from Bére and the occasional call from Maman herself. Her phone is by the front door right over the foot of the stairs and to speak for more than a few moments requires her to lower herself down onto the steps and I think she's reluctant to do that, to avoid the painful effort of having to stand up again — so we don't speak for long. Plus I think she wants to keep conversation to a minimum to spare her little boy, and maybe her own dignity. The only place I ever get medical information is from Bére and that doesn't amount to all that much either. I suspect that the daughter doesn't actually listen too hard to what she's told about her mother's condition — she always tells me the latest developments in a voice riddled with shock and consternation, as if she doesn't already know what cancer entails; as if no one had ever told her before that the disease kills you slowly by devouring your body from the inside out. She certainly professes not to remember much about Dad's final decline and I suppose that's likely to be true: she was in her late teens and early twenties at the time and nothing much gets past the guards at that age. I suppose that explains why she sounds so surprised now. 'Oh my God, Guillaume' were her first words to me this morning. I never correct her.

I usually hear from her when I'm on the bus into town in the morning — she knows she'll get me on the mobile at eight thirty-five and in some sort of position to talk, although she has no idea of the figure I have to cut on the bus, my spare hand covering my mouth, my shoulders hunched and turned to the nearest window or stairwell or grab-handle. It's a fatuous effort at discretion and everyone within five feet gets to hear what I'm saying anyway, however much I contort myself. Nevertheless I do think that I should at least make the effort to turn away, to be seen to be trying to spare everyone the latest grisly news. Not everyone wants to hear about the inevitability of death first thing in the morning. Not even in French.

Anyway, round about ten o'clock this morning, soon after I'd settled into the daily routine on the shop floor, I was thinking about Maman and calculating how to find the time to get over there next, when I saw Lucy Taplow going up the escalator in the central well. She looked briefly over at Bedlinen as she went past but didn't see me; or if she did, she didn't show that she'd seen me. She went up the next escalator too, so I immediately presumed that she'd forgotten to get something when she was in a hurry the day before yesterday — something from Electricals or Sporting Equipment (although I have to say that she does not strike me as the sporty type, nor indeed as the sort who'd spend money on a flat-screen TV, not while she's still got an old-fashioned one that works. Oh no. In fact I'd bet you any money you like that she has a small fifteen-year-old tube telly pushed into a corner in her sitting room, with a defunct remote balanced on the top and dust on the screen).

For the next twenty minutes or so I kept an eye on the escalators as I went about my business but did not see her descend. I was just thinking either that I'd missed her while attending to a customer or, more likely, that she'd taken the lift back down to the ground floor, when I saw her hair sticking out in a sort of sunburst on the far side of my colleague Shireen's head, as if Shireen had suddenly become radiant. Shireen's head is conveniently small and you'd have a job conceal-ing a dessert spoon behind it. But there it was anyway, unmistakably, on the far side of Shireen: Lucy's mane, straggling away, an airburst of streaky blonde jags. Some solar flares are probably more controllable. And then all of a sudden I could see half, then all of Lucy's face emerging from Shireen's paltry eclipse and she was looking at me and her hand was pointing. Shireen was turning and saying, 'Yes, of course,' and gesturing for Lucy to approach my position close to the wall-recessed stacks of fitted sheets and pillowcases, where I had just been helping a customer with the distinction between king and queen size.

'Hello there,' she said. 'I wonder if you

39

remember me from a couple of days ago?'

'Of course, madam. You bought a Siberian duck down pillow.'

'Well, it didn't work. The sleeping, I mean.' Lucy did the diagonal thing with her mouth, then reached out with two extended fingers in a sort of apologetic benediction. She stopped well short of touching my sleeve. 'There's nothing the matter with the pillow — don't get me wrong, it's great, really comfy. But I didn't sleep at all the first night and I slept last night only because I completely knackered myself out yesterday. And it wasn't very nice sleep. More like being dead, to be honest — felt absolutely shocking when I woke up, although I do realise I should be grateful for small mercies.' She half chuckled, making a sort of *unh* sound. 'I do think I'm going to have to go to the doctor, though; can't see any way round it — although I am very, very reluctant to go down the drug route. I'm rather hoping they may have other suggestions to make first . . .'

She paused and studied my face for about a second and a half, maybe to put a stop to her own rambling. But really looking — not scanning the surface but looking into my eyes, as if trying to hook stuff out with her gaze. She then laughed and coloured ever so slightly, embarrassed no doubt by the candour of her own curiosity.

' . . . None of this is your problem of course. Not your problem even in the slightest. But I did want to ask you one thing in passing, on my way down from up there.' She gestured airily out into the escalator well. 'What do mattress toppers *do*?

40

I don't have one, but there was one on the bed when I tried out the pillow the other day and I quite liked the feeling of it. Can you tell me what they're designed for? What I mean is . . . I'm only asking in the desperate hope that you'll tell me that research shows that mattress toppers get good results among insomniacs. I'm hoping you'll tell me that one will fix my sleeping.'

She grinned.

I looked down to give myself a moment to consider how to tackle her question, and as I did so she said, quite unnecessarily, 'Silly, I know.'

'No, it's not at all silly. But having said that, mattress toppers are not designed with anything else in mind other than to bring warmth and extra comfort to the sleeper. In the old days — I mean the really old ones, hundreds of years ago — feather beds, as they were then called, were constructed to enclose the sleeper from underneath. You'd climb into your four-poster or your cot and sink into a great big thick feather-stuffed bag arranged on top of the mattress, if you had a mattress. A pallet if you were a peasant — and if you were a peasant your *édredon de plumes* was actually full of straw . . . Anyway, blah blah. I presume you'd then draw sheets and blankets over the top, as necessary. But it was the feather bed, a sort of thick under-duvet, that did most of the work in keeping you warm, because it enclosed you, a bit like bathwater I suppose. They say that the extreme loft in old-fashioned feather beds is quite an effective summer coolant too, allowing air to circulate and so on . . .'

An expression of deep interest crossed Lucy's

features, as if the very idea of a feathery coolant was intensely appealing to her. She nodded. I went on.

'Well, mattress toppers are modern feather beds, really, only thinner and probably more efficient. Ours have two layers. The top layer is seventy per cent down, thirty per cent feather; the bottom all feather. Warmth and comfort and a sense of extra support is what you get. Really nice actually. I think mattress toppers are great . . . '

'Do you have one at home?'

'Certainly do, yes, and I'd heartily recommend it as a warmth and comfort thing. However, I wouldn't go so far as to suggest that they're a cure for insomnia — more that they promote healthy and comfortable sleep. It's a distinction I feel morally bound to make, if you know what I mean.'

I could see that she did. She was looking at me intently again.

'I . . . I . . . ' she started, then thought better of whatever she was trying to say. 'I think it'll have to be the doctor then. How much are these? Ninety-five quid? It's a lovely thought, it really is, but I have spent an unbelievable amount of money on my bed in recent weeks and it has to stop somewhere. But I really appreciate your help, and I can see I'm going to enjoy the pillow I got from you the other day. But not until I've got the sleeping thing fixed and I have a horrible feeling it may take a while yet, though heaven forbid . . . Can I ask you one more thing?'

'Of course.'

'Have we met before?'

Suddenly her eyes grew much less intense; you might even say that she looked bashful. Her gaze dropped to the floor and then bounced back up again. 'It's just that . . . well, you seem very familiar. The thing is, I don't think I know any Williams — or have ever known any. Bills, yes, but no Williams. You're definitely not the Billy I used to know, for instance. But you're really familiar . . .'

She let that assertion hang in the air, dropped her hands and took a step back.

'Really familiar.'

How does one respond in such circumstances?

Was this flirting? If she were a man it would have been flirting. But she's not a man and it didn't feel remotely like flirting, sadly. It felt like uncontrolled and rather intense curiosity, born out of a wish to have an awkward question answered at whatever cost to her composure in the moment. How warm. How likeable. How *relational*. I considered her question as rationally as I could but I must have paused too long because Lucy took another step back, or rather hunkered back onto her heels, as if receding a bit. She smiled and held up one hand in another sort of benediction with her fingers slightly spread this time, the tips curved as finely as grass blades, like the archangel in an Annunciation. I must have recoiled like the Virgin Mary because, without apparently moving at all, her facial expression suddenly double-declutched into a new, rather surprising blankness.

'I'm sorry,' she said, dropping her wrist to her

side. 'You look horrified and I'm not surprised. You . . . you're . . . You must just look like someone I know. Or maybe I've seen you in here before and not registered you consciously — I've shopped here for years and it's the only department store I ever use. So please don't think I'm bonkers.' She smiled at last. 'And please don't think I'm a bedlinen groupie . . . '

And at last I found a way to laugh. It came out a bit too loudly and I tried, too late, to make it sound kindly and empathetic, although I know my laugh is not an attractive one. ('Hydraulic,' someone once said.) Yet it seemed to match her slightly manic smile comfortably enough and I felt the embarrassment turn to vapour.

Groupie?

Arf.

I never got much in the way of groupie action, back in the day — we really weren't that kind of band; never sparked much in the way of female interest at all in fact. But I did get just enough no-strings musicianly sex to know that there is always a difference between the pathologically needy and the compulsively curious. Groupies are always needy, that's why they're groupies; whereas those women who occasionally sleep with musicians, because they're turned on by the thought, are compulsively curious — and usually much better at sex than groupies too. Also, unlike groupies, you always got the feeling that such women think of themselves as the subject of the sexual event, and in no sense the object. You, on the other hand, are their swain, their foible, the peculiar little *fetish* which proves how

44

separate and individual and special they are as people; you're the specially-made-for-them dish under the lid at the far end of the breakfast sideboard that nobody else is allowed to touch. And yes, you'd be surprised at how often those women turned out to be posh.

However, all of that being said, Lucy quite obviously belonged to neither subset of womankind, and it behoves me on such occasions to remember that I no longer belong to the musician subset myself. Which, in the present context, raised another question. Do department-store retail executives have groupies? Not in my experience. In which case, could there be a subset of womankind who are not groupies but who nevertheless find themselves drawn to bedlinen salesmen as a result of an insatiable *curiosity*, an irrepressible desire to peel forbidden fruit, perhaps as a mark of such women's withering, uncompromising, stark staring individualism? Well, I suppose it partly depends on whether you regard bedlinen salesmen as fruit. But, in general, I incline to the view that even allowing for those succulent figures among us who can claim to have enjoyed an exotic past, none of us can lay claim to forbidden status. Not really. We're not forbidden, we're just invisible.

So not flirting, no. Just curious. But why? Even if our paths had crossed before, it must have been quite clear to her that she wasn't ringing any bells in me, so why bother to embarrass herself with the question in the first place? Why not just let it go? I would have. But then perhaps there was something in her — a tiny, wriggling worm of duty — telling her that it's important she find a place for me in her personal story, either for her own benefit or possibly even for mine.

No, no, no! Christ, no — say it ain't so, Joe. Make it like she doesn't *feel sorry* for me . . .

Back in the world, Lucy was speaking.

'OK, thanks for all your help,' she was saying. 'Must be going. Sorry to be a bit silly. Wish me luck with the sleeping.'

And she positively rushed out of Bedlinen before I'd had time to wish her luck with anything at all. I watched her go until the last of her hair sank out of view on the escalator. I felt ineffably sad and like a total fucking klutz. Like a repellent. Like a toad who was once a man and had forgotten how to be one.

And it was while I registered this heartening emotion that I remembered where Lucy and I had met before, and on what occasion.

6

Dogs

Lucy shoved the needle hard into the fabric adjacent to the parted seam on the inside-out sleeve of the bolero jacket, the one she'd been promising Steve she'd fix all month. For the third time she felt the brocade repel her effort. For the third time, the head of the needle skewered the meat of her thumb.

'Fuckety *fuck*,' she mouthed. She knew she had a thimble somewhere in the flat. Somewhere. She also knew that if she didn't get this small sewing job done now then it would quite possibly never get done and Lucy was weary of the whine in Steve's tone. Now was the time to do it, right now, not even in half an hour after a sit-down and a cuppa.

The knowledge that Steve was currently on his way over to her flat lent more urgency to the situation. So she grabbed the least bendy teaspoon from the cutlery drawer in the kitchen and used its concavity to ram the needle through the fabric, back and forth. Ten minutes later the job was done and Lucy rewarded herself for her imaginative diversification of the cutlery by making tea. She stood in the kitchen sucking her ravaged thumb while the kettle rattled. Christ, she was tired. Without looking properly at what she was doing, she reached up to hoick the red bush out of the wall cupboard and lost control of the box, its contents promptly emptying themselves all over the kitchen floor, the tea bags skittering hither and yon to form islands in a dusty rufous sea. She was still on her hands and knees when the doorbell rang.

She clattered downstairs.

'How's it going?' said Steve on the doorstep. Once upon a time it would have been 'How's it going, babe?' and before that 'How's it going, madam?'

Lucy had known Steve for years and was fond of him, essentially, despite his grouchiness. He, like her, managed a 'portfolio' of work and they had jointly adopted the term, with heavy irony, one busy Saturday morning on Camden Market while reflecting on the curious similarities of their patchwork lives. They occasionally wondered, lightly, whether they would be lugging their portfolios to their graves. 'I'm going to be one of those old women who keeps everything in a shopping trolley,' said Lucy, 'for ease of mobility and for structured support.' Steve was a year older than Lucy and equally inclined to drift.

They'd met soon after Lucy had moved into her flat. Steve was the local painter and decorator deemed most suitable both to her decorating needs and to her personality and he'd spent an extravagantly long week doing the scruffy bits of the flat and drinking tea at the kitchen table. He'd charged Lucy for four days' work rather than five — 'To be honest with you, Lucy, I've spun it out cos I haven't got anything else on the go at the moment' — and that honesty, in addition to his resolute refusal to recognise the formal nature of the transaction in hand, had endeared him to his client. The one time Steve had ever addressed Lucy as 'madam' — on the doorstep when she opened the door to him the first time — the quotation marks attached to the word had been so explicit that Lucy had laughed out loud and decided there and then that this was the decorator for her.

Then, on that Friday night after agreeing his invoice, Steve had stuck around for a bite to eat and he and Lucy had gone on to the pub, from which they'd reeled several hours later, firm friends. Firmly curious. Two weeks later, following another pub night, they'd slept together for the first time and Lucy, without realising it, had embarked on the most sustained sexual relationship of her life — with a man whose sincerity she did not doubt but whose company she did not always treasure.

Steve was as slippy as she was, though from less advantaged beginnings. He was the only child of a suburban upbringing in Barnet, educated to A level, endowed with certain obscure qualifications to do with the insurance industry, but only in a position to claim thirty months' actual experience as a Man From the Pru. Since the demise of his insurance career in his twenties, he'd managed the comings and goings of a would-be stand-up comedian he'd known from school, then tried the stand-up game himself ('No good — I'm about as funny as a wanker'), ditched comedy in favour of glorified hod-carrying for the firm of posh builders preferred by successful north London stand-up comedians, then, following a resentful confrontation with his employer over money and time, set up on his own as a painter and decorator. But what really endeared the ever-practical, profoundly unpoetic Steve to Lucy was his unexpected eye for a vintage frock and his truly amazing talent for rooting frockly gems out of the old-lady wardrobes of south-eastern England, and then flogging them with gusto — and even a hint of style — at a regular pitch on Camden Market. He'd done it 'for ever', as he put it. 'For ever' meant since he was a retrobilly teenager in the late 1980s. Vintage frocks were what Steve did for poetry.

'So this isn't some passing fad, then, Steve?' she'd said in her lightest possible voice. 'It's a real-world, manly, not-at-all camp passion, then, is it?' To which Steve had looked her in the eye and said 'Yes' without apparent rancour.

'And you don't wear them before selling them?'

'Not all of them.'

They'd been dating satisfactorily for about six months, sleeping together half the week, pubbing, clubbing, going to the cinema, gigs and the countryside in Steve's untended Transit, when Steve first invited Lucy to join him properly on the stall at the weekend. He was offering a full share in 'the business', as he put it, supplying the quotes with his fingers, and no strings attached — she could walk away any time she chose, provided she didn't expect to take any part of 'the business' with her.

'Let's give it a go, at least? I've done the sums. It'll be fun.'

Lucy had only recently left the 'comms' department of the NGO, her tail between her legs following a thoroughly unsatisfactory trial period — 'It's not working out, Lucy, sorry. Someone of your talents . . . we think you're probably better suited to other work environments' — and she was virtually penniless. She had also just launched her career as a part-time baker. Steve's offer made a rather compelling kind of sense, especially the no-strings bit of it, and, despite Lucy's authentic ignorance of the finer points of mid-twentieth-century fashion, beyond the basic lineaments of the New Look and the relatively austere forties styles which had preceded the New Look so much more attractively, the overriding feeling in her chest was one of relief, even gratitude, that anyone should think she was worthy of a business partnership, however disadvantageous the terms. So she'd said yes, with the faintest violet tinge of a misgiving playing across the horizon of her sense of principle. And it had been fun for a while, and also worth it in terms of tax-free pocket income.

They'd worked it all out on paper one wet evening at her kitchen table. Steve would do most of the sourcing, Lucy most of the fronting, but they'd cover each other's backs in all eventualities: they'd share any necessary needlework, provided the needlework was not too taxing; they would never fail to take account of each other's needs in the moment, with either time or money. They would strive for balance and generosity in all things.

It all sounded immensely feasible, even hearteningly fun, and so it proved for some months. Through that spring and summer and into the first grim shifts of autumn, Saturdays and Sundays were a riot of coffee and commerce, fun and lip. Hard labour too, especially when it rained and Lucy's knuckles would redden and crack. 'Frankly, my dear,' Steve liked to say at the end of a long day, over the first pint of the evening, 'there's *nothing* like retail. So pure. So clean.' And Lucy would smile as brightly as she could while secretly trying to expel from her mind a saturated-colour image of Vivien Leigh coming apart at the seams in an amazing dress.

But that was then.

Now, Steve plonked himself down heavily at the kitchen table while Lucy scooped up the remaining tea bags and swept up the dusty red sea. She kept her head down and didn't know why. Even now, more than two years after their 'separation', Steve gave off a faint heat of resentment. He radiated it persistently and evenly but at such low levels that it was perfectly possible for Lucy to tell herself she was imagining it. But it was never a good idea to look him in the eye too starkly. His wasn't the febrile anguish of the smithereened lover, broken apart and then scattered by the force of Lucy's rejection. Nothing so shrill or poetic or dark or disintegrated. Rather, he just carried on as he always carried on, simmering away quietly at the irrationality of the situation. He just couldn't for the life of him see where the common sense lay.

'Have you done it?' he said as he stirred his tea.

'Nope. Couldn't be bothered,' said Lucy, sitting down opposite him with her mug. She then relented. Steve could make hangdog really sing. She held up her mangled digit. 'Of course I have. I ruined my thumb doing it but it's done. Good as new. Well, almost.'

'Thank fuck for that,' said Steve. 'I'm sick of making promises and then having nothing to deliver.' He looked up, suddenly aware that he might have walked into a trap of his own making. Lucy appeared not to register the possibility, however. 'But thanks. I'll see who wants it most badly. There's a waiting list, you know, you idle woman.'

'Anyone I know?'

'To be fair, I can't remember. They're all a blur to me these days, Luce. All a blur. But there's at least three of them, I think. Should be good for a scrap.'

From which Lucy deduced that Steve was going to stage an auction for the jacket between the three women to whom he'd virtually sold the thing already. He loved what he called 'a scrap', not because he was greedy — it was his greatest virtue that he wasn't — but because he loved 'the purity of combat', whether it was men fighting for physical mastery of each other or women fighting, metaphysically, for the glory of a rare vintage piece. Lucy had once called him on it; suggested that he got his biggest kicks from watching women go at it. 'Just be honest, Steve: you're a perv. You should go to mud-wrestling clubs — and take all your filthy mates with you.' But he insisted, through clouds of quivering mock indignation, that that wasn't in fact the case. It didn't get him off, he said, gnomically, it got him *on*.

'Conflict is life,' he'd declared, shifting his position in bed to a more oratorial one, one hand cupped behind his head. 'Conflict is evolution. So what you need to do, given that it's unavoidable, is do your conflicting in such a way that no one gets hurt. Really hurt, I mean. There's nothing wrong with bumps and bruises. I reckon it should be looked on as a form of exercise, conflict. It's *good* for you. It gets the crap out of your system and it can be fun. Like sex.'

He'd then tried for the third and final time to persuade Lucy to go paintballing with him that Sunday afternoon — and, to his visible surprise, succeeded. Lucy, for her part, had agreed to it in a storm of weird guilt. And afterwards, after they'd staggered back to his flat tired and sore — and in Lucy's case thoroughly browned off — she'd told him that she'd always love him but she felt the time had come for them to stop having sex together, or going out on dates, or acting like boyfriend and girlfriend, or shooting people. But that she wanted to remain friends and business partners — if he did too. And listen, there wasn't anybody else in the picture, really there wasn't — but, well, it had been *how* many years now? And she felt stuck and depressed and as if she had nothing to offer Steve any more other than friendship and loyalty of an entirely platonic kind, and that she wanted to do this now rather than let their relationship descend into the kind of poisonous trough she'd got wedged in before — she had too much respect for him to let that happen — and, anyway, her portfolio needed simplifying.

She immediately regretted the joke but had needed it in the moment to change the curve of her speech, to bring it back within the scope of their regular, knockabout way of talking. What she did not tell Steve was that she had only gone paintballing with him in the first place just to work herself up to making the speech — for her, the afternoon's entertainment had been penitential, a *Heart of Darkness*-style expedition upcountry in the Transit into the heart of sylvan Hertfordshire (The horror! The horror!), and, yes, she had met with something there, outside Tring, which had darkened her for ever, possibly. She finished by explaining that she could not foresee a future in which they lived together and had children together and ran a joint bank account together — not that she wanted children anyway, and she knew that Steve did. So there was a problem there too. 'I'm nearly thirty-six now . . . ' were her final words before she broke off abruptly.

Steve had not broken down, nor wept, nor raged. Nor had he become remote, hard and cold, which was what she had feared the most. Instead he'd hung his head. He let it hang like a dead weight for several seconds more than were comfortable. When he lifted it up again he looked her in the eye.

'So you see me as part of your portfolio, do you?'

'No, of course I don't. I don't know why I said that. Well, I do — I wanted to make a joke to change the . . . atmosphere, and it just came out. But it was the wrong joke and if you're angry with me I can see why. I'm really sorry. I'm really sorry about everything, including the fact that I hate shooting people . . . '

'Ah. So you're saying that if I didn't like shooting people things might be different? I could learn, I suppose, to be a man of peace.' He shifted his gaze over her shoulder and out through the window, seeing what? Nothing probably. Steve's eyes were filming over. 'Tell you what — I don't feel like much of a warrior right now . . . '

And so it had gone on, with Steve proving himself to be a far more stylish chuckee than he had been a boyfriend and Lucy deciding that actually, yes, she did love him really, after a fashion, but this was definitely the right thing to be doing and that actually, yes, it was not inconceivable that Steve knew it too. He just didn't want it like this, because it hadn't been his idea.

Nevertheless, Steve had acceded to Lucy's wishes.

And now, back in the present, more than two years on from that tricky, twisty, double helix of a Sunday evening in Finsbury Park, he was still sitting at the kitchen table with the face of a whipped puppy. What had changed?

At least it was her kitchen this time.

'Lucy, it isn't working,' he said abruptly.

'What isn't?'

'Our arrangement.'

'Arrangement? What arrangement? I mean, what part of our arrangement?'

'Any part of it, really. Any and all of it,' he sighed. 'Such as it is.'

Steve's hangdog look was mutating into an expression of unadulterated misery. Everything in his face was tending towards the floor. He scratched with both hands at the surface of the table, as if trying to remove an invisible glaze. Looked up again.

'I'm not sure I want to carry on the business any more. Not like this, on this basis. It just makes me miserable. I get up every morning feeling like shit and the first thought that goes through my head is, is this a market day or a decorating day? And if it's a decorating day I feel all right — because I know I won't have to feel like shit for the rest of it. But if it's a market day . . . ' He cast his gaze around the kitchen, as if looking for something, and, not finding it, then refocused on Lucy's chin. 'Look, Lucy, I'm sorry. I love you. I'm sorry. But that's the truth. It's doing my *fucking* head in . . . ' He opened his mouth wider for a moment, as if to draw in more oxygen, and Lucy saw something dark caught between one of his front teeth and a canine. 'But you can see my problem here, can't you?'

Lucy considered whether to nod in affirmation and decided not to. She returned his gaze as rigorously as she could. It was like holding up one end of a piano.

'And it's not,' continued Steve, visibly shaking, 'as if I can just walk away with the business — you know: take off with it and leave you standing there. Or fire you. I'm not that much of a shit. I wouldn't leave you on the debris of the Sunday-morning market.' He gathered himself, perhaps heartened by his ability to quote song lyrics even in the rigours of his despair. The shaking ceased in his voice, if not in his hands. 'I know our agreement isn't a legal one and I always said you could walk away, no strings. But what am I supposed to do in this situation? Huh? I just didn't think it would ever come to this. You know, I never thought in a million years I'd want out myself. Be the one to do the walking. Well, of course I don't *want* out but I have to *get* out because something bad will happen to me if I don't — '

'Steve — '

'No, babe, let me finish. I've started so I might as fucking well finish.' He stood up and opened his palms towards her, sucked in more breath so that his shoulders rose and fell. 'I love you, OK? That's a given. That's unalterable. I've always loved you and I always will, whether or not you love me — and I know you like me but that's as far as it goes. You think I'm all right, if a bit negative — and you're right. I *am* all right, if a bit . . . a bit . . . erring on the side of realism. And that's OK. But I *love* you, and that's a big

58

discrepancy. It's like a matchbox stood next to Beachy Head. If you see what I mean. There's a problem of scale there. And it . . . it . . . ' His gaze roved around a little more and Lucy could see Steve's eyes were moving in an effort to forestall the sort of tears that actually fall. 'It hurts me.'

'Steve — '

'No, I haven't finished, Lucy. OK? I'm getting to the point now. OK. I can't fire you. I can't walk away from my own business. It is after all mine and I am at least legally, so to speak, registered as its owner. But you can leave. You can leave, no strings. You can just walk away any time you choose and I won't make a scene. I've always said this and I'm saying it now.' He swiped his hand across his face. 'And I'm hoping you'll take the hint.'

7

Snakes

For a while in the late Sixties and early Seventies, when Bére and I were still children, we used to go on holiday *en famille* to stay with our mother's parents outside St Mathieu for two or three weeks of the summer, depending on my father's work commitments here in London. We'd put the car on the ferry overnight to Caen and drive down in one go, pausing only briefly en route to refuel both car and bodies — then press grimly on, as rather more than half the length of France spooled away beneath our Michelins. To make the journey was to mark the family's frontier.

There was always further to go than I ever wanted — especially over the last couple of hundred kilometres or so, when the distance in front of us seemed somehow to extend indefinitely, while our destination crept closer and closer in increments too small to feel. This may have been a psychological effect created by the arrow-straight Roman road which accounted for much of that long final stretch; either that or, out of sheer weariness and boredom, it may have been a sort of hallucination. At all events, I learned to suspend my consciousness of things until it was over, treating the last leg from Poitiers as time that didn't count as time. And then, eventually, numbly, a minimum of nine hours after clanking off the ferry, we would roll into the farmyard, the early-evening sunlight golden, the shadows long and purple . . . and life would begin again. Food would always be on the table in the kitchen, under a cloth.

Grand-père and Grand-mère seemed pretty redoubtable to us then, although Grand-père did not survive the decade — he was taken down in 1979 in one hit by a massive stroke. Grand-mère then spent another four or so years fading away after he'd gone. But back then they were glorious, my grandparents. Formidable. As silently imperturbable as their geese were rowdy.

Everything about those holidays is now a haze in the memory — I retain virtually nothing of any substance, just vague, scraped-together impressions of sun and rain and birch leaves doing their shimmery thing in the breeze; excited sightings of boar-shaped blots in distant meadows; textures and colours and light; the intimacy of the hedgerows, which seemed so close and so crowded; the food on the table snared under beaded muslin; the noise the geese made as they went mad at every little thing. But nothing much involving people and what they did and how they interacted and so on, apart from the general impression I have retained ever since of my grandparents' formidability. Otherwise, people and events remain an almost total blank.

The one event I can still call to memory was a private one, even though it was an event I did not experience alone. By that I mean that there were other people present, who may have been aware of what was going on but were not moved by it. And I did not actively participate in this event, nor was I technically complicit, nor negligent, nor implicated in any way. Not as such. I merely watched it occur, as a passenger. It involved a snake.

We were driving through the forest, which was pretty much all you could do then in the Haute-Vienne apart from walk yourself to a stand-still under the oaks and birches. The sun was shining, which it didn't always do. Doubtless, we were on our way to the market in Piégut, or perhaps the *lac* on the other side of St Mathieu, and I was kneeling up on the back seat of the family Renault, staring out through the rear window, watching the road as it fled backwards in time.

It was pale and smooth as grey milk, the road, but wide and straight enough in its cut through the forest to allow my dad to put his foot down, which he liked to do as a treat to himself, and in spite of the fact that the car was a dull family estate. It made a tremendous fuss over any kind of exertion, that Renault: the acceleration always seemed pathetic given the hullabaloo created by the engine. Odd that I can remember it at all, really. But I can certainly still feel in my water the inertia created by the soft, slingy suspension as the car made its effort that morning, my belly pressed into the spongy curve of the seat-back, looking out at the virgin road we'd just used up. What I can't feel — any more now than I could then — is the car undulating minutely as it passed over the body of a snake, which had chosen that moment to cross the road. But it must have done so. We must have run it over because I heard my father say 'Blast!' and then 'I think that was a snake' in the same stretched instant that I saw the stricken reptile begin to throw agonised shapes, like letters of the alphabet, black as ink in the road behind, as if spelling out with its body an accusation for the benefit of my eyes alone. It spasmed and twitched and curled and flicked and, at one point, appeared to part company with the road surface altogether in a violent jackknife — a letter U which joined momentarily at the top to form a lozenge-shaped O. Whether it died or lived on I do not know, obviously, but I felt at the time that I was watching its last throes. A spastic squiggle and then nothing. Death as a thing of passing insignificance in the landscape, like a soldier shot in the background in a war film. Like Icarus by Bruegel.

I said nothing and I don't know why.

I was haunted for nights afterwards by the message I was convinced the snake was trying to spell out to me, the one witness to its death. The guiltless passenger. Some nights, instead of sleeping, I found myself seeing through the dying reptile's eyes, watching my own blobby head in the rear window of the Renault, getting smaller and smaller and dimmer and dimmer as vision clouded and the snake's consciousness departed, and I, the killer blob, carried on down the road to the rest of my life.

I must have been twelve, maybe even thirteen. The snake haunted me for days, weeks and possibly even months. And although it doesn't haunt me now, it remains the one clear memory I have of holidays in St Mathieu. The one memory that has a beginning, a middle and an end and comes with its own calligraphy.

★ ★ ★

I still have a few snaps from those holidays, stashed in tatty Boots photo envelopes in a folder in the bottom drawer of my old desk, the cheap but surprisingly solid and not entirely unattractive desk I was given for my fourteenth birthday by my parents in the outspoken hope that it would help me to focus my mind on my O levels. It didn't. But it's a good desk and I like sitting at it still, even if it is a bit on the small side and my knees press against the underside of the work surface when I put my feet on the footbar.

The desk is about the only thing visible in my flat left over from my childhood, and that's for a reason. I do not wish to be reminded of my childhood, any more than I wish to be reminded of all the other things I fucked up. The desk seems to me to be a reasonable thing to have retained on the basis that it symbolises the effort of others — at the time disregarded by me — to help put childhood behind me. Plus it performs a useful function. But there's nothing else in the joint that would give you any sort of clue as to the fount from which I spring. No pictures, that's for sure, apart from a couple in my bedroom of my mum and dad as young marrieds — before me.

I'm sitting at the desk now. My knees are comfortingly restricted. The red faux-leather sticky-backed plastic on the top has come unstuck at the edge and is curling up at the corners. The surface area feels fractionally too small for comfort, which is probably good because a small surface means that I can't build up distracting deposits of crap on top of it: papers, books, CDs, cuttings, pictures, printouts, batteries, scissors, pens, postcards, spectacles, wires . . . the slippy-slidey shale of chaos which I am given to cultivating as a projection of my untidy mind. And no, I do not feel as if I am doing my homework at last, after all these years.

On the contrary, I feel as if I am doing something I want to do, although it's every bit as hard as homework, just not as onerous. You might even say it's liberating. That's the theory anyway. Liberating like throwing up is liberating.

Actually, no. Scratch that. Anything as controlled as writing at a desk isn't like throwing up at all. And of course you can't put off throwing up indefinitely, not like you can put off writing. Either you're going to do it or you're not. It's not up to you. So not liberating like vomit.

Liberating like a sound decision.

I can still distract myself, though, despite the smallness of the work surface, and that passive activity can keep me from what I'm supposed to be doing for hours at a stretch. For instance, I can sit here after a hard day's work at the store, in irregular urban quiet, and think about the triumphs of my career. The great duvets I have

65

sold. The great solos I have played. The beautiful, willing women I have wanted to caress on soft sheets with my artistic hands but never quite managed it because someone else got their artistic hands on them first. *Mais bien sûr*, I can spend hours of an evening with my head back and my mouth open, legs straight out in front of me, heels hooked comfortably on the footbar, considering those triumphs.

Then there are the triumphs of acceptance, which have required the exercise of less and less resolve as the years have warped into full-blown middle age but have achieved a quality that feels to me like the opposite of passivity. Yes, I am almost Buddhistic in my capacity to accept. I accept as I breathe, sometimes deeply, sometimes shallowly, but always effectively and without unnecessary thought. I only choke when I get overexcited at the thought of my enormous capacity for acceptance, and that doesn't happen all that often, I am glad to say. Do I sound like a self-pitier? I am not one.

It's all good really.

I like to think that my flat in fashionable, edgy Dalston reflects this. Not for me the starkness of minimalist living — the empty walls, the prairie floorboards, the laptop, the telly, the MP3 dock, the statement furniture, the framed poster/ photograph/painting not hanging but leaning; the anti-decor which says 'This space is a tasteful frame to my sumptuous personality', as if one's personality were a crafted likeness of one's preferred self.

Oh no. This space is not a frame. It's a space.

It's the void in which I have made the absolute most of my discount in the furniture department at the store and in which I dispose the accumulations of my adult life. It's a receptacle.

It has the usual shit in it. Sofa, table, chairs, carpet, curtains, shelving, free-standing unit containing gorgeous valve amp (valves exposed, like beacons), CD player and, on top, turntable; knackered leather pouffe, on which I put my feet when watching the telly I got at less than cost from the electrical department when they were selling off the last fat tellies. In the bedroom, a bed and a wardrobe, which I inherited when my dad died — the only sticks of furniture in the joint (apart from the desk) that didn't exercise my store card.

What else? Three or four feet of vinyl, still used not infrequently. Five or six feet of CDs, used all the time. Cassettes, books, a couple of framed music posters (one VineHeart, one Coltrane), a reproduction of van der Weyden's *Descent from the Cross* bought from the Prado where the real one is; a not-bad watercolour done by Bére of the main barn in St Mathieu from an interesting angle, ceremonially pre-sented to me on my fortieth birthday; and, in the corner next to the desk facing the small rear 'garden' window, two guitars on stands: an ancient acoustic Gibson and a scuffed but still gorgeous 1950s blond Telecaster with a lot of the original bits still on it. I've been told it's worth getting on for twenty grand now.

I live with most of my past.

But not all of it. I contrive to *not* live with the

worst of it most of the time. It's a trick I perform. I do it every day, the contriving — it takes breathing and activity and paying attention to the moment, to the exclusion of all other things, so that the thing I can't live with seeps into and then out the other side of whatever I'm doing like thin rain. It goes through; it touches the sides — it must do — but so finely that I don't notice. I function. Can't begin to explain how. Matter over mind, I suppose. Every day I distract myself with what I'm supposed to be doing.

But if you've killed a child, then you never escape the words, even if you do manage to pretend that the deed itself does not sit inside you like a tumour. They are everywhere, the words, in every format on every platform. I am writing them now.

It was an accident of course, by any definition of the word. I did not intend to kill him, nor, in the moment, could I have avoided doing so — in fact I was not even aware that I'd done it, not till some time afterwards. But the moment in which the event took place certainly happened. Whether or not I was conscious of it taking place at the time, as an event, is neither here nor there. The moment happened. It swelled up and burst into reality. Made a disgusting mess all over everything. In another universe perhaps the exact same set of contingencies would have lined up in that moment, in precisely the same order, and the child might not have died. But how many universes would we have to examine to find those conditions and result? A number close to infinite, I imagine.

The point is this: the moment would need to have been composed of only slightly, fractionally, minutely different stuff for the killing not to have occurred. And I was responsible for putting quite a lot of that stuff in place. The child was responsible for some too, as were chance and the wind, and possibly even his mother — although I have always felt that to include her in the deal, even technically, is not just. One thing is unavoidable though: my actions cannot be ruled out of the equation. The equation of his death.

It was me who stormed out of the soundcheck and stomped up the metal staircase from the club basement, rampaged a dozen yards up the road to where the car was parked and threw my guitar case onto the back seat with enough force to instantly make me wish I hadn't. Even then the Tele was precious. Then it was me who hustled round the front of the vehicle, clonking my hip as I did so on the front wing, yanked open the driver's door, chucked myself into the driving seat and then slammed the car into gear, unrelenting and virtually blind. Blind with what? Blind with rage, for sure. Self-pity, no doubt. The wish to hurt, maim, kill?

I'm afraid so, yes.

Whom did I wish to kill? I knew the game was up with VineHeart and I knew that it was partly my fault. But I was also sure that it was not my fault entirely; that stuff had been done to me, if not out of malice then certainly out of transactional expediency. It's the way it goes and has ever gone, in everything, not just music. Shafted again. The way of life. But I could not hide from the fact that I had contributed my share to the conditions which enabled the shafting to take place, and I knew it. I had spent more time than I should acting like a cunt — a righteous cunt but a cunt all the same. And the knowledge made me a killer. So I bashed the car into gear with the heel of my palm, yanked the wheel round with my other hand, squirted out of the parking space and then dragged the gearstick back into second with a hooked fist while the car hopped up the road, the suspension bucking, the synchromesh squalling, the clutch making its usual representations. And it was while this spastic sequence of lurches evolved that the car hit the child.

As with the snake, I felt nothing. But this time I saw nothing either. I did hear a tiny double pop, which I only registered as such twenty yards further up the road. It was just that: a pop-pop. Two separate but connected and utterly distinct sounds with a cardboardy timbre, like an upturned white-goods box bopped lightly with a drumstick, one bop slightly harder than the other. *Pop*-pop. *Punk*-punk. It probably sounds facetious, fretting over the exact description of the sound the boy's head made on impact with my front wing, but I don't mean to be facetious. The opposite is what I feel. As you can imagine, I have been in search of exactitude for twenty years now, and I still can't get everything to fit precisely. Sometimes I think exactitude is a luxury available only to those who can afford to tell lies; sometimes I think it's an unattainable abstract, like perfection.

But in the moment I felt nothing and I saw even less. I literally did not see the child. I did not see his head, shoulders and body appear suddenly between the parked cars as he chased his wind-snatched crisp packet at an excited, pell-mell, headlong scramble, oblivious of everything around him apart from the Golden Wonder bag in its swoop out into the road, and then totally insensible from the moment my car stoved in his right temple and jawbone and sent his body twisting and crashing round and backwards into the side door of the parked car, so that the other side of his head made an indentation in the metal the size and depth of a soup bowl.

I stopped the car four or five seconds later not because I had begun to register what had just happened but because I suddenly became aware, through the windscreen and then through the side windows, that people all around were starting to register something. I felt this happen at first; I didn't see it. I became aware that people were stopping in their tracks, then running. That hands were going up to faces. That cars were stopping suddenly. My first thought was, 'What's happened?'

And then I looked in the rear-view mirror.

And I somehow knew. Although, equally, I had no idea what.

★ ★ ★

I got there as quickly as I could. I did not walk briskly; I ran as fast as I could. I knew. I knew, although I didn't want to. And I was met by faces and hands which did not part to allow me access to whatever lay on the ground next to the dented car. I had to fight through — and it was my right to do so, although the owners of the faces and hands clearly thought it was not.

He was engulfed. A man was on his knees, bending over him. Of the child I could see nothing at all above his knees. But I knew now that it was a child, from his tiny feet. I saw the man's broad back. I saw a woman, white as chalk, squatting on the other side of the man, whimpering, while another woman, bending at the waist, one hand pressed like a poultice between the first woman's shoulder blades, spoke calmly and soothingly to her. She was saying 'I know, I know' over and over again. In response, the chalk-white mother emitted incoherent sounds. There were shouts and there was crying all around in a sort of carousel of alarm. The usual 'Oh my God' and 'Jesus' and 'Has anybody called an ambulance?'

I stood and watched mutely, and in what seemed like no time at all I heard a siren. I was not alone in hearing it. The man bending over the child pulled himself up and stood tall, as tall as he could go, onto his toes — it seemed to me that he was trying to make a lighthouse out of himself for the approaching emergency services, his head rotating until he got a fix. And in that moment I saw the child's head, hard on the ground, misshapen, bloody at nose and mouth and eyes and ears. But misshapen. Distorted. Not as smoothly round as a child's head should be. I thought I could see him breathing. His eyes were closed and the back of his head was on the tarmac, which must have been cold and gritty through his fine child's hair. My second thought: 'He needs a pillow.' And then the man turned back to him, hunkered down and seemed to put two fingers to the child's neck.

The man's shoulders squared. The child's mother let out a stream of noise I cannot begin to describe, except to say that it went on for far too long. I never wish to hear a sound like that again.

I turned to face the approaching uniforms. No one was showing the slightest interest in me.

And it was at this point, as I was grappling with the realisation that I was not the central figure in this drama, that I felt a sharp prod on my arm, just above the elbow. I somehow stopped myself from ducking reflexively, then half turned to face my assailant, my head cocked back as if on a spring.

It was a young girl in her late teens, open-faced with wide blue-grey eyes and a mass of unruly off-blonde hair, like straw. She did not look as if she was about to arrest me or slap me or put me in a headlock. She said: 'I saw what happened.'

8

Dust

Lucy slept like a log. She came to the next morning feeling as light as a daisy and as delicately petalled. She showered and breakfasted, enjoying every minute of both experiences, and then picked up her mail from the doormat as she skated out of the flat to the Jones with an energy she did not recognise.

She could not see why she felt so good. Not really. She was not delighted by her final parting from Steve. Not at all. In fact she was first shaken by it and then reduced to nothing — she had lain on her new pillow after going to bed a bit pissed and listened to the impossibly small sound of her tears plipping one by one from the rim of her ears onto the crisp cotton of the pillowcase on either side of her head. Plip. Plip. And it was only when she turned onto her shoulder for the final drift off to sleep that she realised quite how many tears she'd shed: the pillow was not merely damp but wet to her cheek, and slightly slimy. She had felt obliged to change the pillowcase.

But now, as she moved through the morning, a contrary river of relief flowed through her and around the ache in the pit of her stomach, and she knew that the right thing had been done. The right thing for her, for Steve, for them both: they

74

would no longer be each other's ball and chain; no more would they drag each other down into the silted depths she had come to recognise as their natural habitude. Lucy felt buoyant. Her morning's baking was going to be a pleasure from start to finish, with or without exposure to Oleg's conviction that tart-baking is a mournful undertaking and, as such, requires of the baker an undertaker's solemnity.

It was later in the morning over mid-shift coffee across the road that Lucy remembered the post in her coat: a bill and a letter, stuffed unexamined into a pocket so that the envelopes curled into a flattened cylinder. The bill was red; she didn't bother to open it. But the letter looked interesting. It was not often that items of post qualified for that adjective these days, but this was unusual: a handwritten address on a franked envelope. The script was handsome and rounded and written carefully in old-fashioned blue-black ink. The letter, stretching evenly, slowly, methodically over three sheets of single-sided A4 typing paper, was not headed with a return address.

Dear Lucy,

This may seem strange and I hope you don't think it's inappropriate. I am the chap who sold you a pillow a while back in Oxford Street, and explained at no doubt tedious length all about the history of feather beds. I managed to convince you, I hope, that mattress toppers are a very good thing but not a cure for insomnia.

Nevertheless I hope your sleeping is going better on the new pillow.

The reason I'm writing is this. The second time you came by the Bedlinen department you mentioned that you thought you recognised me. You asked me if we knew each other and I said that I didn't think we did. In the moment I thought that was the case, I really did. You looked a bit embarrassed for asking but it really wasn't necessary to be embarrassed. I was perfectly fine with you asking. However, I now realise that, contrary to what I thought that afternoon, we have met before, I think — if you can call it a meeting.

And this is where *I* become rather embarrassed, because I'm not sure I want to remind you of how and why and where we 'met'. It was a very bad occasion, one I'd ideally like to forget, but can't. On that occasion you were a great help to me and did stuff that saved me from a fate worse than the one I ended up with. It may or may not be worth pointing out that our personal contact was, to say the least, minimal. We are acquainted, but in no sense could we be said to have enjoyed any sort of relationship.

Why bother then? Why not let it go? I hear you thinking. To be honest, I'd think that too if I were in your position. If it's such a bad thing, why not just leave it? Why rake over old coals and risk stirring something up?

Well, the fact is that I never thanked you

for what you did. Worse, I didn't realise I'd never thanked you until I remembered who you were the other day. And now I really want to say it. I am desperate to.

Thank you!

I suppose the omission at the time was all due to the horror of the situation and the shock. It's a fact that, for a long time afterwards, I wasn't myself. I couldn't be. I don't want to claim post-traumatic stress disorder as an excuse or even as a reason for not thanking you — I'm pretty sure I wouldn't have qualified for a PTSD diagnosis at the time, either clinically or morally. But put it this way: I didn't speak to anyone about anything apart from the very basics for more than a year afterwards. Two years actually. Twenty years if you're talking about the event itself. Twenty and counting. I still haven't talked about it, because I have nothing to say.

The event? I am of course wondering whether what I've said already has jogged your memory. I'm hoping it has, because I don't want to write it out. I'm pretty sure you must have got it by now, so me giving even the barest outline of what happened is probably redundant. But I'm hoping this will do: you were a passer-by in Newman Street off Oxford Street, and you witnessed something terrible happen for which I was directly responsible . . . Got it now?

You must have.

Anyway, whether you get it or not, it's

true to say that you saved my bacon legally. But equally importantly, I think you saved my bacon psychologically. Your testimony helped me to see that there was another way of looking at what happened, other than the one I had in my head. A different, less punishing version of events. One which didn't let me off the hook completely but which enabled me to see what happened literally from a different point of view. So I want to thank you on two counts.

Thank you. Thank you.

It was very nice to see you again after all this time, even if I didn't twig it was you straight away. I know I must look rather different now to how I looked then and I have tried to match that difference by becoming a slightly different person. I have tried to retain the good bits of my old self and get shot of the less good bits.

Anyway, you don't need to hear about all that. I just want to thank you, is all.

No need to write back, but do come into Bedlinen and say hello next time you're in the store. It'd be lovely to thank you in person too. But only if you feel like it.

Very best wishes,
William Carberry
(formerly known to you as Guillaume)

Lucy did not finish her coffee. She spent the last ten minutes of her break marching briskly around the block. She then finished her shift at the bakery without thinking about what her hands were doing, somehow managing not to empty flour onto the floor or drop mixer blades onto her feet. She barely noticed Oleg's atmosphere and did not force her customary smile in his direction as she left the bakery by the back door and clambered clumsily onto her bike. Ten minutes later she found herself in her kitchen staring vacantly into a cupboard full of tins and jars and packets held shut with postman's elastic bands.

William Carberry aka Guillaume Carberry . . . The rocker-cum-snivelling wreck she'd last seen twenty years ago in the West End. Then, he'd been a spectacle: a broken stick man, white as a sheet, trembling, unseeing in his effort to compute what had just happened to him. She remembered his hands, clenching and unclenching. Spastic. The memory of his hands was the most vivid thing of all. But the rest of the episode was not hard to summon. It came back to Lucy without effort of will.

She'd been eighteen years old and getting ready for college: working as a gofer for a West End rag-trade wholesaler to scrape some cash together for her departure. It had been late afternoon, at least an hour after school chucking-out time, and she was returning to base after running an errand to a client in Soho. Just walking. Walking on the pavement without much care or consideration, but with a large cardboard box of surprisingly heavy samples held at right angles to her abdomen, the joints and sinews of her arms and back getting tired and hot on the inside. She was just walking, and then . . . It had all taken place in front of her, unfolding like some barely plausible TV melodrama — but secretly, for the edification of her eyes alone. At that moment, there must have been at least half a dozen other people walking on that stretch of Newman Street, going about their off-Oxford Street business. But she was the only one who witnessed the entire sequence of events from start to finish in detail. The only one. The solitary all-seeing eye. And from the first moment, she had felt involved, tied in, complicit, as if she were a protagonist.

She was *in* it. She saw and felt it all, like a temporary god. From the moment the rushing, obviously furious form of Guillaume had disturbed Lucy's airspace on the pavement, nearly but not quite touching her — his turbulence was such that she'd half dropped her box of samples and had to stop and cling on inelegantly as the thing slid down her thighs — to the moment perhaps ten minutes later when he more or less threw himself into the arms of an approaching policewoman; and then to the last blue shriek of the ambulance as it conveyed the inert form of Samuel Wheating to the place in which he would draw his last breath — from all of those moments, and from the sliding pell-mell of moments that separated them, Lucy drew the conviction that she had a role to play. This was not a story belonging solely to Samuel and his mother and Guillaume and the paramedics and the guy who tried to comfort Samuel and the woman who tried to comfort Samuel's mother — it belonged to

Lucy too. She was in it up to her neck, whether she liked it or not.

Twenty years. She contemplated the debris in the kitchen from the night before and decided to do nothing about it this instant. Then changed her mind. She crashed about the space flinging bottles into the recycling box, wiping surfaces, flushing fag ends, ash and cellophane into the bin, sweeping the floor and cursing out loud as she chased the elusive, shifting constellation of dust and debris into ever-diminishing lines with her dustpan and brush. Good grief. It hardly seemed possible that the day after severance from Steve — *the very next day* — something like this would turn up out of the blue. It was a real knife-twister. What were the chances? What did it mean? What *could* it mean . . . ?

Oh, come on, get a grip! It doesn't mean anything. She swished the last fine line of unsweepable dust under the cooker with a couple of angry flicks of the brush and slumped back onto a kitchen chair.

But what the hell did *he* mean by writing to her? Stirring it up again, just as he said. What was his point? What was he after? She'd done her bit back then. She had told the truth both to the police, who'd wanted to prosecute 'the driver' for manslaughter from the moment Samuel had died, and to the Crown Prosecution Service, who'd materialised like ghouls soon after little Samuel's expiration. And it had taken some doing, doing her bit. Particularly annoying had been one officer with a pink, shiny face and pendulous lower lip — he was oddly like a younger version of the current government's Education Secretary, now she came to think about it — who had pressed her insistently for her *impressions* of Guillaume's behaviour in the seconds before he'd got into his car. Over and over again. 'How did he *seem*, Miss Taplow?' he'd said, eyebrows up, lower lip pushed out, expectantly emphasising key words, as if they were the ones she was forgetting — through no fault of her own of course. 'Would you say he was *enraged* or *out of control* in any way?'

She could tell what the guy had wanted: just one overripe adjective, a single descriptive word expressing a degree too strongly an emotion she did not really feel; something colourful and rich on which a position might be hung, an incrimination . . . But she had stayed resolute, helped to a large degree by the fact that the officer was such an obvious, screaming creep.

Yes, Guillaume appeared to be in a rush. Yes, she did get the impression that he was upset. But no, he hadn't seemed 'out of control'. Yes, he pulled away from the kerb abruptly — but not 'aggressively'. No, she was absolutely certain that he had not been exceeding the speed limit or driving carelessly. It had clearly been an accident. Awful, terrible, shocking, violent. But an accident resulting from happenstance, not carelessness or negligence. Look, if anyone had been out of control it had been the child . . .

Lucy realised that she was sitting with her mouth open. She shut it and went out.

In Mr Rustem's she bought a pint of milk, a tin of chopped tomatoes and a newspaper but not toilet roll, which had been the reason she'd come out in the first place. She got most of the way back to the flat before realising she'd forgotten it and had to turn round. Some things can't wait to be picked up next time.

Back in the flat she returned almost immediately to Newman Street. She was revisited by how she'd avoided looking at the stricken Samuel, by taking a single step back so that the wing of the nearest parked car masked his position in the road. She remembered the wind that afternoon — its strange, gusting violence in the high-sided gully that was Newman Street. In particular she remembered how, before the impact, a few yards ahead of her on the pavement, the wind had snatched the crisp packet out of Samuel's hand and sent it bulleting between the parked cars and out into the road — and she remembered how Samuel had taken off after it, as if carried by some inner wind. She remembered the sound over her right shoulder of Guillaume's engine revving, his gears clashing; and she remembered, abruptly, the tiny, choking moment in which she knew what was about to happen but had no time in which to do anything about it. She remembered how, as soon as she had taken her single pace backwards, she had frozen and had been unable to do anything at all.

9

Air

The tickles left me alone last night, which they do periodically. I have no idea why. Sometimes they do, sometimes they don't. I've tried hard to find a pattern but I don't seem to be able to make anything stick. At one stage I was fairly convinced that it was a dietary thing and that I was reacting to sugar or wheat or lactose or any of the other popular scourges of the middle-aged. But no. My controlled experiments with diet only revealed that I was addicted to all the main food groups in most of their subdivisions and that, whatever I did or didn't do at meal-times, the tickles would come and go as they pleased. Perhaps I was an inconstant lady of Aquitaine in a former life.

Pretty much anything is possible, I sometimes think.

What I do have to admit is that I feel kind of lightened as a result of writing to Lucy Taplow, fatuous as it may seem. Could that be the reason for the untickly night, I wonder? Possibly. I followed my usual bedtime routine: *Newsnight* until boredom set in, accompanied by the regular late-night struggle to suppress the desire for a spliff, which was then palliated with a mug of peppermint tea, as per usual, plus my ritual *dégustation* of something choice from the deeper recesses of the record collection. Yusef Lateef was last night's lucky star and he mesmerised me in a bedwardly direction (while in no sense reducing my desire for a burning spear). I read for half an hour and went to sleep like a baby. I did not even yearn for someone to knead my thigh.

I dreamed about love.

Then woke up feeling sad. I don't think I've had enough love over the course of my life — or at least not enough of the kind I'd like. I was loved by my parents all right, in their rigid, reductive, recessed, post-war way. And I received acceptable amounts of admiration for VineHeart, before the admiration turned to weariness and diffidence. Looking further back than VineHeart, memory tells me that I was not deeply unpopular at school — and at university I might be prepared to admit that I cut something of a dash, until I dropped out. I did get a reasonable amount of sex while VineHeart lasted, although that, I always felt, had more to do with the looks and charisma of a '54 Telecaster than my own.

Then there was Mireille. Mireille and I were locked into some terrible pavane of love and death for half a dozen years, until the accident killed it for good. I don't know whether I loved her or not. I don't think I did, not really. No, of course I didn't. I'm pretty certain she didn't love me either. But it rumbled on regardless, sometimes 'lovingly', more often resignedly, frequently with neither one of us treating the other very well at all.

For most of the duration, Mireille feigned a

hippyish acceptance of my 'creative soul' and its needs, which included the occasional sexual outpouring with another woman. But it was feigned, her acceptance. I think she hated my outpourings. Who wouldn't? And all that pretending that she didn't mind was actually a fat part of the big, fraudulent construction of her love for me, which began with bullshit and ended in utter contempt. The whole edifice of our relationship was held up with scaffolding made of dried bullshit, which appeared to lend rigidity and strength to the structure but in fact was just a brittle outer cladding of narcissistic invention. If I tell you that our relationship began one addled Friday night with, as she put it, 'our destinies being entwined in our French names and our beautiful musical potential' then you will begin to get a sense of what this scaffolding was made of. Stinky stuff. Cringy stuff. Mireille was not actually French — she was a Jaguar dealer's daughter from Surrey — but she often used to wear sunglasses at night.

Her musicianship was conceptual rather than actual. It was founded on a sort of Francophile romanticisation of the individual creative spirit, in which any old shit will do, provided you do it with commitment and proper equipment, which includes the right clothes. So Mireille was always buying ethnic drums and cheap synthesisers, often with my money. She'd then conceptualise her inability to play anything cogent on these instruments as a mark of her freedom from the tyranny of technique. Then take loads of drugs. Then pass out. The important thing to her was to *feel* like a musician. She was, I believe, remarkably loyal to me throughout VineHeart's lifespan but then dropped me like a hot turd the minute the band ceased to exist.

I can't really blame her. By then, not only was I out of my mind but I was also determined to go into bedlinen. I expect I was no longer matching even the merest of M's expectations as a lover, either.

Why did I go along with the Mireille fraud for so long (we can all perpetrate a fraud over short distances — but *six years?*)? Because it suited me, of course. She was rather better-looking than is usual in the girlfriends of uglies like me. She laughed at my jokes. She trailed around after me as if I was important. She turned a blind eye, whenever she could, to my wick-dipping. She asked only for money, sex and unengaged proximity. And did I mention that she was good-looking?

In the end she left me for some proto-mash-up mix-artist/producer type — a shaven-headed knob-twiddler, basically — and finally got herself into a proper studio to make guttural noises and play 'found percussion' on an album of caterwauling by a white thirty-five-year-old trustafarian who lived in North Kensington. Last I heard — which would have been fifteen years ago if it was a day — Mireille was in Hong Kong taking drugs at somebody else's expense. Her new husband's, I think.

I didn't give her diamonds but neither did I give her disease. I gave her pretty much nothing, apart from an opportunity. She made much the same sort of offer to me, except the opportunity was of a different character. And when she disappeared from the flat a few weeks after the accident it was with a gesture that brought me great relief, such was its dim-witted self-dramatising crappiness. She wrote on our bedroom mirror — in lipstick, if you please, and in double quotes: 'I LOVE YOU, BUT . . . '

You could see where she'd had trouble getting the lipsticked dot-dot-dot to take on the surface of the mirror and had pressed too hard. I left the inscription up there for months afterwards out of sheer idleness and amusement rather than as a caution. I always read it as I LOVE YOU, BUT SPLODGE SMEAR CRUMBLE.

To be fair, when she wrote it I hadn't spoken to her for a fortnight.

The question is, though: would I recognise love if it came my way? Is love even recognisable to one of my experience and disposition? I am more than half a century old. My legs are thin and my stomach is not flat. I have a purplish spot on the back of one hand. I have a narrow jaw which has left me vulnerable to jowliness. OK, I am jowly. Furthermore, I have no soul. (This I try to disguise with a large pair of heavy-rimmed spectacles which I know make my eyes look big and alarming.) Who on earth is going to love a soulless bespectacled man with thin legs dressed in a polyester blazer and slacks?

In my love dream I was Welsh and I had only limited time in which to finesse an arranged marriage with a Welsh woman. The main drawback was that the terms and conditions of the arranged marriage required me to be in love with my intended, even though we had never met — and the consequences of not being in love with her did not bear thinking about, or so I was given to understand by both her father and mine. The tantalising thing was that I knew her address — her street was but a short bus ride away — and yet I kept on getting on the wrong bus.

I woke up sweating, without a hard-on.

★ ★ ★

What is wrong with my generation?

Nothing at all is wrong, of course. We just think so. Well, we suspect that it might be the case.

We may not be babyboomers with enormous pensions to look forward to and paid-off mortgages and an evolved appreciation of how fortunate we are. But we are all right really, relatively speaking. Historically, we have nothing to complain about. We were offered a decent education — I certainly got one at my Home Counties grammar school. We have had the opportunity to get mortgages on reasonably affordable property (provided you got your timing right, and I did). We benefited enormously from the shared feeling that it was possible for the world to get better. We didn't grow up scared that everything was shit and only going to get shittier — not unless we were personally unlucky. Nor did we have to grow up — and this I deem significant — having to pretend that everything was great, for getting-ahead purposes. I never thought for a moment that my future would depend on the spin I contrived to put on my present. For God's sake, we grew up with and then survived nuclear angst, which was our normal. It scared us, right enough, the nuclear stuff, but it didn't bend us out of shape or force us to make stuff up about ourselves to make ourselves into marketable commodities: nuclear angst *was* our shape. Duck and cover, protect and survive. Brown paper Sellotaped to every window. I'm generalising massively here, of course.

In fact I think it's true to say that anyone born clear of the bottom couple of rungs of the social ladder in the decade between 1955 and 1965 was handed a pretty reasonable deal, socio-economically speaking, and a cracking one culturally — not least during our teens, when the gap between the richest and the poorest was at its smallest ever and we were still young enough for the economic shitstorm of the 1970s to be experienced as an annoyance and a worry, and often as a stimulus, rather than as the all-out devastation of a way of life. Our parents had to deal with that; they were the ones who had to shoulder the implications of manufacturing decline, expensive oil, bad planning, inflation, union power and so on. Mine were mostly dumbstruck by it all. But we roaring teenagers were lucky. We had choices, ways out; as yet, we had no fixed way of life to lose, because we were still kids. Skinny ones, mostly, with plenty of energy — most of it undirected, because a lot of us didn't know what to do with ourselves, or what we were *for*.

I sometimes think of us as the scatter of debris left behind when the tide of the 1960s receded. The tidemark. We didn't actually experience the 1960s as 'The Sixties' — you needed to be at least half a decade older than us to be able to make that claim, and possibly even more than that (I was twelve when the Sixties ended) — but we were, as a generation, all but issued with pass-out documents as a birthright: invisible dockets which confirmed that you were fully socially mobile and that you could do what you want with your life, provided you're creative, you work hard and you're considerate to others. Do those things and there *will* be a place for you in the world. Furthermore, there is a chance for happiness because, demonstrably, the world can be changed by force of will, goodwill . . .

That was the Post-War Consensus speaking, I suppose. It was certainly the Post-War Consensus which prepared and rubber-stamped those invisible pass-out documents. No one ever told me that I was the holder of such a thing but I grew up convinced that I had one, that I was entitled.

Hah.

I'd love to have met the Post-War Consensus, if not over the kitchen table then down the pub or in a tea room in some childhood dream of a seaside resort. I imagine he or she was a very agreeable person in his or her distillation of things upon which we may all agree, and did not resemble in the slightest a person who works in the financial services sector. I imagine him or her to be understanding and soft-voiced but firm, clad in stylish but not ostentatious work clothes made from the very best fabrics of English tradition, mixed with a little American. Corduroy and denim perhaps. Elegantly frayed. I imagine him or her to have many things to say worth hearing but also to be a good listener. In fact that would be his or her primary function. Listening. S/he will have recognised the importance of money but would not have been interested in money as an end in itself — only in the good it can do for the world. S/he will have been everywhere present, a little like God. Yet deeply secular.

But of course the great P-W Consensus is dead and has been ever since I was old enough to be actually socially mobile, as opposed to theoretically so. And old enough to vote.

My parents were not lefties. They were not 'political' at all, in any overt sense, and certainly did not discuss politics over the dinner table, as some of my friends' parents did (by which I mean the friends I met at university rather than the ones I made at my grammar school). But they were consensualists, my parents. The consensus was for them a dignifying veil which they were able to draw over what they stood for and *where* they stood in the political spectrum, if indeed they could be said to stand anywhere. It would have been vulgar to do otherwise. Your vote is the next thing in your heart to your religious belief and the number of your bank account. A secret thing. What they were able openly to agree upon was that these new things were GOOD THINGS: the welfare state and nationalisation and kindness and tolerance and the joy of having come through the war together.

My dad met my mum when his Signals unit found itself bivouacked in the boarful glades of the Haute-Vienne in the year following VE Day — cleaning up, basically, south of Oradour-sur-Glane. He was a very young lieutenant; she was the even younger daughter of a moderately successful goose farmer. Their hands touched once on the handle of a pail and that started it. It was a slow business. He averted his gaze when she stuffed the gullets of the geese. She averted hers at his attempts to flirt in his schoolboy French — a thing he felt obliged to do in his role as a military insurgent, putting himself in mind, as he blushed and twinkled, of Olivier in *Henry V*. It was the highest expression of his patriotic duty.

They enjoyed a chaste, inarticulate, for a while virtually wordless courtship, which was interrupted when the Signals departed and my father enlisted in the Civil Service in London, with 'a big job to do' in getting the country out of Austerity. But he went back for her. By his twenty-eighth year he was deemed mature and responsible enough for his troth to be accepted and then settled upon. They were married in 1953 and set up their first home in St Albans where they lived childless for five years before giving rise to me. Bérengère came along two years later. It remains the most romantic true story I have ever heard.

And I have never felt able to live up to it.

Do I mean that? Yes, I do. I really do, even though it's taken me until now to realise it.

I do wonder how many other fifty-three-year-olds have had the same thought.

In fact I often wonder whether the whole thing we did — the music, the politics, the sex, the artisticness, the disdain for the corporate, the obsessive contemplation of our individuality, the principled rule-breaking, the desperate scrabbling for *charisma* — wasn't out of some latent sense of destined inadequacy, some terrible inbuilt feeling in our guts, our thighs, our hands, feet and ankles and hearts as well as in our brains, that when you got right down to it, we were never going to measure up. We were trivial by comparison. We grew up knowing that big things had been done in our name and that those big things were big enough — that you can't get any bigger than that, not meaningfully. That the big stuff has been done. And that however hard we tried to make our own lives big, it would never amount to more than a giant, bouncy, inflatable bigness. Hot air. We grew up listening to the golden stories of our parents' childhoods: their suffering, their resourcefulness, their triumph, their modesty, their unique historical scale. We also grew up listening to the distant rumble of somebody else's Sixties, just out of reach beyond the mountain range of puberty, where everyone's having a great time and an important time — but sorry, no tinies allowed. We didn't signify.

The myth is that we never measured up in our

parents' eyes. But this is rubbish. We didn't measure up in our own. Someone else did the Fifties and Sixties. Someone else did the War. What did we do?

We benefited of course.

But what did we *do*?

* * *

So no tickles for a change, which is convenient. Something to be embraced, like sleep and love. A comfort even. But I should be careful about how I phrase that. Convenience? Comfort? Not to be confused!

Don't get me started.

Actually, do.

Here's a question. Is it just me, or has the difference in meaning between the two words 'comfort' and 'convenience' actually narrowed? I don't think it's just me. I think that, to most people, they mean more or less the same thing, because they so often go together in the way we think about the world. It's as if the two concepts have been married off — the Mr and Mrs of the feelgood world: 'May I introduce FG Factor Esquire and his good lady wife! For your comfort and convenience!'

Things are done on trains, on planes and in public spaces 'for your comfort and convenience'. 'Your comfort and convenience' is a euphemistic device deployed to disguise a play for our business. It's a phrase that comes without thought, a mantra. 'Well,' we are meant to intuit in response to it, 'if our comfort and convenience is such a priority for these service providers, then what else will they have to offer? Just how well attuned are they to my needs? Not to mention my desires and my sensitivities! What next . . .?!' Sometimes, of course, 'your comfort and convenience' is a cover for unpleasantness, as in sickbags on planes. So it's about euphemistic niceness too. It's the new genteel, from the same stable of gentility which permits tennis players to leave the court for 'a comfort break' instead of a wazz in a convenience.

After fifty years of intensifying, competitive, life-defining, all-out thermonuclear consumerism, 'comfort' and 'convenience' are strangely blurred, which is odd bordering on the outrageous given their mutual non-dependency, semantically speaking. Perhaps it's just that we feel such a sense of entitlement to both comfort and convenience in the modern world that the two things blur in the mind: they are constituent parts of what we think of as 'normal' — as our entitlement. Comfortandconvenience.com, *c'est moi*!

But they are not the same thing at all, not even close. Nor should they be allowed to get any closer in meaning. In fact it is almost the last political conviction left to me that it is our moral duty to preserve the distinction between comfort and convenience at all times and in all practical and philosophical contexts. In the same way that we preserve the distinction between bread and foie gras. One is more or less essential to life; the other a grace note, an indulgence.

But then I would think that.

I spoke to Bére again this morning. My mum is not in good shape. 'I just can't get comfortable,' she says. Her body is, she thinks, forgetting how to *be* comfortable. I can see that at some point soon this is going to become very inconvenient for me.

10

Pig

'Steve. No!'

Lucy put the phone down. She wasn't cross but she was irritated. If she'd been truly cross she would have talked it out there and then; taken the sting out of the issue at least, if not out of the feeling. But the fact was that she wasn't cross; she just wasn't in the mood. She was irritable. Her mind was elsewhere. Everything was jagged.

Everything was wired differently now. That was how it felt.

Yes, she *was* cross, actually, now she thought about it — but not with anyone in particular, despite Steve's best efforts to make himself the object of her ire. This was his third phone call about 'the practicalities' of their separation. No, she was cross with the awkward position she found herself in, all adrift like a soggy paper boat in a sink of sadness, disorientation and, for heaven's sake, inflamed curiosity. What was going on? How had this happened? What was one supposed to take from it all, this chain of discrete but linked occurrences? Lucy supposed she ought, at the age of thirty-eight, to be able to cruise her own backwaters smoothly enough, modifying her rigging at will according to prevailing conditions, changing tack, dropping anchor, launching the cutter, her moods serenely unaffected by whatever fate or the weather or the barnacles on her hull had to offer in the way of drag. Wasn't that the point of being grown up — that you were in control of, if not events themselves, then one's own reactions to events? Shouldn't one, at thirty-eight, be one's own helmswoman, navigator and captain? She stopped herself from sighing out loud but couldn't forestall the sour reflection that *that* was all very well, but how you performed in your multiplicity of sought-after executive roles still depended to a large extent upon the state of your backwaters . . .

Yes, well, all right, she was cross. Above all, she was cross with Guillaume/William, who really ought to have known better at his age.

What was that all about then? His letter?

Sex, probably. Middle-aged men who work in department stores probably don't get much.

But then again, men who do that for a living possibly don't need much either, otherwise why would they work there? Or was that his subtle secret . . . ? Work in bedlinen; become expert in the uses of bedlinen — what better way to meet women? Women who are thinking about bedtime.

She made a 'thth' sound in the cavities of her face which might have been the beginnings of a laugh, and then wondered why. She really ought to be shuddering.

What was it he used to do? What was his job?

He was a musician! That's what he was. A guitarist and singer. He had a band she'd just about heard of with a name that was a bit

. . . gypsy. A London band; been around a while. Played pubs and clubs and the occasional support slot with bigger bands in bigger venues. Fairly successful, she supposed, but by no means a household name. A cult band. She recalled the afternoon of their first encounter: his thin legs in their narrow black jeans; his black denim jacket. The pointy boots. Wrangler! That's what the jacket had been. A classic Wrangler dyed, unforgivably, the colour of wet ash. The dishcloth knotted round his neck, which was probably supposed to be a reckless scarf. The look of animal terror in his face. Shocked hair. His hands.

So yes, maybe sex. Or perhaps not. Perhaps sex for him had never been an issue . . . No, not plausible. No one would be in a band with a gypsy name if they didn't want sex. No, hang on, no, not gypsy, but to do with drinking and nature. VineHeart! That was it. She'd listened to their one and only album at the time after she found out what Guillaume did for a living and had been disappointed — not because it wasn't any good — it clearly was 'good' — but because, well, because it required such a lot of effort to *enjoy* what was going on, music-wise. She remembered it as a brambly thicket. There were tunes in it, she supposed, but you had to dig them out of a tangle of guitars and drums whose primary objective seemed to be to obstruct access to the tunes. She remembered feeling simultaneously both over- and underwhelmed by it. Plus she hadn't liked his voice much. Too reedy. She realised that she had no memory whatsoever of what the songs were about.

So why bedlinen?

I know I must look rather different now, he'd written, *to how I looked then and I have tried to match that difference by becoming a slightly different person.*

Come on, Guillaume. A name change. A job change. A look change. A whole-new-person change. What's that about? Isn't that what teenagers do when they aren't getting enough traction in their scene? Isn't that what criminals do when they're hiding from the law? Well, perhaps you hadn't noticed, Guillaume, but you got off. You faced the music and you walked free. You are an innocent man. Totally innocent. You had me to thank for that. And you're not telling me that grief over the accident caused you to effect such wholesale changes in your life, because, because . . . well, because I'm not buying that. A life cannot be defined by one event. Nor rejected on the basis of one event. You can't ditch an entire life story on the grounds that you didn't like a turn the story took — that is ridiculous. No, it's worse than that. It's pretentious. It's childish. It's insulting. Insulting to everyone else involved in that story . . .

Lucy realised that she was writing a reply to Guillaume/William's letter in her head. That's the trouble with letters. They want answering.

Well, not this one.

Unless she were to write to the store to complain about Guillaume/ William's clear breach of his professional code — and probably of some privacy law — in sourcing her address

101

from the store's data records. She could do that.

Oh, come on, who are you kidding? You're not going to do that . . .

The phone rang. It was Lucy's mother, wanting to catch up on Lucy's news, or so she said, but also to recount the latest outrage from the riot-torn streets of Aldeburgh. Lucy thought she'd better make her own news punchy so that they could cut quickly to the important part of the conversation.

'Mum, Steve and I have parted company.'

'Oh. Really? But I thought you did that years ago?'

'We stopped our private relationship two years ago but we stayed in business together. You knew that.'

'Oh yes, I suppose I did . . .'

'And now we've decided not even to do the business any more. It's OK. We haven't fallen out. Well, I hope not. But Steve is finding it harder to let go than me, I think. I'm fine about it, but . . .'

'Oh, darling, I am sorry to hear that. Although, as I'm sure I've said before, I've never been sure that Steve was really the type to be getting into bed with business-wise, any more than he's the type to get into bed with . . . well, you know what I mean. Nice enough boy, but I always thought he was a little lightweight intellectually for you . . .'

'Mum.'

'So how have you divided proceeds, as it were? Is it much of a carve-up? Do you need advice? Tell me there isn't debt! Would you like your father to look at it, discreetly? I'm sure it must be possible to audit the situation . . . remotely. Let me have a word with him when he gets back with the dog. It's the second time he's been out with Archer today. He's letting off steam, I'm afraid, and possibly looking for someone to have a fight with. You wouldn't believe what happened outside the butcher's this morning . . . '

'Oh, I'm sure I would, Mum.'

And on the monologic conversation rolled, according to firmly established precedent. Lucy's parents had moved to Suffolk from Finsbury Park when Lucy followed her brother out of the family home, not long after the Guillaume incident in fact. Her parents were academics; not particularly high-flying ones. The move was designed to change the pace of life yet allow for more 'wriggle room' in the diurnal round. And yes, Martha Taplow had indeed taken the opportunity to continue to write slender, footnoted books about aspects of female life during the medieval and pre-medieval periods, which achieved very little in the way of a popular readership nor much academic esteem, but kept on coming nonetheless. She was currently attempting to piece together a life-and-myth of Etheldreda, the seventh-century East Anglian princess — saint, and was struggling. The latest dismal news was that she hadn't been able to sell the idea to her most recent publisher.

Lucy's father Robert, meanwhile, continued to teach the rudiments of business studies on an ad hoc, peripatetic basis, although he'd been technically out of the academic loop for a decade, having taken early retirement at fifty-five following a heart scare. They'd moved out to Aldeburgh, the Suffolk seaside town of Martha's childhood, and were constantly in a state of towering dudgeon over the 'hooligan behaviour' of the town's newest demographic wave — 'new' in the sense that the numbers constituting the wave hadn't amounted to a wave thirty years ago: then, the *arrivistes* had merely amounted to a slow drip, persistent but not disturbingly so. Now the wave was crashing on the shore, destroying the coastline.

Martha was just getting into her long, raking stride.

'. . . quite extraordinary,' she was saying. Lucy settled back on the kitchen chair — this could take a while. 'Dad's ankles were actually locked, as in *physically trapped*, between the footplates of two giant, multi-storey baby buggies from hell, with a third one apparently waiting on the flank like Stanley at Bosworth, poised to swoop in and finish him off once his ankles snapped through and he fell to the ground, defenceless. Dad had to physically push the two buggies apart just to free himself, and all that did was elicit scowls from the owners, who seemed to notice him for the first time when he laid hands on their personal property. They seemed quite ready to report him to the local constabulary for it. Did they apologise for virtually chopping his feet off? Did they hell. Did they ask after his well-being after he'd extricated himself, poor man? No, they looked at him like some lower form of life, some scrofulous insurgent from beyond the exclusion zone who'd dared to intrude upon their exclusive . . . *dimension*, and then went back to talking about whatever it is these people talk about. House prices, no doubt, and school fees. Oh no!' Martha paused, as if stricken, which is a difficult trick to pull off convincingly on the telephone. 'Silly me. Of course they don't talk about school fees, do they, because if you do that, it runs the risk of suggesting that you don't have enough money . . .'

And on Martha raged. It was clear that unless Lucy stopped her, she would carry on indefinitely. Oh well — let her have her rant. The daughter had long-since learned how to tune out the mother's tone, if not her content.

The truth of it was that Lucy felt sympathy with the content, she really did — just couldn't stand the sound of it. After all, Lucy was herself dismayed more than a little by what had lately become of her favourite childhood holiday destination. Dismayed? No. Revolted. But it wasn't only the colonisation of Suffolk's prettier locales by regiments of 'Cameronian good-lifers' that had kept Lucy off the trains to the coast in recent times, but the chopping, metallic *snitch* of her mother's tone when complaining about them. Lucy heard garden shears.

'I really think,' Martha was saying, 'that we will have to consider selling up *again* and going back inland, to Saxmundham or somewhere like that. Bungay even. Beccles! Norwich, if it weren't so ludicrously far from civilisation. Somewhere these people haven't yet bought up and turned into Notting Hill-on-Sea. I really do, mad as it sounds. Be cheaper too. Because it's really not doing your father's health any good, getting into a state like this over the purchase of a microscopic bag of hand-crafted sausages. It's just not worth it. And I'll tell you something else for nothing . . .'

And Lucy just rolled with it. The truth was that she did rather enjoy the details of her mother's 'social cleansing' riff. Not just the knockabout observational stuff about rapacious, self-serving, sharp-elbowed bonus boys in pink polo shirts, their dead-eyed women and their giant SUVs which blot out the very rays of the sun — Lucy had on her phone a rather cleverly taken picture of two such vehicles, parked nose to tail, appearing to tower like Blenheim Palace over the hunched little shop frontages in the high street. But also — in fact more so, because it honed a real edge onto their joint indignation — the serious stuff: the stuff about what happens to a local economy when it is colonised by an aggressive tribe with money to spend on anything they can think of that will give them a sense of insulation from the lower orders. Historically speaking, Aldeburgh, Southwold and Walberswick had scarcely been bastions of Anglian *sans culottage*, yet they had always in the relatively recent past — well, the twentieth century — been places which catered amicably enough to all comers and at least allowed all comers to feel relatively at ease in their timeless purlieus; as if all comers might *belong* here, if only on a summer's lease.

But now . . . Well, put it this way, Lucy would

106

not be surprised in the nearish future to see checkpoints sited strategically on the undulating, gorse-edged causeways which conveyed the columns of Range Rovers in and out of their coastal destinations; checkpoints manned with screw-eyed farmers' sons toting shotguns half concealed in the folds of waxed jackets, requiring all drivers to show documentation of their old school and college, their current firm and family title (where applicable) before granting them leave to enter the scrubbed-twee streets of the town in which you may purchase handmade monogrammed organic sausages from The Butcher Who Saw You Coming.

★   ★   ★

The riff had still not reached its final cadence some quarter of an hour later, when Lucy forced the issue. 'Mum. MUM! I've got to go — I'm expected elsewhere,' she'd said, conjuring in her mind a large, ugly rock perfectly designed by nature for shoving between the snapping blades of a pair of shears. 'I'm already late,' she further lied, and then regretted saying it. Still, the fifteen minutes-plus already swallowed up by Steve and then the further thirty-five consumed by her mother constituted the best part of an hour she'd never see again, and neither exchange had been bringing light to the world, let alone real edification to Lucy. It was all just time used up, as far as she was concerned, and she'd already expended far too much of her life on the bootless activity of making time pass.

107

She looked at the clock. It said nine thirty-five. She thought, *Oh God, well at least I'm still alive.*

Then wondered why. What was that supposed to mean? What new existential horror-stroke-pretension was this? Had she begun to narrate her own observations and thought processes back to herself, as if she were outside herself and looking in?

And then realized that the thought came with a fragment of melody . . . It was a song; in fact an inaccurately recalled lyric from a song by David Bowie, about the mocking, curiously flexuous properties of Time.

Lucy smiled briefly. A good song was always welcome and this was the kind of incursion from the past that she really didn't mind. Perhaps this is what it is to have grown up: it's when your whole life is constantly re-invaded by its own past, as a reflex, on a loop, like some sort of automatic digital-marketing thing, day by day by day . . .

She reflected upon how she'd been far too young for David Bowie at the time of his greatness but had fallen obsessively in love with the earlier records as his career had taken its decisive turn for the less-than-great in the 1980s — the decade of Lucy's teens. Retroactively, *Aladdin Sane* and *Hunky Dory* had thrilled her but *Low* had been the one that changed her life. She'd borrowed it one summer from her schoolfriend Delilah — who'd inherited it from an elder brother — and it had seized Lucy's imagination like a disease and not let go for many more summers.

108

The seizure had been a freeing one — a sort of liberation. The sealed, air-conditioned, single, blue room-space described by the music on *Low* had allowed Lucy to unclothe her covered-up self in perfect safety and discretion, or so it seemed to her, and she had loved *Low's* author frequently in there, usually wordlessly. She had spent many hours with him contemplating life as they lived it between their four windowless walls and had swallowed the pleasure of it all like milk.

The phone rang again. It was her mother.

'No, no — I won't keep you! It's just that you were in such a hurry to get away just now that I forgot to get round to the reason for ringing you in the first place. My birthday this year. We'll do the usual, if that's all right with you — the weekend, if you can spare the time, but just the day if you can't face the Zed bed. However, now you're no longer needed on the market, I expect it won't be quite so awkward for you to get away. I've spoken already to Oliver and it's all right with him — he's bringing the kids, but not Jude. She is of course in production. I have told Oliver we won't have room for the nanny, whatever her name is, and frankly I think it'll do him some good to do some proper hands-on parenting for once — I don't think I've seen either one or both of them with the kids, in any permutation, without some trailing entourage of staff of one kind or another, not in *years*. I do find it shaming.' Martha sighed. 'But if I can tell him you're definitely coming, and occupying the Zed bed, then it is obviously completely impossible as well as unnecessary for Whatsernanny to come too — and he doesn't need to know that you may not be staying overnight. You could always come together in that ridiculous vehicle of his, I suppose, if you can face it.'

'Mum . . .'

'Good that's settled. See you in three weeks. We'll confirm how and when and for how long a few days before, shall we? Byee!'

PART TWO

11

Lunch

Jolly Bizzle is back in town. Well, he's threatening to be. Which is all right. He was the one member of VineHeart I kept in touch with afterwards, for quite a while, although that was because he was the one individual in the group who appeared not to despise me. I say appeared because I mean appeared. But I trust him. I would even go so far as to say that I like him. Always did. He was the one I liked, despite everything.

As a social group, bass players are universally inscrutable and invariably more tolerant and thoughtful and measured than the rest of us in their responses to what goes on, and so I suppose it's probably fair to say that a fundamental bass-player virtue is that they allow guitarists and drummers and singers to be themselves, without let or hindrance. They keep the world safe for fly boys and fuckwits. Sounds like a generalisation, and it is one. But it's also true. I have never met a decent bass player who didn't cut slack for others, usually with a suppressed sigh. Having said that, it's also true to say that I never met a bass player who wasn't also a secret moralist and sometimes a little fond of heavy footwear. Comes with the territory. It's what happens when your whole existence is governed by the need to land with absolute precision on The One. Bass players can never be late without causing offence, most especially to themselves.

Jolly Bizzle is a fine bassist and a good guy.

Is?

Was a fine bassist. He was a good guy last time I saw him.

But I don't think he's picked up his instrument for money in ten years nearly. Maybe more. And that's the point. He's back in town because he wants to get it out again. He turns fifty in a couple of months and, for the occasion, he wants to form a Fiftieth Birthday Band to play at his birthday party, which is to be held at a former working men's club in north London, close to where he grew up and not that far from where I now live. Wants to reconnect with his north London friends. My roots, he says, 'in the words of the cliché'. And for the climactic feature of the event, the big finish, he wants to re-form VineHeart. The whole escapade is designed to map his career trajectory from the mid-Eighties, when Jolly was the far-too-accomplished twenty-two-year-old bassie in the worst ska band in London (where I spotted him), through his VineHeart period (which, if I may say, was where his reputation was built), to his post-VineHeart activities as a classy session-eer — and that means inviting everyone he ever played with down to the club, including a couple of names, to jam onstage while he does his timeless impersonation of James Jamerson Jr to the acclaim of roaring crowds. Mr Funky Reliable.

Mr Fucking Deluded more like. Sounds horrendous, the whole concept. We can assume that the names won't show up. That's a given. But anyone from the ska band who's still alive will be no more capable of disciplined skanking in their dotage than they were in the prime of their youth, and they were rubbish then. Then there's the sessioneering, which finally broke Jolly's heart, as proper bass playing became a marginal art in a rhythm world increasingly dominated by pinky-programmed sequencers. He attended many, many really quite impressive sessions in the Nineties — going 'plunk', basically, within the rigid matrix of a pro-grammed beat — which paid OK but screwed with his love of music, until the day dawned for him when he could stand it no more either, and he finally deposited the last of his eggs into the basket he was originally trained to nestle in at some reputable provincial art school. After maintaining a casual and not unprofitable sideline throughout his music career, Jolly became a full-time graphic artist, bunged his session money into it and launched a company with a mate. They operate out of some new-build office space in south London and have a staff of five, who wear strange, overtight clothes with tiny collars and too many buttons and speak the language of digital youth. Talented, bright, go-getting guy, Jolly.

But deluded guy.

Re-form VineHeart? Even for a night? I cannot begin to think how I am going to explain to him that I would rather die than drill into that

115

hornet's nest with my penis. He's coming up west to 'lay the groundwork', as he puts it, which will include a brief, persuasive visit to the bedlinen department en route to N16 where the club is (he has been reliably informed that you have to schmooze the club's management committee live and direct if you want the booking of your choice together with agreeable treatment on the night). I have no idea whether he has contacted the other members of VineHeart yet, but I'd be very surprised if he had. Last I heard, Simon was teaching in a posh boys' school in Guildford and Godfrey was nowhere to be seen, possibly even dead, after disappearing to America a dozen years ago at least, without his drums. At all events, none of us are musicians any more. Not properly.

But the Jollyman, Jolyon Bizzle Esquire of the London Borough of Bizzlington, is a man I will be delighted to see, for all my sense of impending horror at his fell purpose. I just hope he continues to not live up to his name: never was a man more inappropriately abbreviated than Jolyon Bizzle.

Jolly?

Not on your nelly.

★　★　★

And here he is. Shambling along the carpet causeway from the escalator, cutting corners, raising both his eyebrows in my general direction although not smiling, and then, yes, a hint of teeth when he sees me smiling at him. Then a giant hand extended out in front of him like a pincer. It's great to see him.

Actually, he doesn't seem quite as tall as he used to and, obviously, nothing like as scrawny. I suppose the slightly thinned hair ought not to be a surprise but the grey beard is. Last time I saw him, the beard was pretty much black and much more sculpted. Not now. He is lugubrious, contained, condensed, weighty — the fully-fledged Bizzle. It is surprisingly difficult to see in him the mantis-thin, slightly twitchy kid I first encountered nearly thirty years ago disdainfully anchoring the Worst Ska Band in London. It is as if that Jolly had never been.

But then look at me.

And that is exactly what he does, without smiling. He is as inscrutable as ever.

'How long's it been, Gil? William, sorry.'

'No idea, Jolly. But a long time. Seven? Eight? Nine?'

'Must be.'

'You well?'

'As can be expected.'

'You look well.'

'I am.'

'Business good?'

'Yep.'

Well, at least some things haven't changed. Jolly was always a minimalist small-talker — as in subatomic. But he does look pleased to see me, as I am to see him. He is slightly early for our appointment but instead of offering to wander round the building for a browse, he takes himself off to lean quietly against the glass wall next to the escalator, thirty feet away. As I work through the last ten minutes of my shift, he barely shifts his weight from one foot to the other; he doesn't even alter the arrangement of his upper limbs. He might be part of the display; the first mannequin of colour in the store.

'So tell me why not, William,' he says twenty-five minutes later in Affamato, a pseudo-Italian coffee and pasta bar down the side of the store, over a chop. 'Where's the harm?'

We have discussed his family, his business, our respective health concerns and we have carefully steered round the subject of what remains of his unofficial love life, which was always more extensive than he was able to deal with comfortably. I have also told him, straight up, that the circumstances do not exist in which I would consider re-forming VineHeart. I have reminded him that VineHeart was technically 'my' band and that he does not have the moral right to re-form it himself.

Jolly will not express disgust, not as such, but he will convey a sense of exasperated disbelief at my trickiness. He obviously sees in my resistance a pose, a vanity, a dramatisation of self. The idea of his Fiftieth Birthday Band Reunion Thing is nothing more complicated to him than a goodwill gesture towards the rest of mankind. A bit of fun. All right, it's a slightly narcissistic bit of fun but it is, in the end, *only* fun. He thinks that it is pretentious and, yes, quantifiably much more narcissistic to consider his proposition in any terms other than those implied by the words 'goodwill' and 'fun'. And he knows he has me there. He knows that I know that I look like a fatuous curmudgeon, and he is playing me, the soft-tongued devil.

But I will not budge.

The exasperated disbelief shades into a smile at last.

'You know what, William . . . ' says Jolly, and then visibly changes his mind. He's not going to tell me that I am a shameful, cowardly, self-pitying tosser and then laugh. He's not even going to cannonade me with euphemistic psychobabble. Not his style. 'You know what? If you didn't eat children's food you might not feel so much like a kid yourself.'

I stare at him. My pizza quietly cools on its plate.

'Don't get me wrong — I'm not saying I think you're childish for being so stubborn. But I think you'd feel less childish *yourself* if you didn't treat yourself like a kid. I mean, really, man.' Jolly shovels oily potato into his mouth and sits back to chew, raises his eyebrows to their highest feasible elevation. 'Anyway, come on, what's eating you? It must be twenty years since . . . the band. The bullshit explosion. The meltdown. The . . . bad vibes. The accident. So that's e-*nough* of that shit — time to be moving on, don't you think? Wassup? Is you lonely, bro? Is you sore? Or is you just stuck in a rut?'

'Now, Jolly — '

'And you can wipe that indignant look off your face. This is coming from a loving place, not an angry one or even a slightly pissed-off one. It might sound a bit patronising, I suppose, what

I'm saying, but you leave me with no alternative — you've handed me not just the right but the duty to be patronising. And I'm buying lunch, so . . . ' he leans forward and speaks out of the side of his mouth, conspiratorially, ' . . . you can fuck off. I will always be grateful to you, William,' he says, looking at me sideways as if to emphasise the drift of his sidelong speech, 'so believe me, it is quite easy for me to find it in my heart to tell you what's what. Quite easy.'

'Jolly — '

'No, let me finish.' He holds up one palm, halfway between his face and mine. 'I can take the sheets and pillows and solitariness and introspection and all that, but I'm not talking about that — and you know I'm not. It's the rock-star attitude, man. The big artistic posture. It just doesn't go with the sheets and pillows. It doesn't go with the reformed-bad-guy stick or the plain-living retail-executive-forward-slash-martyr image. It doesn't go with anything in the grown-up world. It just doesn't work as a vibe, man. I mean, where's it going? How does it end? Way I see it . . . ' Jolly looks down at his plate for a moment while formulating his next aperçu, then up again just in time to stop me from butting in (I am dying to tell him, just for starters, that the word is 'schtick', with a 'sch'). 'You can't have it all ways and expect people not to . . . react. Especially the people who love and respect you. Huh? You can, of course, butter your bread on both sides, but it will leave a smear on your face, somewhere. Always. You hear me?'

He takes his hand away and sits back in his

seat, evidently fairly pleased with his Ciceronian flourish. I look at my pizza, which is now emitting the vibe of an overfilled food-recycling bucket.

'I hear you, Jolly. And you're probably right.' I realise that I am in danger of starting to look pitiful and that Jolly is doing his best not to pity me, and this is not how I wish to be perceived — so I may as well back up the feeling with straight talk. 'I *am* lonely. I *am* stuck in a rut. And I'll take it from you this once. But listen: fuck off to you too. It's my rut. My loneliness. I live with it, not you. And that's the way it is — same way it's the way it is in your way of life. I wouldn't *dream* of telling you about yours. Look, I'm really pleased the business is going well and I'm delighted you want to do this Birthday Band thing. Delighted the family's well. Delighted you can tune in to your past without feeling anything other than delight in it. You are a lucky man. But I'm not doing the gig. I couldn't. It's not rock-star bullshit. It's me. Just me. My life. I own my life and I own VineHeart. I wish there was more to it than that.'

The Jollyman is impassive, but he is at least listening. I go on.

'Look at me! I am a middle-aged bloke who works in a department store — who likes working in a department store. It's what I do. My job. And I like it, even if, as a way of life, working in a department store doesn't amount to a socially desirable 'passion'.' As a reflex, I supply the quotes with two forefingers and then wish I hadn't. 'OK, maybe that makes me a

121

failure according to most value systems. Well, most TV-calibrated value systems, and I realise that they're the ones that count. But I don't give a *shit*, Jolly. I have stopped — as in completely stopped — feeling like and being a cunt, and that matters much more to me. It may not make me ecstatic, but it doesn't make me miserable either. And anyway, what the fuck is a 'passion' when it's at home? Eh? It's just a way to get around, if you ask me. A fucking trolley. A free ride on something. I do not and will not subscribe to the view that you are who you can persuade other people to believe you are. That is pernicious, lying shit and you know it is.' I realise that I am pleased with my own Ciceronian flourish and, worried that it might be visible, I quickly change down two gears. 'It's also a fact that I haven't kept my chops up — I last picked up the Tele just before Christmas and it was like blundering around in a cellar with the lights off, hideous and disorientating and depressing and I couldn't wait to get out of there. A bit frightening too. Left me a bit bruised.'

Jolly is opening his mouth and raising a knife, furtively, like a periscope, an inch at a time.

'No, Jolly, shut up and let me finish. Yes, I could practise — I could probably get up to snuff in a month or so, and it would probably do me good to do it. Yes, I could do it out of love and respect for you and for what the band stood for and for the sheer bloody pleasure of playing again in what I can see would be a pretty stress-free environment. I can see all the advantages or whatever you want to call them.

122

It's a sweet idea. But I can't go there. It doesn't mean I don't love and respect you or have forgotten the good things about VineHeart or any of that stuff — of course I haven't. But that isn't the point. The point is that the tide has gone out. And it isn't coming back in again. Ever. Gravity won't permit it. It's gone down the plughole.'

'You are a coward, you know that, don't you, William?'

'Look, I don't care — '

Hang on a minute!

'Shut up, Jolly. Shut your fucking face. Don't go there, all right! I'm not one of your boys and you don't talk to me like that, even out of love. OK? Ever.'

'OK, I take it back — '

'I should hope so.'

' . . . but I'll tell you what you're stuck in, William. I'll tell you it for nothing because it's true and there's no way I'm going to let you cuss me for it, because you know it's true too. It isn't a rut you're stuck in. It's a comfort zone.'

And we both sit back in our seats simultaneously with some violence, so that the front legs of our chairs lift off the floor and then land again with a surprisingly loud double report. Blat-blat! We both then lunge forward over our plates so that the table shifts and an item of cutlery crashes to the floor.

We speak simultaneously too, in voices compressed into razored whispers — but my whisper wins the battle for airspace. I do not hear his.

'Listen to me, you *fucker*,' I hiss through bared teeth, suppressing the urge to jab my finger in his face while pretending not to notice that the dozen or so other faces present, distributed randomly around the seating in Affamato, are turning in our direction. 'I *was* going to say to you that I'd lend you any support you like for the do — anything you like. Apart from VineHeart. I'd do technical stuff. I'd help with the set-up. I'd turn up and join in with the thing from the floor in the spirit *you'd* wish me to. I'd round up the natives. I'd make a fucking speech . . . '

'Oh, don't bother, Gil. Don't put yourself out . . . '

But he is too late because I am already dusting myself off and moving to pick up from the floor what turns out to be a fork.

'And I'll tell you one more thing I was going to do.'

12

Ices

The weather in Suffolk was its usual dry, gusting self. The wind made its way straight there from the Urals without hindrance, or so Lucy's mother Martha liked to claim. Lucy didn't doubt it for a moment. Even inland, in bright sunshine, six or seven miles shy of the coast in the car park at Saxmundham station, the wind slapped her around. She sat on a disintegrating pebbledash bollard and waited for her father's car to approach their agreed rendezvous point on the roadside, thirty feet away. The birthday present Lucy had bought for her mother sat between her knees in its wrapping paper on top of her overnight bag. It had happened before, this moment. Perhaps a dozen times on and off over the past twenty or so years. Maybe more.

It would have happened every single year if Martha had had her way. She did not like her birthday to pass without 'a family moot'; and when the tribal gathering did contrive to depart from traditional pattern by so much as a turned hair, then an inquisition would follow hard. What had gone wrong? Was the family disintegrating? Would we ever pass this way again? We really must resurrect the tradition next year, without fail — yes? And everyone present, Robert, Oliver and Lucy (and Oliver's wife Jude, if she wasn't 'in production'), would assent as if their future happiness depended upon it. For in repetition Martha found stability and comfort, and was fond of saying so — although not in so many modern English words. 'In rited acts plumb we the deeper sooth,' insisted Reginald FitzUrse in 1170, after spreading Thomas Becket's brains around the stones of Canterbury Cathedral with the toe of his mailed foot, or something; and Martha had certainly said the same thing over birthday breakfast several times since.

Lucy looked up. The small blue Ford was drawing to a protracted stop on the double yellow line on the road which ran alongside the station car park, and she hurried to intersect with it before its driver had time to grow anxious, carefully inserting her baggage onto the back seat and then flinging herself into the front with an enthusiastic exhalation.

'Haaaaaaah. Daddy, hello.'

'My darling girl. Strap yourself in. It's going to be one hell of a ride.'

And they peeled slowly away from the double yellow and began the epic third-gear pootle to the coast as if sailing reluctantly in a small, slow boat towards the very edge of the world.

★　★　★

At the edge of the world there was already an atmosphere. Lucy's brother Oliver had driven up from Islington with the kids (but without the nanny) the night before and Martha's serenity was under siege. Little Eds, eight, and even littler

Edie, six, had declared themselves officially bored that morning, shortly after breakfast, and were filling the gaping hole in their lives by emptying their grandparents' downstairs cupboards and then fighting over ownership of whatever worthwhile booty they found there, before marching upstairs to deposit it in proprietorial heaps on their respective beds. The ransacking of Martha's barbican was almost complete and it was obviously only a matter of time before the Visigoths moved into the streets of the city and torched her inner well-being for good measure.

'Jesus H. Christ,' she muttered into Lucy's ear beneath the sound of wailing from the top of the stairs. 'You'd think their father was some sort of child-rearing *eunuch*. He's just *terrified* of those bloody children and all squeaky around them. Can't say no to them; won't raise his voice — runs away when he can . . . '

'Hello, Mum, nice to see you. Happy birthday!'

'Yes, yes — thank you: lovely to see you too, darling. But you wouldn't believe what it's been like here since they arrived yesterday. They're worse than ever — a total living bloody effing nightmare of bad manners, worse discipline and absolutely no sense of where boundaries are or even what a boundary *is*. They wouldn't know a boundary if they were garrotted by one. No one ever says 'no' to them, ever, as far as I can tell.' She batted away an invisible fly from her swag of gunmetal hair and closed the kitchen door. 'And yet we appear to be required to find them *charming*. If I had any wits left, I'd be at the end of them and it's only Saturday morning. They riot all the time over everything on grounds of simple entitlement — they're efficient little Tories in the making, I suppose — and Edie seems to win the riot every time purely by dint of being able to shriek louder than anyone else and grab harder . . . and then everyone is apparently supposed to just stand back and laugh while she gets her own way. Oliver seems to admire and worship her for it. 'Ho-ho-ho,' he says out loud so that the bloody child can hear, 'Well, Edie certainly knows how to get what she wants' . . . '

'Mum, it's lovely to see you and I promise to impose my massive will on the children as soon as I'm sorted. But please make me a cup of tea, then sit down and tell me your news while I drink it and I'll tell you mine. And then I'll have a wash and take them out to the beach or something. Where's Ollie?'

'Oh, he's out making important phone calls . . . '

★ ★ ★

Within the hour Lucy found herself walking a couple of paces behind her niece and nephew towards the ice-cream parlour on the high street. The children appeared to be conferring rather than bickering, their words inaudible; not only could Lucy not hear what they were saying but, quite clearly, she was not meant to — their hands occasionally strayed reflexively to cover their mouths and then the sound of their voices was wholly engulfed by the wind. Lucy could not find it in herself to believe that an eight-year-old and a six-year-old were actually conspiring against her, but she could certainly countenance the notion that they were comparing notes — perhaps doing a joint inventory of what they proposed to get out of her on this short and obviously extraneous walk to the shore and back 'to see the Maggi Hambling'.

She didn't like them, but she felt a shaft of pity go through her all the same: poor kids, she thought, they are so fraught with an unnameable desire, a desire which twists and plaits and knots and thickens in them like hair, that even full-grown adults with no real interest in them suspect them of deviousness and conspiracy.

What must it be like to be that young and yet that unsure of what love is — of what it entails, what it requires? At that age, she thought solemnly, the one thing you ought to be able to take for granted is the uncontingent presence of love. Yet she'd always got the impression that both Eds and Edie knew little of love's essential, ever-giving balm, or of its reliability. Instead of a balm, love was a trophy to be won — a love-shaped *thing*; something winnable, exciting, rare, *bestowed*, which resulted in enhanced status and roaring delight in the moment but got passed on, soon enough, to the next winner. Love was not a warmly constant breeze engulfing the children. It was a gift given by hard-working parents — usually in the form of absolute acquiescence to the children's material wishes on those occasions when they, the parents, were around to acquiesce — in the expectation of forgiveness in return. Lucy did not doubt that Jude and Ollie loved their children, but their children were not accustomed to *getting* their love as a matter of course, and certainly not in any form other than as an act of compensation.

Love. Parental love — the only kind that really makes a difference to anything, she thought. Lucy herself had certainly been the recipient of plenty, in the slightly bracing style with which her mother and father had administered it. Bracing or not, she had always felt confident of its uncontingent presence. It was available, a constant, a *certainty*. So if she believed in that kind of love, why not the other? The glamorous, tinselly, thrillsome kind that also gets you fucked . . .

'Auntie Lucy,' said Eds, turning, stopping and then falling in beside her. Lucy stopped too. They were about to cross the road to the ice-cream parlour anyway.

'You don't have to call me Auntie, Eds. Lucy will do . . . '

'OK, Lucy,' he pressed on, surprisingly meekly. 'Are you a lesbian?'

Edie extended a hand for Lucy to hold while they crossed the high street. Lucy took it and they proceeded with perfect orthodoxy across the ribbon of tarmac to the opposing pavement, then squeezed sideways between an immaculate German bumper and the towering frontage of some sort of Rover. (Land? Range? It was as big as a stately home, whatever it was.) Lucy let the children's question percolate — and then

130

percolate some more while they decided on flavours in the retro-vitreous world of handmade ice cream.

'Do you think that's a polite question, Eds? The one you asked about what I am?' she said as they emerged from the parlour and started towards the beach. No response. Lucy changed tack. 'Have you been learning about gay and lesbian stuff at school?'

'No. But I know what a lesbian is.'

'Well, I'm glad to hear it. And what is one?'

'I know too,' interjected Edie. 'It's a — '

'It's a woman who doesn't like men,' said Eds first. 'Like a racist.'

'What do you mean, like a racist?'

'Well, lesbians don't like men, in the same way that racists don't like black people. Lesbians only like other women in the same way that racists only like other white people. Sorry if it's rude. I . . . I . . . '

'It's all right, Eds. It's not rude so much as not very respectful. And you haven't got it quite right either — lesbians don't dislike men, necessarily, but they do definitely prefer women, for, for, well . . . mostly for love. And I'm not one, since you ask, Eds. I like men and women the same, but prefer men for love . . . '

She let it hang and watched both children wrestling with what to say next, before giving up and returning their attention to their ice creams which appeared to be melting fast in spite of the wind. By now all three of them were trying to establish traction on pebbles. The Maggi Hambling was a good couple of hundred yards away up the beach, tiny and inconsequential at this distance, and it seemed like unwonted labour to get there in this gale, with ice creams. To hell with Maggi Hambling. Lucy followed the children to the water's edge.

'But if you're asking whether I'm a lesbian,' she yelled above the elemental din, 'because you think I ought to have a boyfriend or a husband, then I suppose . . . I suppose . . . ' This of course was not a conversation you could have with eight- and six-year-old children and she fell silent, leaving the elements to complete her sentence. Where had this lesbian idea sprung from? Was it something the children had overheard on the back seat of the car, or over the dinner table, or earwigged from a phone conversation? Or, more likely, was it something they'd construed for themselves from their fund of worldly knowledge, to ingratiate themselves? One thing was for sure: you'd never get a straight or comprehensible answer out of them.

Perhaps this was the reason she didn't really like children — and why she was quite sure that she did not want to have any of her own: because there were things you couldn't say to them, even if you did propose to love them unselfishly. Because you couldn't tell them the truth. Or at least, even if you did find a way to tell them the truth, you had to embroider it so that it made a nicer picture than the one you wanted to show. The honest one. The true one. The one that made everyone hurt and not want to forgive everyone else.

Perhaps that was it. Perhaps she resented

children for their entitlements. The abstract ones — their entitlement to love, primarily, but also to innocence.

It would be nice to have abstract entitlements.

* * *

By nine thirty that evening the Taplow moot was going tolerably well. It was traditional that birthday presents would be forthcoming after pudding but before the toast (dessert wine doing the office of mead), which was always proposed by Martha and which invariably took the form of a brief sermon on a theme taken from antiquity — usually based on a quotation in Middle English. Lucy suspected that Martha made most of the quotations up.

At Oliver's earnest behest, the children had been allowed to stay up until the end of the meal and, in truth, they had not behaved excessively badly at the table. Edie had tipped the contents of her water glass all over Robert's dinner plate, causing him to abandon his fish. It was not clear whether she'd done it on purpose. Then Eds had interrupted a hesitant discussion about health care in America by speaking in tongues. But that had been about the limit of the kids' transgressions, apart from much fussing over whether the food was edible or not. 'But I don't *like* peas,' Edie had insisted repeatedly and not very plausibly.

'Gub-gub-gub bub-gloooble waaaaaaaargh,' Eds had then bellowed, disgorging fragments of pea in a variety of directions at high velocity.

'That's right, you tell 'em, Eds!' Ollie had said.

'On second thoughts, don't,' Martha had said.

'Waaaaarf-waaaaarf aaaargh-a-bub-bub-a-booog-aaaaaah!' Eds was warming to his moment.

'Come on, Eds. Tell us what you want, but in English, so we can all understand,' Ollie had said.

'Waaaaaaaaaaaaauuuuurgh.'

'I think it's probably time for bed, don't you?' Martha had turned to face her son, and for a moment it appeared that Ollie thought she really meant it: that it was time for Ollie to climb into his pyjamas. But of course not. Not really. Ollie had looked panic-stricken nevertheless.

'Come on, you two, time for bed, I think,' he'd said, flapping his hands across the table as he'd pushed back his chair, and to everyone's manifest surprise Eds and Edie had descended from their stools and allowed their father to shepherd them 'up the wooden hill to Bedford Square' without so much as a peep. The whole operation took no more than forty minutes and Ollie reappeared at the table looking less hunted and entirely pleased with himself.

'Crikey, that was smooth,' he said. 'You must have knackered them out on the beach, Luce. They didn't have much to say about what you got up to, even though I gave 'em the third degree — all very mysterious but obviously successful. And I managed to get away with one story and only a couple of songs. Suffolk air, eh? It's a first, I think. Edie's out for the count — '

'Very good,' interrupted his mother. 'Now, before we get on to my few words, how about

134

giving me a present or two? Well, two. Robert, the bottle!'

And so while Robert busied himself pouring, Oliver disappeared outside to his car and Lucy fetched her gift from its conspicuous hiding place under the chaise longue in the living room and made her offering to her mother with due ceremony. Martha accepted it graciously with a small gasp and used the scimitar-shaped cheese knife to slit the tape carefully at each folded end, then slid the box inside from within its armature of paper as if removing an ancient volume from a damask sleeve in a library vault. What emerged from the box was a tasteful ceramic vegetable dish, green-blue, divided in the middle.

'I know you cracked yours,' said Lucy helpfully. 'And I know they discontinued that line, so I thought I'd replace it with something that would go just as well with the rest of the set, even if it's a different colour and style. It's still a divided one — and about the same size as your old Denby. I think it goes rather well, but if you don't like it I can always change it, no problem.'

Martha did not speak immediately. And then she did.

'Darling, it's very well chosen and I appreciate your thought. In fact it's rather nice and I would love to keep it anyway, had I the space in the cupboard. But guess what? There's a Denby factory shop in Southwold — well, not a factory shop but a place where they sell off discontinued lines cheaply. And I found a perfectly un-shop-soiled one there at half the price of the original, two or three weeks ago. Oh, darling, I'm so sorry.

The best-laid plans, eh? And so thoughtful of you. Would you mind awfully taking it back?' She fixed her daughter with a suppliant eye. 'I have no plans to come down to London in the very near future, so perhaps . . . In fact, if you're taking it back to a kitchen shop I can drop you a couple of hints of things you might like to exchange it for . . . '

There was a thump against the closed dining-room door and the door handle rattled. The rattle was accompanied by muffled cursing. And then the door flew open and Oliver struggled into the room bearing a lamé-wrapped gift the size, awkwardness and weight of a modest altarpiece.

'Good heavens,' said Martha, looking worried. 'Don't tell me you've been shopping again at the Unaffordable Art Fair.'

13

Mercy

It was bright and blustery when I went out this morning to get the bus. There's a short walk to the bus stop from my flat and I love the procedure when it's bright and blustery — that sense of collective physical instability, of a world teetering like a drunk on the border of the out-of-hand. In those conditions, the world makes itself a servant to hazard. Cyclists wobble, awnings flap, coat-tails snarl, hair snaps like washing on a line — and it is on such mornings that I am especially grateful to have kept the vast majority of mine, so that it can lash around my head like drying pants.

And then there's the joyful problem presented by things snatched from their moorings by the wind. Plastic bags pursuing each other in vortices too close to your mouth, ears and eyes; cardboard boxes that scuttle along the pavement in cephalopod bursts, pursued by tradesmen or, more often, not pursued at all, just getting in the way and under wheels. Grit. Smuts. Bits off trees. Wisps of other people's hair. Crisp packets everywhere.

Wind-borne crisp packets, you'd think, would upset me. But you'd be wrong. They don't. They always cheer me up. They might remind me of the worst thing that ever happened, but they also plug me into the crazy, untameable energy of a mindless thing in flight, the randomness, the compelling, surging, dipping, swooping, looping wandermania of a thing which has no power to think and feel, but has the power to move like a jet. Wind-borne crisp packets are expressive. Of course they are. What do they express? They express that it's *random*, life. It's compelling! It's exciting! Small boy, come on, chase me . . . So if I am going to be reminded by fate of what I hate and fear, then I am content to be reminded like this, with energy and spectacle. Makes sense. It's better than feeling the weight of what it's like to want to kill someone and finding yourself doing it.

I was feeling good this morning actually. I had slept well again. I had the iPod on, set to Shuffle, and my mind was rejoicing in the commentary on routine life provided by Radio William. Iggy Pop out the door and down the road, then, and into the newsagent's and out again. William's got his Oyster sorted; Iggy's the chairman of the bored. Then down the high street towards the junction and the bus stop outside the new station, with a horny exultation by Ray Charles about girls . . . But long before I get to the bus stop, Brother Ray gives way to 'Erbarme Dich' from the St Matthew Passion, and I'm trying to guess, from the solo violin, which version it is before the voice comes in: Hertha Töpper, Elisabeth Schwarzkopf or Michael Chance? I know it's going to be Michael Chance instantly, without having to think, because even against the bedlam of the morning traffic I can hear it's John

Eliot Gardiner's 'authentic' *St Matthew*, on sticky period instruments with funny tuning in a funny key, all *cranky*, rather than the big smooth Romantic panzer-orchestra German versions from the Fifties and Sixties, which are great too but always miss the point for me . . .

And the long unwinding loop of Bach's melody is beginning to have its terrible-but-thrilling way with me when I see Shirley Crabtree maybe twenty-five yards up the road on the other side, conversing with someone in a doorway next to a building site, where a betting shop used to be (lots of ugly buildings round here were flattened and 'regenerated' in time for the Olympics, on the off chance that one day someone from elsewhere might get off the train at the new Dalston station). I keep walking. The angle to the doorway is too acute for me to see who Shirley's talking to. Nevertheless, the music takes on new feeling.

Shirley Crabtree is the name I have given, perhaps not that wittily, to a local big figure, a figure as anchored into the local environment as the heavier street furniture. I think she's a he, but she could equally be a she. It's six feet plus of one, half a dozen feet plus of the other — I really can't tell. The important thing is to recognise that she wants everyone to treat her as if she's a she, even if she isn't one technically — and in spite of the fact that we're not really sure, and she possibly knows it. I call her Shirley Crabtree privately because Shirley is usually a woman's name but sometimes a man's, most famously in the case of the wrestler Big Daddy,

139

whose name really was Shirley Crabtree. Dalston Shirley is almost as vast as Big Daddy and very nearly as masculine in deportment, but she wears a minidress with a plunging neckline (she has magnificent knockers), big clumpy heels and thickly approximate make-up. Her eyebrows look as if they were fired at her with a catapult, her lipstick applied with a shovel. Plus she wears blingy, multi-pointed specs, à la Edna Everage. Her panniers of bleach-blonde hair jerk spastically around her chops as she chats.

Michael Chance is singing in German. I happen to know how it translates: 'Have mercy on me, Lord, in my bitter weeping.' And the English Baroque Soloists are climbing their rope, hand over hand, inch by inch — 'Erbarme Dich' is surely the most prayerful expression of pity in the Western canon, and the most dignified. Peter has just denied Jesus for the third time and the crucifixion is now as inevitable as dawn. Meanwhile Shirley rabbits away with her invisible chum in the doorway, shrugging her heavy shoulders and raising a finger to wag in her interlocutor's face — with irony, or is it now with menace?

I begin to wonder if this situation is going to blow up and I make sure, as I cross diagonally from the island in the middle of the road to the kerb, a dozen paces from Shirley's position by the doorway, that I am able to cut a path through the pavement rush to within earwigging distance of Shirley's great debate. Some of the passers-by turn to slide a slippery eye over her as they go about their business, but mostly they hurry straight past. And it's as I draw within spitting distance of Shirley's huge left shoulder, close enough to see the tip of the lightning tattoo peeping from the cuff of her three-quarter-length sleeve, close enough to hear her voice when she raises it and the jangle of the bangles on her flapping wrist, that I am at last able to see right into the doorway and to observe that the scuffed and dust-streaked door within the embrasure is closed, that the embrasure is otherwise quite untenanted and that Shirley is talking to empty space, clearly for the benefit of the rest of us. To show us all that she has friends, perhaps. Or perhaps for secret reasons.

Have mercy, Lord. I wonder how many kinds of loneliness there are.

I get on the bus with the last bars of 'Erbarme Dich', which promptly gives up its seat, so to speak, to a chirpy, woolly soul from New York called Anais Mitchell singing an awfully beautiful song about what it is to be a sheep farmer. Before we've even turned off Balls Pond Road, the phone rings.

It is Bérengère.

* * *

I find that you need to exhibit infinite patience with bedlinen customers. They expect it. But for the most part they expect it in a nice way; not hoity-toitily but meditatively, with real concentration and often with a sort of theatrical grace, as if enacting a ritual. In my view, anyone who buys a sheet quickly and without considering

141

their options with Epicurean intensity is not doing the job properly, and probably has hidden mental-health problems he or she is trying to deny. Sleep is too important to throw away — even when we're wide awake.

But imagine throwing sleep away when you're actually asleep. How crazy is that? It is certifiable. We all do it, though. We do it when we force ourselves awake from a dream we can no longer sleep through. The old forced quit. I don't have them often, those dreams — I don't sleep that often. But I do have them. I won't bore you.

Bérengère says that our mother now wakes herself up virtually every night to get away from her dreams. Maman is exhausted but she has to do it, can't stop herself from doing it — and she won't go back to sleep, not if she can help it. Most nights, she says, she gets up, creaks down the stairs and sits on her hard wooden armchair in front of what embers remain in the kitchen stove, forcing herself to stay awake for as long as possible by using the pain to fight dormition. What kind of crazy inversion is that?

I'm going to have to go over soon.

But for the meantime there are sheets and duvets and pillowcases to be sold to customers straining bravely for the comforts of comfort. They're entitled. We're all entitled. Comfort is not a privilege; it is a necessity. I really don't mind people taking comfort seriously. Makes a lot more sense to me to do that than to make an almighty hoo-ha over buying and preparing food, an activity which is essential obviously but, when exhibitionistically fussed over, is really about personal status; or to make a song and dance about convenience, which is really about personal status in its relationship with bone-idleness. No, we can't all rise to Egyptian cotton — not even our own-brand variety, which is really quite affordable these days — but the sun should never set on anything less than cotton percale.

Some of my happiest moments have been spent appreciating the cleansing solace of fresh sheets.

But I was not thinking about that when Lucy walked into the department. I was thinking about how I should talk to Shireen about her competitive attitude. She's been with us a year now and she still thinks that the bedlinen department is the Colosseum and that pillow sales are an excuse for a fight to the death, with tridents and nets and short stabbing swords. I was just fixing her with my most remotely forbidding paternal eye, prior to offering her the benefit of my best and gentlest advice, when she did what she always does when she sees a potential new mark approaching over the carpet. She went rigid, like a cat. My forbidding eye could not hold her.

I turned to see the object of Shireen's attention and found myself mere feet from the grinning visage of Lucy Taplow, who was marching towards our position next to the payment station and appeared to be clutching a specimen from our kitchenware department in its box, like an offering. Like a cake.

'Is that for me?' I said, stepping towards Lucy and extending my hands, partly to put a distance between myself and Shireen and partly, I have to confess, to blot Shireen out of the picture.

'Don't worry, William,' said Shireen simultaneously, emerging from behind me with a startling display of acceleration from a standing start, 'I'll take care of this.' And she actually put out a hand towards me — flat, thumb down — to indicate that she was taking care of this.

'Good morning, madam,' she said effervescently. 'Can I help at all today?'

'Actually,' said Lucy, 'it's William I need to talk to.'

Rather deftly, she turned sideways, as though showing me away from the scene, and I took the opportunity to smile, to step back in front of Shireen and to lead Lucy to a more congenial spot for conversation behind the pillow stacks. This was a simple enough operation to accomplish technically: one foot in front of the other and so on. But for some reason my whole body seemed to evaporate into the moment, like tiny popping bubbles; I felt as if I was pulse and nothing but. Pulse and electricity. What did Lucy want? I thought: This could go one of several ways — and I wasn't even sure which way I was keenest on. Actually, that's a lie. I was very sure. I just wasn't at all confident that it would go that way.

'How nice to see you,' I said. 'I really wasn't expecting to . . . '

'Thanks for your letter,' she interrupted, as if it had arrived that very morning (it can't have: I sent it weeks ago). 'Look, I'm on my way to the kitchen department to change this.' She raised the box in her hands. 'But I thought I'd drop by to say hello, as you suggested, and to say 'Thank you, but it really wasn't necessary'.'

'What wasn't?'

'To say thank you to me, for doing the right thing twenty years ago. I'd do it again — any half-decent person would. Although perish the thought that I'd ever have to see anything like that again.' She dropped her shoulders and flashed a stern look at me. 'And you know you shouldn't have written to me, don't you?'

Her gaze was rock-steady but I did not feel that her heart was. Out of the corner of my eye I could see Shireen at the till, studying something in the air over the escalators while leaning, ear first, in our direction.

'Well, I'm not so sure . . . '

'But it's OK. I don't mind that you did. In fact I enjoyed your letter, if that's not a weird thing to say about something so . . . so, well, *strange* and out of the blue. And I kind of presumed that you had stuff to talk about still, from the incident. To say to *me*, because I was there at the time.' This was getting harder and harder to read. I began to wonder if Lucy herself even knew where she was going with this; whether this was a prepared speech or whether she was busking it. 'I mean, that's why I don't mind that you wrote, because I can see that you needed to . . . *express something* . . . to someone who would know not just theoretically but *actually* what you're talking about. Well, I was there, and I'm here now.' She shrugged. Locked her gaze on again. 'So express away.'

'Well, I — '

'Or has it all been said now? What do you think? Have you said everything you want to say about it, or is there something else you want to say? You know, that you couldn't say in the letter? Something challenging or unexpected or forthright or something? I'm all ears. I'm a good listener, and once I've replaced this elegant vegetable dish with a convenient and desirable new ergonomic stick-blender, then I'll have the rest of the day to listen. I'll be five minutes.'

'But I — '

Lucy held up her hand and hunkered back on her heels. Shireen had now disappeared completely from view — where the hell was she? I manufactured an airy glance around the department, without rotating my head further than would seem entirely casual. Just a quick, responsible glance.

Nothing. The floor was clear.

'But I have to work,' I said, sounding as lame as a schoolboy.

Lucy's hand came down and hung by her side. She exhaled. Her eyes softened and misted. Greyer than grey; not a trace of blue. I inhaled. For the first time in our several encounters, I noticed what she was wearing. I noticed possibly because she was wearing noticeable clothes for the first time: an obviously authentic black vintage belted PVC raincoat, a blue-and-white hooped jumper and red neckerchief, jeans and clumpy boots. A black beret. Matelot-style.

She said: 'I know. I'm sorry. I was being facetious.'

'OK, I probably shouldn't have written to you, technically. No 'probably' about it actually. I just shouldn't have. But I hope you can see that it was . . . that it was a sincere thing. I really didn't expect a reply or for you to come here — and I said so in the letter, as I remember. I meant it. It was just incredibly overwhelming, in a really nice way, to remember who you were all of a sudden and to recognise maybe for the first time just how significant a figure you had once been in my life — and that that had never been acknowledged. I didn't even acknowledge it to myself, I suppose. You really did save me from a terrible fate, psychologically as well as legally, and you did it without having to change the facts of what happened that day: you didn't make it all right by changing reality to suit my needs or your needs or anyone else's needs, but by telling it like it is. Was. Sorry, I'm babbling . . . '

I put one hand on the perspex rim of a pillow stack and then to my forehead. Lucy had an opportunity to say something, but didn't, which I felt was a shame.

'And to be fair, Lucy,' I continued, suddenly able to be a little more cogent. 'To be fair, you did ask me first whether we knew each other — you were the one who crossed the line first . . . '

'The fourth wall of retail,' she said.

'Eh?'

'Never mind.'

'No, go on, tell me . . . '

'It really doesn't matter — it's a thing from when I was a drama student. The fourth wall . . . It's the wall which divides the reality of the auditorium from the made-up reality of the stage: you're not supposed to breach it; not according to the old rules. I was being facetious again. And the reason I was being facetious was because you're right about me crossing the line first. I did. You're absolutely right. I take all my facetiosity back.'

I think I smiled at 'facetiosity'. I know I did. I'm pretty sure I showed most of my teeth, which is never a good idea.

'Look, I really ought to be getting back to work.'

I don't know why I said this — Shireen's tiny head was no longer visible, unless she was concealing it behind the digital read-out stalk on top of the cash register. Lucy and I were quite alone in Bedlinen. But I wanted to get away, to not have to say anything else. We had said enough.

Lucy seemed to think this too.

'I know, I know. And I have to get my stick-blender.' She half turned, then turned back. 'But is everything all right? Am I forgiven for being . . . *a bit like that?* I really didn't mean to be sarky — it just came out because it came out. Are we friends?'

'Oh, I hope so, madam.'

She held out her hand and I took it. She smiled quickly and not, I thought, without a hint of embarrassment. I knew that I would see her again.

★ ★ ★

I saw her again almost exactly ten minutes later. Nine, actually.

She sauntered across the carpet wagging her stick-blender in its box like a trophy.

'I got it,' she said. 'It's incredibly ergonomic.'

'Well done.'

'And so easy to use. It says so on the box. Soup is a doddle.'

'Better and better.'

She breathed out again. Her hair seemed to map the burst-pattern of her exhalation, sending flares out in all directions despite the restrictions imposed by the beret. 'I'll be off then, back to sunny Brownswood Park,' she said. 'You can write to me any time you like, William.'

'I might just do that, madam.'

And instead of telling her that I knew perfectly well what a fourth wall was, I just smiled again and hoped that it wasn't another mistake.

14

Twilight

Lucy studied her reflection in the front window on the top deck of the bus. She had somehow managed to get herself onto a front seat — an unexpected bonus at this time of day — and the near-silhouette of her head, neck and most of her torso faced her down from the angled plane of the glass like a shadowy twin, its features only hinted at, expressing nothing, a hole in the blur of light and angles and juddering movement which composed the reflected interior of the rest of the top deck, everything tilted up and reversed and drained of colour. A ghost interior. Outside, the afternoon was drawing in. A darkening blue. Through the Lucy-shaped dark blue hole, Tottenham Court Road was a torrent of lights and churning shadow. Tottenham Court Road was real all right.

Lucy sat back in her seat and refocused her mind.

Well, that had been reasonably satisfactory. The vegetable dish had been replaced with something her mother actually wanted, plus there had been change for Lucy. Then William Carberry had been bearded in his den and no one had got hurt. In fact they had moved on rather efficiently, the two of them. Lucy had been both gracious and bracing (although she

150

regretted her sarcasm, which had just slipped out, defensively, in a panicky moment); William must have felt both told-off and forgiven, which was entirely appropriate given the circumstances. It had been quite sweet, actually, his reaction. A job well done. Well done, Luce.

She stared at the glass, and then through the glass, and then back at the surface of the glass again, at her own dark reflection and the reflection of the rest of the bus interior. Then out again at the surging traffic. She tried to do it seamlessly, making her gaze travel from one point of focus to the other smoothly and without jerking, trying to spot the moment of crossover, from outside to in and back again. But she couldn't get it; it wouldn't work. Once, twice, three times she tried — but there was no biting point. There was only a vague, achy sense of evasion as her retinas strained to accomplish her mind's desire, and failed. This was not a natural thing to be doing. Enough of that.

She resettled her gaze on the traffic; watched it do its thing in a kind of trance. Tottenham Court Road is a broad, rushing, one-way thoroughfare and the only illumination you ever see out of the front window of a bus or the windscreen of a car is red tail lights. Red tail lights competing after dark with street lamps and the halogen blaze from the shop interiors on either side of the road. Gadget shops, sofabed emporia, upmarket burger bars, *Time Out*, Habitat, Heal's. Plus traffic lights and the frantic winking of emergency vehicles. Everyone going the same way, but not *in* the same way; some going at it quietly, some generously, others not so much.

Lucy watched as a gap opened up in the flow in the wake of a bus leaving its stop, and two cars dived simultaneously for the new space — not advancing significantly at all, but *moving*, moving into a looser, more congenial lane. A gain of sorts, a real gain. But, of course, two into one space won't go. The loser of the duel then braked hard and issued into the space just vacated by the winner and continued hunting for new gaps, nosing forward like a shark unable to withhold its forward momentum for fear of its own death. Oh yes. Traffic, like Nature, abhors a vacuum. Traffic *is* Nature . . .

Lucy already knew that she quite liked traffic — or at least that she quite liked observing it. She did not own a car herself but she liked to imagine that she did and would sometimes amuse herself by picking out a particularly rampant-looking example — a lowered-suspension BMW, say, or a big chromed-up SUV — and putting herself at the wheel, just to see what she did with her machine; to see, as it were, what kind of mood she was in today and what kind of person. 'Go on, my son,' she would mutter under her breath. 'Go on: go for it!'

One rainy afternoon on the number 29, she had even attempted to devise a vicarious traffic game with a points system: points awarded for displays of unbridled aggression, then taken away for graciousness or generosity — the point of the game being to finish as close to zero as possible, or lower.

But it hadn't worked as a game and it had not

survived the bus journey home. Its ironies were too complicated.

★ ★ ★

She got off the bus at Finsbury Park and headed briskly east towards the barriered side streets which led to home. The wind, which had gusted and howled all day, was now sharpened with a hint of rain but seemed less blustery. Nevertheless, Lucy felt herself pushed across the zebra, her hair in her mouth.

Her thoughts were hard to bid in the wind. They pressed themselves on her, whether they were welcome or not.

Why in heaven's name had she told William he could write to her any time?

Eh?

That was just stupid. Nice guy and all that — and certainly harmless. But why do the reaching-out thing when it wasn't necessary? He was interesting, but not *that* interesting, even if it was kind of extraordinary that he'd swapped, overnight, the world of sex and drugs and rock and roll for the world of sheets and duvets and crimplene slacks — and then stuck with it for twenty years. Twenty years! How weird was that? Perhaps he wasn't as harmless as he seemed . . .

Don't talk rubbish. He's perfectly sweet and actually rather funny, in a slightly hollowed-out and dry-as-a-bone-dry-gulch kind of a way. And his shoes are pointy. She imagined he'd be fun to while away a weekend with. But those teeth. Crumbs. Talk about period teeth: they were like

153

Bowie's but more so — not particularly large but snaggled and incisive-looking and crammed into his mouth like New York into a satchel that has seen better days. Kind eyes too. When he does get round to looking, he looks *at* you, not all over you or through you. Lucy wondered how old William must be and then realised that she already knew — she knew from back then, when she'd given her witness statement. She had no memory of how the information had been conveyed to her, but the phrase had stuck. Then, he had been a 'thirty-four-year-old male driver'. Now he was a fifty-three-year-old department-store salesman.

What had become of his guitar? And his filthy scarf? His band?

What else did she already know? How much had she forgotten?

Halfway down her own street she saw a familiar figure lumping a buggy down the short flight of steps that led from Lucy's shared front door. Darkness had properly fallen now but the lamplight was good, and this was one of those figures that you can always identify at distance, just from the way they move — a picture of diligent application; an emblem of dynamic labour uncontaminated by self-pity.

Lorna.

'LORNA!' Lucy called, as loudly as felt seemly, but the wind was too strong and Lorna had made it through the gate, oblivious, and was now struggling womanfully with her car door while trying to soothe the child in the buggy. Lucy could now see that Lorna's other child was present too, concealed by the hood of the buggy, just standing there mutely, one hand in his mouth, dejected. Probably knackered. God, what was his name? Something weird . . .

So Lucy broke into a gentle trot, her shopping bag whanging against her knees and calves, her hair back in her mouth.

'LORFFF-NFFF! LORNA!' she shouted again, having first removed the wedge of hair from round her molars with her spare hand as she ran. And this time Lorna looked up and saw and waved, and relaxed her body from the braced posture with which she was attempting to prise the writhing, mewling Paisley from his shackles in the buggy in order to lash him into his car seat. Paisley and Shankly, known as Shanks. That's right. Both of them boys, Shanks being the elder of the two. That was it. It was something to do with football.

'Lucy, hello! Wondered if you'd be in — I was just passing with these two and thought I'd drop in for a cuppa, on the off chance. Didn't see you in the Jones earlier, so I thought you might be at home . . . '

Lucy liked Lorna, although she wasn't always all that convinced that Lorna liked her. They'd known each other since school but had never been close, and it seemed to Lucy at least that what relationship they did now possess was predicated entirely on the fact that they were the only two from their school year left in the area — so, well, yes, they might as well be friends. Why not? They got on with it amiably enough. Lucy did most of the laughing.

155

Lorna was as charismatic now as she had been then, despite being burdened with the multiple encumbrances of two small boys, a large mortgage and an extremely demonstrative husband, an architectural something or other from Liverpool.

Both boys and girls had loved Lorna at school, and everyone loved Lorna now — something to do with her wolfish good humour and energy and enterprise. And her hair, which was amazing. She seemed undauntable somehow. She'd been an architecture journalist for some years — quite a hot one in the early Noughties when young, female, charismatic architecture journalists had been about as thick on the ground as hot male ballet critics — but had given up her staff job to have children when newspapers hit the skids, mid-decade, and architecture journalists of any gender had become rather less desirable, certainly less affordable. She'd taken redundancy at the first opportunity, boffed out Shanks and Paisley without much fuss, carried on freelancing as a writer and had since set up shop as an importer of cheap but highly desirable vinyl floor coverings from China. She was, if not making a packet, then certainly 'getting around, y'know', as she liked to put it with a deprecating shrug. Lorna was said to be a marvel. But then people had been saying that since she first wowed the first year at secondary school with a few well-timed tosses of her continent of impossibly thick cave-dark hair.

'Come in, then,' said Lucy, slightly out of

156

breath. 'I can give the boys a bicky or something and I could do with a chinwag . . . '

'Nah,' said Lorna, with her usual cogency. 'I was pushing it a bit stopping off here in the first place, and the childminder hasn't given them any tea — so I'd better get 'em home for a feed and a hose-down. But listen. I did want to tell you that Steve's been round, ostensibly to buy some floor but really, I suspect, to talk about you.' She folded her lower lip over her teeth and tongue and hunkered onto one hip, one hand resting with masculine aplomb on the top of the car door. 'I thought you said it was mutual?'

'It is. It was.'

'Doesn't sound like it to me. Poor bloke's changed his mind, I reckon, not just on the business relationship but on the whole lot of it. Couldn't stop going on about you and why it went wrong and how you love each other really underneath and so on. On and on. Really quite twitchy too; his hands look red-raw, like he's been picking them or something? Oh dear. I can see that's not what you want to hear. But what you ought to know on top of that is that he asked me — he actually asked me — if I could arrange some sort of casual, semi-accidental meeting between you . . . '

'Oh fuck, Lorna . . . ' She clapped a hand to her mouth. 'God, *sorry*.'

'Oh, that's all right.' Lorna flapped one hand at the buggy wherein Paisley was visibly zonking; Shankly had already installed himself in his seat and was looking vacant and mumbling to himself. 'They're so far gone they won't even notice . . . And they hear it all the time at home. But I thought you ought to know about Steve — that you'd want to know. I of course told him that I'd do no such thing and to get himself a life and move on and all that shit. But he had that look in his eye: persistent pitiful pup.'

'I know the look. Oh bloody hell. Thanks, Lorna. Don't worry. We occasionally speak and I'll give him what-for when we do. You get off home with the boys and forget all about it. Thanks. You did the right thing. That's if you're sure you won't come in . . . '

'Really sure. But we should catch up. Maybe next week? Gotta go. Bye!'

And so, having frontloaded the limp Paisley into his bucket, Lorna climbed into the driving seat of her fiercely nondescript car — Gavin drove the family Audi — and inadvertently elbowed the horn as she turned to aim a few succinct words at the boys in the back, before slamming the car into gear and roaring off down the road as if her life depended on getting to the junction before the wind.

But actually, as Lucy was just noticing, the wind had suddenly dropped and everything was now calm in the early-evening darkness. Leaves were barely stirring. It had all been a lot of fuss about nothing.

15

Electric Dark

Jolly Bizzle on the phone.

He's giving me the smooth shit; the 'great to see you still got fire in your belly' dung. Like I can't see through him.

He's also apologising for speaking out of turn at the fake Italian cafe — but hey, man, he says, it was worth it to see the 'flash' of my old anger. Apparently that proves something, although I'm not sure what. Jolly reckons it proves I should still be 'getting out there', which I interpret to mean showing up and plugging in at his God-awful half-baked reunion of VineHeart, as some sort of birthday present to him. But he insists he's not going to pressure me about that — he respects my decision and knows I'll come to righteousness in my own good time. I tell him not to be an arrogant fucker and he ticks me off for language unbecoming in a distinguished sales executive in the bedspread trade.

I call him a fucking cunt.

I do like him. Always did.

His persistence is part of his charm of course. That's how he managed to make basslines roll like a tsunami, even the ones with only three notes in them. Repetition as pleasure. And that's how he's built a pretty respectable business, I suppose, from unpromising beginnings, learning not only the trade of the trade but also the art of it, including all the new digital stuff. And just *not stopping* for anything or anyone. Plus he doesn't have anger issues — just lets bad feeling drain out of him through his heels, through force of gravity and with the passage of time, in addition to his persistent refusal to allow his mood to be altered either by injustice or by contractual bullshit, management duplicity, the unfathomable behaviour of narcissistic visionaries or chlamydia, to all of which he was a martyr in his younger days. Jolly is as Jolly does. And while he is seldom jolly, he is always, indefatigably, Jolly.

So I tell him again that, no, I will not participate in some kind of phoney reunion of the band, even if it does make him feel special for a day. Nor will I give him permission to reconstitute the band out of inferior, inauthentic parts, even if he has managed to track down Simon at his private school in Surrey and retrieved Godfrey from among the dead of New Orleans or wherever it was he breathed his last rank breath. Boy oh boy. *There* was a drummer who, far from sounding like a man building a shed, actually was a man building his own coffin. I have said enough. It ill-behoves one to speak ill of the probably-dead, even if he was a drummer.

But — and it's a big but — if Jolly will promise not to treat his do as a VineHeart reunion, then I in turn will promise to buff my chops and show up to play some old chestnuts for the pleasure of rocking with him again. 'Mustang Sally' or something. Maybe a couple of tunes. 'Barefootin''? A nice, fleet, tricky shuffle. We used to do 'Barefootin'' as

160

a rehearsal warm-up, just to get everyone light on their feet. Ready to jump. If there's one thing I'll say about VineHeart it's that we never wore big boots and that's partly down to 'Barefootin'', which we worked to exhaustion as a warm-up. I was a bit nutty about it actually. I'd make the rest of them jam on it — or play it over and over again — until I could feel both the flow and that lift under your elbows and armpits which tells you that what you're doing is . . . well, that you're *taking off*. No, really. You could actually feel the music pushing *up*, like when aeroplanes go down the runway, or what geese must feel in their armpits after lumbering across a field for forty-five seconds with their necks out and their wings flapping. Lift. Used to drive Godfrey crazy because he always wanted to get down to what he called 'the real work', so that he could then clear off again and start doing what he really liked doing. But 'Barefootin'' was the real work, in my estimation; or at least the start of it. I never liked a rhythm section in hobnail boots.

And I am secretly hoping that Jolly gets someone in instead of Godfrey who has got the ability to achieve that lift, otherwise it won't be much fun. Not for Jolly, not for anyone. Roy Dodds might be around, I suppose.

But listen to me. I'm talking like I'm fully committed. Like it's my gig and I'm responsible. Old habits die hard, even after they've been officially declared dead, had unguents shoved up their nose and been humped into a sarcophagus.

It's like a reflex. But maybe that's why I had to detach myself completely in 1993 — because I knew then that if I didn't turn myself into a bedspread sales executive I'd remain an impoverished, misanthropic, musicianly miseryguts for the rest of my puff, forever disappointed, forever angry, forever dying the squelchy death. A toad. Spare me. I can't imagine, I really can't, what it must have been like to be a pro musician over the past twenty years, observing the evisceration of the industry from the inside, with no power to change it and having no other choice but to participate — and ageing while I did it. Ugh. Unimaginable. A fate literally worse than death. Although Godfrey might not agree.

And it's not just the nature of the work and how it's changed during that time that makes it unimaginable. It's how people in general think about music, and even how they feel it; certainly how and why they spend money on it (or not, as the case may be).

Of course people still *feel* music, of course they do. Privately. Discreetly. Even publicly, where, no matter the context, it is now a requirement to put your hands in the air and go *wooo*, to show what a good time you're having, because showing you're having a good time is now the whole point of existence. So, yes. Quite possibly people still think about music, and feel it, perhaps more honestly than they used to when music seemed important in the world (I'm pretty sure that there's much less *pretending* about it than there used to be). But I am also sure that there is much less value attached to music than there used to be: obviously in the money sense, but also in the philosophical sense and the emotional sense and the social-change sense and the sex sense and the freeing-up-your-soul sense. In every sense that's worth a damn.

Music used to be *about* those things, all of those things; not necessarily explicitly, but certainly intrinsically. Music wasn't just a thing you had around in your life for convenience's sake, like furniture and drugs and gadgets; something to consume idly, to use without thought. And you didn't have to coerce people into believing that it meant something either, by putting it on telly all the time and by telling music's story. People just knew, without having to be told. The usual wisdom is that music was the means by which two, maybe three generations of postwar people got their first little taste of how important it was *not* to see the world as their mums and dads saw it. The more refined point, to my mind, is that music was the best means available for those people to tell themselves that it *is* OK not to have lived through the Second World War.

And so on. Blah de blah. Yadda yadda etc. What am I going on about? Ranting again. Jolly would approve, of course — Jolly despises theory but loves a rant. But, actually, I am not one of those old farts who thinks everything was better then because it was then, and everything is rubbish now because it's now. By no means. That would be shoddy. Obviously many, many things are better now than they were then. Obviously. Just not music. Well, not even music per se — there's loads of music being made right now that is very fine indeed. But what music *means* to us — what we use it for, how we value it, how it shares our living space . . . those things were better then, no question. Music remains. It is adamantine in its staying power; it's only our attitude towards it that has been subject to corruption — which in turn does something back to music. I suppose what I'm probably driving at is the same old saw: I am a stuck record on an old-fashioned turntable, really I am. I suppose what I probably mean is that I think that music has crossed over, like so many things, *to the other side.*

Music is no longer a vital comfort to us. It is merely convenient.

★ ★ ★

But the big news, so far as Jolly is concerned, is that he's found Simon in Surrey and Simon has said yes. Simon will knot a spotty handkerchief round the end of a stick, bung some sandwiches in it, get on a train and convey himself, plus Strat, to north London for the gig next month, and when he gets here, he will plug the Strat in and be Jolly's wingman for the duration, having kept his hand in playing in local bands (and in the school music room) ever since he jacked it in professionally in the Nineties. Makes me wonder what they're teaching in private schools these days.

PPECB, perhaps. Philosophy, Politics, Economics & Chuck Berry.

Imagine, a prime minister who understands the greatness of 'Nadine', leading a Cabinet entirely composed of posh boys who may not know the price of a pint of milk but can do a structural analysis of 'Let It Rock'. 'Quentin, we've got an off-schedule recession coming two miles out. Your thoughts, please, and a paper by the end of the week. Now, on to the railways and this question regarding the provision of steel-driving hammers . . . '

Simon.

Last time I saw or even spoke to Simon must have been the last time Jolly tried to broker an agreement between the three of us, with a view to reforming VineHeart a dozen years ago, under a different name and with a different drummer. 'You know, man, as a fun thing on the side, to scrub the cobwebs outta y' caaarners.' Jolly would always adopt his mother's accent when trying to be persuasive.

In response, one could only ever say, 'Yeah, yeah.'

Godfrey had already gone missing and Simon was in the latter stages of his teacher training by then and no more interested than I was in revivifying a dubious past. He was nice enough about the idea, but as diffident as I was furiously resistant. It's hard to see how such a fundamentally edgeless, slippery, aloof individual as Simon could play the guitar as passionately as he did on his good days, but again, maybe that's a public-school education for you. On his good days, of which there were many, he combined grace and bite and fluency and feel in a way that I could only dream of on my very best days, which were rare. He could play my arse off, if truth be told — a lot of the time I'd feel like Bob Weir in a cutting contest with Jerry Garcia: just not suitably equipped. Next to Simon I was a category error (although, like Bob Weir, I have other virtues). And then, afterwards, he would unplug and mooch away with his girlfriend and get on with his life elsewhere, as if his genius were a small thing; a thing of *some* account, yes, but not the key to life. Good heavens, no. I imagine he's an unflappable teacher.

I don't know whether they are going to do any actual rehearsing together, prior to the Great Event. But I imagine they will. And that will be tricky since, by my calculation, the gig won't fall during the school holidays and, anyway, isn't Simon a 'housemaster'? Isn't he supposed to be available at all times to tend his flock at the boarding house? Or have I just made all that up out of my prejudices about private education? Surely, in private education everyone's either a future Chancellor or a prefect or a fag or a housemaster or a dimwit antiques dealer/estate agent in Dorset who just doesn't know it yet . . .

They *must* have to rehearse. Simon and Roy Dodds are good, but they can't just roll up and deliver a full Personal History of Jolly set without prior research — and without first having had some sort of violent disagreement about tempo and changes and where to stop and so forth. Just for starters, they would have to practise playing out of time to get the vibe right for the reconstruction of the Worst Ska Band in London. That takes talent *and* rehearsal.

Then there's the question of which of the

'names' on Jolly's list are going to turn up on the night — my guess is none — and if any of them do show, which of them is going to be bullied into getting up onstage and acting the goat on Jolly's behalf. Plus — and this is the biggest doubt of all — he's now talking about opening the gig up to the public, and charging something nominal on the door on the night for walk-ups. Plug it to the locals on Facebook. 'Create a buzz.' 'Your chance to rub shoulders with Weller for a fiver.'

Weller my arse. Jolly did one session with the Great Man a decade and a half ago, and it didn't get used. If Weller shows up — never mind gets onstage — I will personally autograph his penis, or at least offer to. I love Jolly Bizzle but he is delusional.

But then again, I don't for a minute think that he's going to pull off any of these stunts or even try to. He is only really delusional in the sense that he appears to be. It's all smoke and mirrors. It's the cloaking Bizzly mist which allows him to conceal his true motives, his real moves.

I know he's shooting me a line because he wants me to get a hard-on for this gig. But I won't. I just won't. I can't.

★ ★ ★

When I was a kid I was quite good at what is now called creative writing. I wrote stories both to amuse myself and to get ahead. Some of them were all right. That's why I ended up doing English at one of the snootier red-brick universities: by dint of lots of creative writing and a certain amount of last-minute swotting. It's also why I dropped out after two terms. After six months of trying to think about Thackeray and Hawthorne as if they somehow amounted to a lively contribution to the world we all inhabit, I came to the conclusion that I would be better served by putting flesh on the stories boiling formlessly in my own head. They seemed so very much more real and vivid and to do with the world I actually lived in. And not as long-winded.

My parents were quietly appalled. But because they were quiet about it, as parents of that generation often were about the besetting existential issues of modern life, I did get down to my new work straight away. Didn't mess about; acted on conviction. I got a job, wrote songs and started a band in St Albans. In due course another, better one followed. I suppose you could say that VineHeart was the culmination, the *dénouement*, of the biggest fiction of all: Guillaume the energising suburban visionary.

But before then, back when I was a teenager and full of it — and when I wasn't hunched over my guitar (and sometimes even when I was) — I wrote like a demon. Enhanced creativity is perhaps one of only two known side benefits of being unattractive to girls. And there was in the 1970s enough romantic mythology still clinging to the figure of the solitary boy in his bedroom with a cheap Gibson copy and a ream of scattered foolscap to grease the vision and administer some shove, whatever form the vision happened to take. And so I plunged into the life of the rockin' wordsmith and actually stuck with it. It certainly saved me from making an arse of myself with girls. This is an irony I can stand to contemplate now I'm in my fifties.

Mostly I wrote what used to be called speculative fiction, and for all I know, still is. By and large these stories would turn out to be short, pacy narratives energised with a clever twist written in humming neon — 'Hey, look at me! Pfff zizzz crackle!' — concerning the contradictory/ impossible/absurd nature of existence in the contemporary or near-future world. For a while I thought of myself as a near-future Ray Bradbury or Harlan Ellison.

One story survived my adolescence and somehow contrived to stick with me like chewed gum in a pocket lining, which is perhaps apt since it was resolutely adolescent in conception. Actually, probably *because* it was adolescent in conception. I began it when I was fourteen or fifteen and finished it for the first time that same summer — but was never happy with the ending. I wrote several more endings over ensuing years, just to try to break the back of it, to lock it down, as it were, and to get it out of my system for good. But I never really nailed it. Used to drive me nuts, whether actually writing or merely turning the story's parts over in my head while trying to sleep — it was as if it were chucking me off, bucking me like a bronco. It didn't appear to *want* to have an ending and was grimly determined that, for as long as I continued to hunt down a conclusion for it, it would continue to throw me off the scent. I eventually named VineHeart's one major-label album after it: *Electric Dark*.

'Electric Dark', the SF story, concerns the efforts of a man to preserve his sanity and indeed the sanity of the entire world following his invention of the eponymous bulb-like electrical device which, when installed in an ordinary light socket and switched on in a sunlit room, would plunge that environment into sudden darkness. The electric dark.

I did not expend many words elaborating on the technical achievement that such an invention represented. The switchable electric dark had to do, technically, with quantum physics, obviously, not to mention negative charge and photons and reversed polarity and so on, and I vaguely recall trying to find a role in the story for Schrödinger's cat, but failed on account of the fact that I didn't fully understand the point of Schrödinger's cat, let alone the physics (I just liked the paradox of a cat that can be both alive and dead at the same time). But I have always been an enemy to bullshit and so I chose to leave the technical details to greater minds than mine to speculate upon. Besides, what I was really interested in was not paradox or quantum mechanics but what happens to people when they are granted the opportunity to do 'impossible' stuff as an everyday consumer choice. What happens when you can get freaky shit from the corner shop?

I suppose that, really, I was expressing curiosity about drugs.

The story made no mention of drugs. It merely anatomised the electric dark's implications for the world, a world in thrall to a thing that served very little practical purpose but nevertheless turned people on, fascinated them, addicted them and drove them crazy with unending rapacious desire. The pleasure, the compulsion, was not to be found necessarily in the darkness itself, but in the fact that you could have darkness any time you chose — and everyone else in the vicinity would just have to go along with your choice.

I imagined streets full of darkened houses on summer mornings. Black-hazed tower blocks (escaping particles of e-dark would form an anti-nimbus around any building in which it was being used); rooms in buildings vast and small where only sound told any kind of a story and to touch or be touched was to be electrified with fear and excitement. I wrote about murder and out-of-control sex and the mistaking of identity, all of it acted out in pitch-black rooms by perfectly nice people bent traumatically out of shape. (The nicer the person, the worse the trauma — or so you'd think; but not always.) I conceived of mass etiolation, stubbed toes, heightened touch and smell and hearing and, yes, taste. I feared the mole, as one always fears one's most dangerous rival. As electric dark was put to greater and broader uses in society — and it began to chew at the roots of the world's economy, invoking new legislation — I proposed a new social-evolutionary step in which the naturally blind became masters of all that could be seen and blinding became the fashion, so that nothing could be seen, ever. In due course it became more than the fashion. It became liturgical. At thirteen, when once upon a time you might have celebrated your bar mitzvah or confirmation, with a book or a candle, now you were put to the Anoculus, as a sign of your readiness for maturity. It was a brief ceremony and a beautiful one and was only painful if you had not learned your catechism. The darkness that followed Anoculation was all you could ever have hoped for . . .

But I couldn't finish it. It was a story without end. It wanted to go on for ever and I could never arrive at the kind of terminal cadence I wanted, not because I couldn't imagine it, but because I just couldn't get there. I couldn't cover the terrain.

16

Starless

Dear Lucy, [it said, in handsome blue-black fountain-pen script . . .]

Very nice to see you this morning in Bedlinen. Thanks for stopping by. I'm glad you did. But I never got round to asking how the sleeping is. How is it? I do hope the pillow is doing some good, if only to make the wakeful hours less harsh. But I'm hoping you're sleeping properly now.

As you're a local, I just thought you might like to know about the following. You know Bellsmith's Working Men's Club down our end of Green Lanes, before you get to the green itself? Filthy great red-brick Victorian civic pile? Of course you know it. Well, there's an event taking place there in a couple of weeks on the 3rd, which ought to be a lot of fun. It's an old bandmate of mine celebrating his dotage and he's pulling together a mighty cast of great and not so good figures from his musical past; they're going to play his greatest hits, along with those of Wilson Pickett and Jackie Wilson and — who knows? — Wilson Phillips. I might even join in myself. Been a while, but it might be good for me. Everyone involved gets to bring three guests and I rather wondered if you'd like to be one of mine. Then you can tell me all about your sleeping, before I send you off into the land of nod by leaping onto the stage and rolling out my fabled impersonation of Steve Cropper in 1967, or somesuch.

Jolyon, whose 'party' it is, has also threatened to awaken some sleeping musical giants of his former acquaintance to join him in the spotlight, although frankly I think he's barking up a died-back ash with that one. Paul Weller? My Great-Aunt Francesca!

But I do think it might be great fun — the drinks'll be free for a while, I believe, and you can always bugger off once you've had those. You never saw my band, did you? Well, here's your chance to see three-quarters of them, aged beyond repair, a fraction as well rehearsed and nowhere near as visionary or brilliant — and not even playing the stuff we used to play. But really us. At least more really us than The Who can be really them ever again.

What do you say? Here's my mobile number: do phone or text. A syllable will do.

Best wishes,
William Carberry

Lucy stuffed the note and its envelope inside her bag and afforded herself the merest twitch of a smile, then dragged her tired body up the stairs to her flat. It had been a long shift at the Jones, or at least it had seemed that way. Probably this had been because, in the absence of Nelson's silent gravitas, Tomas and Oleg had been behaving like a pair of princesses.

174

What now though?

What was to become of Lucy Taplow, now that she was down to her last source of income and hadn't the slightest interest in training to be anything that she wasn't already?

There's a question . . . What *was* she already? What did she amount to? Not a lot. What had she got to show for her thirty-eight years of reading and gardening and clerking and baking and acting and charitable bungling and sewing and soft-selling vintage dresses to hungry-eyed women in the teeth of a Camden autumn? Neither the riches of Croesus nor the contentment of the righteous, that was for sure. Nor any depths into which she might drop an anchor. She was flotsam on the surface of life. A drifting clump of accreted experiences, not one of which stood proud enough on its own to catch a breeze and get her under some sort of way. What was that bit of the ocean where everything just *sat*? The Sargasso. No, that's the weedy one, where ships get snarled up with mile-long bladder-wrack. Wrong image. The Doldrums! That was it: the bit near the equator where winds don't prevail. Everything just . . . waits. She slumped in her kitchen and gouged at the grain of her table with a thumbnail. She had nothing to steer by either. No stars. All she could do was drift.

And why did she always think in nautical metaphors, for heaven's sake? She wasn't a sailor. It had been years since she'd read a Patrick O'Brian, and then it had only been to

175

please her mother (although she had rather enjoyed the three or four that she'd finished). So, why? What else? She didn't sleep enough to have oceanic dreams. She had never fantasised about 'going to sea'. She had never nearly drowned or had a thing about dolphins. Her father was bizarrely keen on the idea of the sea dog's life at the narrative level, she supposed, although his limited experience of seafaring — Sea Scouts? — had taken place in his remote past and was only ever alluded to with a slightly specious look in his rheumy eye, as if he were unsure whether he was recalling something real or something that he'd like to have been real.

She boiled the kettle and Lorna came to mind. Lorna didn't think like this. Lorna would sooner dress in Boden knitwear than permit watery metaphors to slosh around the interior of her skull. There was nothing wet inside Lorna, other than blood. No metaphors. Ball bearings maybe, certainly blood, but not water. Indeed, Lorna was no more capable of reflecting bluely on the events and non-events of the past than she was capable of permitting contemplation to take up space in her mind that might otherwise be devoted to the formulation and execution of action. She was a doer, a fixer, a warrior, a creature wholly adapted to maximising her potential within the context of whichever environment she happened to find herself in. Perhaps that was what the hair-tossing was really all about: shaking the wet out of her system.

Lucy filled her mug and plonked herself down again at the table with an abrupt and rather uncontrolled exhalation, noticing even as she did so that the plonking and sighing embarrassed her. She grabbed her phone from the coat she'd flung across the back of the other kitchen chair.

She thumbed a text to William Carberry.

OK. That'd be really nice. That's 7 and a half syllables. Plus 9 more, plus . . . Oh dear. Where will it end? Lucy T.

She then wished that she hadn't said 'Where will it end?' Way too flirty. Christ, she might as well have said 'I hope it'll end with me sleeping with you', and *that* she had no intention of doing. But, well, this birthday gig thing sounded fun, she supposed, and it was only down the road. Fun and weird. Bound to be full of old gits wishing they were young again.

She dialled Lorna's number.

'Lorna, it's Lucy . . . Taplow,' she added, to be on the safe side.

Lorna sounded cheerful but busy. Lucy took the hint.

'Nice to see you the other day . . . You mentioned catching up. Well, I've just been invited to a kind of birthday party-stroke-gig thing at Bellsmith's down the bottom of Green Lanes. I think the drinks are free for a while and it sounds like it might be fun, and as if some famous musicians might even show up. You know — old rock stars. It's in a couple of weeks. Don't suppose you fancy trotting down to that with me? We can always make a ladylike exit and go somewhere else if it's ghastly . . . Yeah. It's on the third. I've accepted in principle and I'll need to check whether you can come too, but I'm sure it'll be fine. He's a nice guy, I think . . . No. No, no, no. But I like him. He's one of the musicians — it's his mate's party. You don't remember VineHeart, do you? . . . No. Me neither. Well, not properly. I was certainly never a fan. I do faintly remember them, from when we were teenagers. Fake gypsies, as I recall. Anyway, William was in them and they're re-forming and there's talk of celebrity jamming and wildness and I just thought it might be nice to at least see how it goes . . .

'Yes, yes. Brilliant. Let me check with William it's OK and I'll text you back. But I'm sure it will be . . . '

And now she thought about it, yes, it would be a very good idea to have Lorna along. She texted William.

Hi. Lucy T here. Wondering if ok to bring chum on 3rd? Cheeky I kno.

The reply was almost instantaneous.

Course. Bring 2 if you like. No problem. Wm.

★　★　★

She lay awake with the lamp on and studied her ceiling. Whitewashed woodchip. Vile. Like acne. Off-white eruptions through a bloodless skin. One of these days . . . But she didn't have the money it'd cost to fix and now she had one less job — and it's only a ceiling: you only see it when you bother to look up, and how often do people look up?

She was looking up now.

Steve always said he'd do it for cost.

He probably still would.

She switched the lamp off and turned onto her side. Listened to the curious scrunchings within her new pillow. Not so new now. In fact the pillow had settled well to its new environment and special responsibilities. Its loft was slightly diminished, but the support it gave was perfect. How come there was so much *noise* inside a pillow? She was lying absolutely motionless, yet the pillow was gurgling away on the inside like a tummy after breakfast. Except it wasn't gurgling. Nothing like a gurgle. More like the sound of a short person fighting their way through tall grass in a rainstorm . . . Perhaps the noisiness of a pillow was how you judged its value. The more 'active' its ingredients, the more likely it was to do the job properly. The noisier the pillow, the better the sleep . . .

No. That didn't make sense.

Tomorrow she'd ask Charlotte for an extra shift at the Jones. Definitely. Plus there was the long-standing idea about 'Jones Delivery'. Or 'Jones on Tap', as Charlotte had preferred. The idea of a bread-delivery service was a couple of years old at least, and a good one, Lucy thought, but it had never got off the ground and Lucy was in an ideal position to offer her services: first to get the operation running and then to do the legwork. In fact she rather liked the idea of tootling around north London on her bike on frosty mornings, laden with loaves and cakes in bulbous panniers, smiling and waving. And it wouldn't take all that much to fix the bike up — the business could pay for panniers and basket and maintenance; Lucy could supply the basic wheels. Plus Charlotte had that van-type thing she used to get supplies in, and Lucy had a pristine driving licence, so once the turnover was up enough to justify the fuel, she could deliver in the van. They could signwrite 'Jones on Tap' on the side — or something better. Jones . . . Jones . . . Jones on Wheels . . . Jones to You . . . You and Mrs Jones . . .

She could see the route. Brownswood Park to Manor Park to Dalston via Stoke Newington in an enclosing cloud of fresh-bread smell, criss-crossing the crust of the morning as if it were a bun.

An envelope.

A pillow.

What could be better?

17

Frost

The Fender Telecaster is one of the perfect things. I say this without the tiniest hint of facetiousness. The Tele is more than a design classic. 'Design classic' sounds a note of preciousness and cleverness that simply does not register in Telecasterworld. Really, the guitar is more a triumph of *thinginess* than of design, because no one would ever claim that a Tele is anything to look at or that its looks had been considered a decisive issue in its conception. Its form follows its function, which is a good thing of course, design-wise. But more than that, its form determines the way its function exhibits character. The Tele expresses itself cogently as a thing just by being so thoroughly, unselfconsciously functional. Beef and twang? Spit and heft? You get all of those qualities and more because of the way the instrument is designed and made and because of the stuff *from* which it is made. Solid, uncomplicated, undecorated. Economical. Functional. A slab of shaped ash devoid of 'comfort contouring'. Were it designed and made another way it would be a Stratocaster, say, or a Jaguar, and would do things differently. But it isn't. The Tele is like it is because it can't *be* any other way. It stands for what it is; always backs itself up. That's its power.

It is a god among things.

Mine's a doozie. It's a little worn now, being nearly sixty years old, as all near sixty-year-olds are. The frets on its lovely buttery neck need doing and I haven't had the bridge reset in years. The strings must be in need of the old heave-ho too. When did I last buy new strings?

But there it is. *Here* it is. Right here.

I picked it up again three or four weeks back and just the weight and balance of it round my neck felt good, instantly. Transforming. I don't want to be overdramatic about this — oh, all right: I do — but once I'd slung the guitar in its rightful place, with its doorstep of a dorsal bout digging under the arch of my ribs and my left thumb hooked over the neck, it felt like a lost limb reattached. I felt remarkably whole, and not in a small way — as if I'd literally got an attribute back from some place I'd lost it. I tuned the guitar quickly and roughly and hit an open G and the chord went through my organs like a ripple. And that was before I'd even plugged it into my little brown Champ, which has had books piled on it for more years than is dignified. The little sweetie. I left the Champ to warm for ten minutes before daring to insert jack into socket, but then, once the Tele was properly tuned, it was ring-a-ding-ding all the way to Memphis for an hour at least. My organs were joined by my soul. They were all jumping together.

I didn't have any chops, mind.

Three or four weeks on, it's a different story. I have chops of a sort. They came back in a surprising rush, in all their paltriness, and are serviceable at least. I won't be making a complete fool of myself at the gig; there's a chance only Simon and I will know that I can't do half as much as I used to be able to. But I think I can get to the leapy feel of 'Barefootin'' and the drive of 'Mustang Sally' without undue alarm. No call for augmented chords in those babies after all — not unless you *want* to put them in there, for fancy-pants purposes.

Doubtless the fresh chops were helped into being in some small measure by the comprehensive service granted to me by an amiable Geordie guitar-tech in Denmark Street ('Whoa,' he said as the instrument came out of its case. 'There's a canny lass!' — which, as I've already indicated, is to gild the weathered blond-and-black lily somewhat: feminine the Telecaster is not) plus a kind of Zen commitment of my own to practice, which entailed wearing the thing around the flat in the evenings like a heavy housecoat, fingering away constantly, ignoring the RSI-type pain at the base of my left thumb and singing. Yes, singing. I found that I wanted to sing all the time.

But I am not going to be pulling up any trees at Jolly's do; I am going to be fitting in.

★   ★   ★

I've been sleeping a little better too. The midgy tickles have not been torturing me and I've found that my usual bedtime routine, of a good listen to, say, Trane or Miles followed by a read, and still no spliff, has resulted in me tripping relatively lightly off to la-la land and not actually waking again till fiveish, tickle-free. Which is great. The key was obviously to give up *Newsnight*. No one should ingest Paxman last thing before bed. You might as well snort neat monosodium glutamate.

I was chuffed to hear back from Lucy so promptly too. Her text must have been sent the day she got my letter. It was rather sweet actually. And quite funny, once I worked out what she was on about. Then there was 'chum'. She said she wanted to bring a 'chum'. Chum is good. Chum is not the same as 'husband' and would only be the same as 'boyfriend' if Lucy were a games player, and I really don't get the impression that she is one. And I've never seen a ring on her finger. In this context, 'chum' surely means 'girlfriend' — and that's good with me, whether there's a boyf in the background or not. In fact I'd rather she came mob-handed. It would feel less like a date. I don't want it to feel like a date, I really don't. I don't mind if she has a boyfriend. I just don't want him at my comeback gig.

So it was Happy William who took a call from Bérengère this morning at eight thirty-five, as per usual on the bus. And it was Happy William's blood which turned to frost as his unhappy sister explained how their mother was back in hospital for one last dose of chemo before they jack it in for good. Before they draw gently up to the buffers at the end of the line and Maman gets off.

'She's . . . she's . . . ' gasped Bére. 'She's not going to live, Guillaume. She's going to die.'

I refrained from applauding Bére's percipience in observing this fact. Instead I made soothing noises and told her to keep me informed of developments — I can always be in Limoges at two days' notice and I want to be there if I can be. I asked her if she needed money, which she declined — unnecessarily testily, I thought. I also told her that she must not hesitate to command my presence if it became essential.

'She wants to go home,' she said, again stating the obvious, reproachfully this time, as if I had some personal investment in keeping the old woman in an institution. 'She really, really doesn't want to be in the hospital or some hospice. She wants to die at home.'

At which point I reminded her that Maman was going into hospital to have treatment, not to die, and that there was every chance — well, not every chance, but a decent chance, albeit a small decent chance — that Maman may be granted many more months or even years of pain-free existence, and Bére was not to prejudge or let herself give in to dark thoughts. It wouldn't be what Maman wanted.

'It's all very easy for you to say, Guillaume,' she said sharply, and then thought better of it, changing tack. She switched to the voice she uses in shops, the emollient sing-song one. 'I think I need to make everything as beautiful for her as it can be. I am planning to stay in St Mathieu until she is either well enough to look after herself or . . . or . . . it becomes unnecessary for me to be there any more.' She permitted herself a beat's pause, then: 'Guillaume, there is no point in you coming now. Well, not right now.'

And that's how we left it.

★　★　★

I hadn't got the frost out of my veins by the time I got to work. And even after an hour on the floor and a couple of modest interactions with customers I was still vexed about my mum in a curiously detached, physically indolent way that I don't recall from the long occasion of my father's decline. So I gave in to it and let it be and did not emerge from my cocoon of self-containment for anyone or anything, even when a woman stood in the middle of Bedlinen and snapped her fingers repeatedly over her head for attention. I left her to Dorcas, Shireen being on her break at the time.

Instead I made the day into a sort of vessel in which to stew. I am good at this. It comes quite easily and, when the conditions are agreeable, I can stew for England as well as for France. I did it as a child as a way of making eventless time seem . . . not exactly lively, but *not dead* — it's where all my stories were brewed and fermented, I suppose. And I've done it as a man. Broodingly and, I dare say, rather self-consciously as a young man; passively and quietly as a middle-aged man. I can function perfectly efficiently while doing it too (I'm pretty sure I turned over my usual daily quota in the department today) and I can even stew blithely when called upon to do so, with a smile on my face and a quip on my lip. Stewing may be a dark art but it must betimes wear a bright social face.

The secrets of good stewing are twofold: not thinking and not prioritising. You can line up your ingredients any way you like outside the pot, before you start cooking, but once they're in the pot, you just have to let them go. Let them do their thing. Pay them no mind, as Americans would say. Real stews do not privilege one ingredient over another, or at least they shouldn't. You can't have favourites. Stews can't be stewarded and they aren't hierarchical — the whole point of a stew is that it is a passive melding process, a textured, symbiotic mush in which one essence involves itself with another and all the essences combine together to resolve into a new and deeply worthwhile concordance. Oh yes. But no, you can't contrive a stew. That would be a fundamental betrayal of what a stew is and how it works. You have to let it do its thing. A good stew does not require the imposition of will or wishfulness or, for that matter, intellect. And certainly not theory. In fact a good one actively resists those things.

And it's not often I have three ingredients to stew. Three! Count 'em: my mum, the gig, Lucy. What larks! What luxury. A triplication of class-A botherations to cook on low for a full eight-hour stretch. And throughout the day I felt the stew stewing, below the level of consciousness, but only just, bubbling and shifting to its own wet rhythm and never coming fully to the boil. I didn't let myself think about my mum, the gig or

Lucy all day; I simply let them brew.

When I got home it was just about ready.

I wanted a spliff, of course. I wanted one like crazy. But I know better. Spliff up on a stew that's ready to roll and what comes out of the pot, so to speak, is invariably a mess: a flavoursome, slightly gamey mess but a mess all the same, fraught with hints of anxiety and overtones of uncertainty and an underpinning subflavour of subtle paranoia. You can never quite trust what you're tasting, even if it's the best taste you've ever had. And the next morning you pay a dismal existential price.

So I spent the evening in contemplation of the contents of the kitchen cupboard and then in their subsequent transfer to my stomach (twenty minutes banging out and then banging in some linguine and passata), followed by more virtuous contemplation of my fingering progress, a spot of telly and a side of Serge Chaloff, during which the stew did its last bit of cooling in the airy vaults of my unconscious mind. And then, and only then, I turned my conscious mind to face what it had spent all day studiously avoiding.

My mum. The gig. Lucy.

In no particular order.

Lucy. My mum. The gig.

A stew is a stew. There are no hierarchies in stew.

The gig. Lucy. My mum.

Doesn't matter how you order the ingredients . . . Yet there are salient flavours in every stew, subtle soundings, timbres even, which bring out tone and shape impressions. They not only lend character but also convey substance, irrigate feeling. And in this one, the newly plated stew steaming in the forefront of my conscious mind was dominated by one theme.

Ambivalence.

No two ways about it: I am a divided soul. Here's what came out of the pot.

The gig: I don't want to do it, but I don't want to miss it either. I don't want to re-form VineHeart, but I would, desperately, love to play in front of people again with what remains of VineHeart. I don't want to make myself that vulnerable; I do want to make myself that vulnerable. Who am I kidding? What a nana!

For fuck's sake.

My mum: I don't want her to die; I do want her suffering to end. I do want to see her; I am frightened to see her.

Lucy: I really, really want to see her; I don't want her to see through me. I do want her to be my friend; I don't want her to be my critic. I do want to sleep with her; I don't want to make an idiot of myself.

I am — to say the least — out of practice in all of these things: in being not see-throughable, being a son, being a friend, having sex and so on . . . In fact, the last time I had sex was so long ago and was so underwhelming as an experience that I can't even recall which year it was in. Sometime in the mid-Noughties, with someone I'd barely been introduced to who mewed throughout like a seabird. Mmmeeee-eee-eeeuw, she went. Eeeeee-eeeeuuuw — not rhythmically, nor with obvious reference to what we were doing, but apparently automatically, at some deep instinctual level, as if calling to other members of her species, perhaps to gather in shapely flittering flocks around pylons before heading south for the winter to the Great Rift Valley. The mewing seemed also to be meant as an act of encouragement to me.

To choke off a laugh I pretended I had a frog in my throat, which evolved, as soon as I thought of it, not into a prince but into an imaginary pubic hair, which I managed to extract from the region of my tonsils with an elaborate mime involving thumb and forefinger. 'One of yours, I believe.' It took some moments to do, but I needed all of them to recover my composure (it's very hard to laugh when you have your own fist down your throat). Then having cleared my airways, I asked my lover if she was all right and she said, 'Don't ask.' Which were virtually the last words we ever exchanged. But she did stop mewing. We finished our business in businesslike fashion and never saw each other again.

Nevertheless, I felt a little jolt in my cock as I contemplated my new inventory of impossible, irresolvable contradictions, and I found myself rummaging with almost indecent intensity for the Miracles and the Moonglows. And then I went to bed.

18

Slime

The foot of Green Lanes has many toes. Odd toes.

There's a baby cafe and an accessories shop for cab drivers. There's an art shop and a hairdresser's and grocer's and fishmonger–butcher's (meat in vacuum packs, fish exceptionally naked), a junk shop, a cake shop, a toy shop and any number of Turkish gentlemen's clubs, most of which deploy net curtains against street windows to conceal the goings-on within from passing eyes. Opposite the baby cafe there is a moneylender's and a pet shop — or at least there used to be a pet shop, thinks Lucy. It would appear to have evolved into another Turkish gentlemen's club. There are also restaurants and takeaways, which change their identity with the season. It's impossible to keep up. And on the site of the old Shell garage, where Lucy had more than once bought overpriced milk and cigarettes in the small hours, there now stands a small 'express' outlet for one of the big supermarket chains, whose custom appears to arise chiefly from the students who occupy the new-build residence on top of it. Although it does have an ATM. There's always a queue for that.

Lucy and Lorna extract cash from the

machine and cross the road to enter the gates of Bellsmith's Working Men's Club (Est. 1878), a forbidding sooty-bricked Victorian pile which takes its place among the other toes like the swollen and blackened victim of a vicious stubbing — outsized, vulnerable-looking, dark, as if asking to be trodden on painfully by the new world economy.

There is no queue outside; very little sign of action on the pavement generally, in fact. But in the two women go, through two sets of doors, the second one aluminium-framed glass, checking Lucy's name with a doorman who, it has to be said, has probably seen better days himself; up two handsome flights of stairs divided by a worn brass rail (funiculated by a heavy-duty stairlift); red linoleum on the floor, magnolia walls dignified with gilded lists on monumental boards of those club members who gave their lives over the course of two world wars. Also a noticeboard spelling out in tiny print club news, rules and regs; agency photographs advertising forthcoming events: a DJ at his console under the canopy of a Seventies 'fro; Kathy 'N Simon, a 'singing duo, for singalonga's and foot-tappa's of every age'; Benjy & Bongle, a ventriloquist and his dummy meerkat, who are virtually indistinguishable from Kathy and Simon in facial expression, the most obvious difference being that one of the four is made of mauve nylon.

Billowing through the heavy swing doors at the top of the second flight of steps, a thunderhead of music. Stevie Wonder, thinks Lucy. 'I love Stevie Wonder,' says Lorna. 'You did say there might be some good people playing . . . '

Lucy and Lorna have already downed a couple at Lorna's kitchen table. They are later arriving than they intended to be. But this is evidently only the disco bit — plenty of time yet for Weller and Primal Scream and Hole and Del Amitri and The Sundays to do a couple of songs each. And maybe Musical Youth. The Youth must all be in their forties now at least — grown up enough to fit right in with the demographic.

David Bowie? Possibly not.

What larks!

They had compared notes about first musical passions over the kitchen table and roared with laughter — not at their choices of course (Lorna's first compulsion had been 'Pass the Dutchie', Lucy's 'This Is Not America') but at the boyishness of the exercise — then trundled down Green Lanes concocting their ideal bill of fare for Bellsmith's tonight in the secret hope that if they built up a big enough head of steam-irony, their evening would not subside into boredom and irritation once it's revealed that William's friend, the birthday boy, Jo-whateverhisnameis, is really a Billy-No-Mates with the star-magnetising power of a chump.

But Stevie Wonder quacking on the sound system . . . That'll do to be going on with. They'll have a drink at least.

It's dark inside, the darkness stippled with light reflected from a mirror-ball rotating above the dance floor in its rig like the most classical disco spaceship ever seen. There are coloured disco spots dappling the floor too, and occasional fierce jets of perpendicular downlight, like tubes. Like reverse thrusters. Close Encounters of a Disco Kind, thinks Lucy. Yes! How long has it actually been, since she danced? There are perhaps a dozen hoofing it self-consciously to the fading tail of 'Higher Ground'.

Quacketty-quacketty quacketty-quacketty — 'Till ... I ... reach my high-er grou-oun'' — quacketty-quacketty ...

They're all middle-aged. All of them. They heave their bottoms around like shopping bags.

Quacketty-quacketty ...

Apart from the ones who aren't quite middle-aged — and they're the same age as Lucy and Lorna. But mostly they're middle-aged. We're the young ones ...

The quacking fades, suddenly, and ...

'Lucy, let me get you a drink!'

It is William, or rather his near-silhouette, grinning fit to bust in the half-light (his teeth and the whites of his eyes are catching the odd photon) and steering her with one finger towards the small, brightly lit bar to the left of the doorway. Then ...

The roar of a revved motorcycle engine. Blatt! Uh-*blatt*! ... The implosive sound of mountains collapsing into a hole ... Plasticised 1980s squelch-funk backbeats pulverise whatever it is William is saying to Lucy and, now, to Lorna too ... Lucy wags a finger at one ear and they shift into a deep alcove waterlilied with tables. The edge comes off the music slightly.

'Thanks for coming,' William enunciates.

'Really pleased you came. Hi, I'm William.' This to Lorna, one paw out, shooting cuffs. William is wearing a sharpish suit with a dark shirt done up to the top, no tie. Lorna introduces herself. Lucy flicks her gaze to the floor but she can't see his feet between the tabletop lily pads. No matter. She knows his shoes will be pointy.

'Drink?'

'Please. Gin and tonic.'

'Lorna?'

'Same please . . . '

'I think they do gin and tonic. Although G and T may be a bit poncey for Bellsmith's. You might have to make do with vodka and orange. Remember the house rule: it's always 1974 in here. Back in a minute . . . '

He disappears and Lucy suddenly becomes aware that, outside their recess, the club is filling up quickly. In the four or five minutes since they crossed the threshold, the clientele has doubled in number, filling space, softening the anxiety that is the natural coefficient of exposure in empty space. The music somehow seems less domineering too, damped by the new press of bodies — shoals of self-possessed but worn-looking men and women holding coats up on one finger and wondering where to put them, clustering, bellowing into each other's ears, eyes widened and glinting in the gloom, turning to the heavenly light of the bar, leaning, even tipping towards it as if tugged by some invisible force.

'No sign of Bowie in that lot, then?' says Lorna.

'No, not that I can see,' affirms Lucy, looking over Lorna's shoulder. 'Not even anyone out of the Wonder Stuff.'

'Christ, this is unimpressive.'

'I'm sorry, Lorna.'

'Oh, that's all right, Luce. I knew what I was getting into when I signed up to this . . . this adventure. I was hoping to see *someone* from the Wonder Stuff though. Or maybe one of their roadies . . . '

'Look, Lorna, I'll make it up to you . . . '

'Don't be silly. It's fun. Look at me: I'm having a laugh, and God knows I could do with one. I'm laughing. Ha-ha-haaah . . . '

'Ladies!'

It is William, with drinks. Stubby cylindrical shorts glasses of the old school, two in the palm of one hand, two tiny tonic bottles dangling dangerously from his knuckles; a pint in the other hand. He doles out the G and Ts.

'Just made it before the rush. They were able to do gin and tonic, I'm glad to say, but made it very clear to me that this was a one-off and they weren't prepared to go out on a limb again. But who's this lot?' he says, flicking a thumb over his shoulder at the milling horde of new arrivals. 'And do they always go around mob-handed? Safety in numbers, I suppose. What's the collective noun for a mob of ancient rockers?'

'I'll give it some thought,' says Lucy.

'A sad bunch of fucks?' offers Lorna.

★   ★   ★

Jolly Bizzle takes the stage some forty-five minutes later to hoots of approval from the dance floor. It must now have more than fifty people on it, most of whom look only too relieved to have the excuse to stop dancing. Many of them are breathing through their mouths and are drifting together again to form clumps, a dew of mild anticipation discernible on their extensive foreheads. One group actually lean up against each other in a sort of stook. They appear to be giggling. All of the tables around the edge of the dance floor remain busily occupied too, ribaldly in some cases, while the swing doors at the back of the hall fire a steady, percussive, almost rhythmic fusillade of hesitant bodies into the fray. With no music on, it is possible to hear the *punk-fwish punk-fwish* of the door. There must be well over a hundred in now. Well over.

Lucy and Lorna have emerged from their alcove and are standing with William a few feet back from the edge of the disco-light pool. The pool is dimming now anyway as the stage illuminations come up to reveal Jolly and a crew of malodorous-looking coves blinking and holding up their hands to shield their eyes from the sudden glare of the spotlights. There are drums, bass, keyboard, sax, two singers and two guitarists, the healthiest, most respectable-looking one of which flicks his guitar lead behind him like a tail and removes a dangle of hair from his eyes with a well-bred toss of his head. His job, thinks Lucy, is to counteract the unhealthiness all around with undiluted essence of public schoolboy — what a marvellously *levelled* spectacle rock music once presented . . .

'Ladies and gentlemen!' declaims a disembodied voice over the PA, slightly distorted.

'Here we go,' says William.

'Ladies and gent-le-*men*. Thank you for coming out tonight in such gratifying numbers. We hope you have a marvellous evening of unrestrained rocking mayhem — insofar as you are able to rock in an unrestrained fashion. May I welcome you all on behalf of the birthday boy — ' there are whoops from every corner and smiles and claps from all the players onstage, except Jolly himself, who is fiddling with his settings — 'and will you please put your hands together for the first of tonight's performing artistes . . . the greatest unsigned ska band of the 1980s . . . THE RUDIES!'

A couple of low-frequency burps emanate from the stage. The drummer drops a stick with a clatter. Nothing much else happens for a few seconds while the players await Jolly's pleasure. He remains steadfastly preoccupied with his amp. A gust from the wings momentarily ripples the glittery streamers which dress the upstage wall. And then one of the two vocalists — a stringy, chalk-white individual in a pork-pie hat and sunglasses — steps up to a microphone and sasses his head from side to side: 'Course we'd have been the greatest *signed* ska band of the 1980s if Jolly hadn't fucked off elsewhere.' He jabs a thumb and grins a toothless and mirthless grin, then qualifies himself. 'Nah, Jolly, we love you, man — I'm joking. We never held it against you. Not often anyway.'

And while Pork-Pie Hat cackles and points at the object of his joke, Jolly turns upstage to face the drummer, with the floppy-haired public schoolboy at his shoulder, and somehow, suddenly the music spasms into life, as if defibrillated. It takes several seconds for the um-cha, um-cha rhythm to settle, and even then it is not a confident groove. But forward motion is achieved. Pork-Pie Hat begins to shout into his microphone while capering from foot to foot . . .

'You wanna watch this?' bawls William into Lucy's ear. 'Or you wanna bring your drink outside with me?'

'I'll come with you. C'mon, Lorna . . . ' Lucy mimes 'drink' and 'outside'.

'Nah, I think I'll watch for a couple of songs,' mouths back Lorna, but then changes her mind and yells: 'Actually, no, I won't. I'm coming too.'

There's a big plastic finger pointing the way to the designated smoking area — it's out the back of the building, the exit to it half concealed behind an old curtain and down a precipitous stairway running beneath the wings of the stage. The three of them clatter down the steps, their feet barely audible in the boom from above. At the bottom, a heavy black fire door is ajar and they push through it to find themselves corralled in a fenced and roofed enclosure, dotted with plastic chairs and the occasional plastic table. There is enough clearance between the top of the creosoted planking walls and the corrugated-plastic roof for the enclosure to count as 'outside', just about, although it must have been a close thing getting it past the council's Health and Safety regulations.

There are three other bodies present. One of them is Steve's. He's stubbing out a cigarette.

'LUCY! How nice. You too, Lorna. What a surprise!'

Lucy does not turn to look at Lorna, as she'd like to — to look at her and to pierce her. No, she greets Steve warmly but holds her ground while he gets up and accidentally kicks over a plastic chair with a crash. He saunters over, visibly drunk.

'Well, as I say,' he resumes. 'What a surprise. I mean, what's the connection — what brings you here, this fine autum'al evening? Are you friends with Jolyon? I had no idea . . . '

'I was invited by my friend William here, who used to be . . . '

'In Jolyon's band! That's right. VineHeart. Always a fan, William, always a fan . . . Though didn't you used to have a French stage name?'

'It wasn't a stage name. It was my real name — I'm half French. But I'm all William these days . . . '

'Well, it's great to meet you, William. Must have seen VineHeart at least twice back in the day, supporting someone, I think, at the Town and Country, back when it was the Town and Country — dunno about the other occasion . . . in a pub somewhere, maybe . . . the Robey, perhaps? And I had a mate who had the album. Nice one. So how do you and Lucy know each other?'

The emergency exit swings open for a moment

to release another small party into the night air and briefly it is filled with clumsy skanking.

'It's a work connection, Steve,' says Lucy, raising her voice but trying not to rush. 'William and I have been doing some business over the past few weeks . . . '

'So what do you do now, William? Are you still playing?'

'I'm playing tonight . . . '

'William's headlining,' says Lucy, before she can stop herself. 'He's doing a couple of numbers. I never saw VineHeart myself, but I certainly heard of them — and in fact William and I have known each other for years. Since *then*, in fact, except I didn't know it at the time. I suppose you could say he's an old and long-lost friend . . . '

'Is 'at a fact?' says Steve over the rim of his pint glass, which he has just raised to his lips.

'I work in retail now,' says William. 'Bedlinen. Not very glamorous. I sell bedlinen in a department store. Done it for years. So much for rock 'n' roll, eh? I know, it's only sheets and pillows, but I like it, like it, yes I do. It keeps body and soul together and it's a fairly stable business to be in, given the economic circs. People will always need to sleep comfortably. I genuinely like it. The bedlinen, I mean . . . '

'Nothing to be ashamed of, mate. Nothing to be ashamed of at all. I sell vintage fashion myself — on a stall on Camden Market and now on the Net, when I can get the stuff that looks good on the Net. Fancy that! Sounds like we're ladies' men, the two of us.' Lucy can see that Steve's

201

combative impetus is beginning to lose out to his desire to be liked. 'So do you miss the rocking and rolling then? I mean, you did quite well for a while, didn't you, with VineHeart? . . . What happened then? Must have been sometime in the Nineties you broke up, no?'

'Early Nineties, yes. Ninety-two. I just got fed up with it, in the way that anyone can get fed up with anything . . . '

Steve is looking at Lucy, even though he is having a conversation with William. She turns to look at Lorna, who has a fixed expression on her face which is evidently meant to be unreadable. Even if Lorna didn't set this up — and Lucy doesn't really imagine that she did — it must be obvious to Lorna how this must look to Lucy. Time to get her involved.

'Didn't you see VineHeart in their pomp, Lorna?' she says brightly.

'Possibly.'

'I thought you said — '

'I remember them being faux-gypsies and my brother liking them, but — '

'We were never faux-gypsies,' says William benignly. 'We were a gypsy-style rock band with Parisian Hot Jazz overtones, which is completely different. But we weren't pretending to be gypsies. We were gypsy-*ish*. We wanted, really quite uncynically I have to say, to leech off the romantic gypsy look to suggest that we were fugitive souls with no great respect for respectability and convention and to cover up the fact that we were a bunch of suburban middle-class boys — some of us from St Albans, for fuck's sake. But we didn't pretend to *be* gypsies. We didn't live in a caravan. We didn't cook rabbits in a pot by the side of the road to prove our authenticity to *NME* readers. We didn't want to be *mistaken for* gypsies, just to look a bit like them. It's a subtle but important distinction . . . '

'And maybe that's why you never really took off properly,' says Steve, not really trying to disguise the triumph in his voice. 'Because the whole point of everything was that you had to *be* whatever you professed to look like, otherwise no one would take you seriously. It was a *cred* issue . . . '

Fwump. The door flies open again, admitting another gust of ska into the smoking area, but no actual bodies, and giving Lucy the opportunity to change the subject.

'Anyway, Steve, what are *you* doing here? How do you know whatever his name is — Joe, Jolyon?'

'Jolly, usually,' interjects William.

'Jolly . . . What's the connection, Steve?'

'Friend of a friend, Luce. Mate of mine said he was coming down to celebrate some rock-star mate's fiftieth and that there'd be drinks and c'lebs and rock 'n' roll and probably lots of falling about and maybe even fighting . . . and I thought, fuggit, why not? No sign of the falling about and fighting yet, but I live in hope — I'm well on the way, so to speak . . . '

'Oh God,' says Lucy to Lorna, turning out a palm, 'Steve's in one of his fighting moods — better call the feds now . . . '

Steve ploughs on. He is beginning to adopt his stand-up comedy persona, as he does when he's had a drink and is feeling the tingle in his blood: the Singing Hodsman. There is a yodel in his voice, to go with his ramped-up cockney cadences. ''Aven't seen too many celebs here yet or 'eard much rock and roll — this band are shite, aren't they? But I did come in at the same time as that guy in the wheelchair, you know . . . Beard. Whossisname? Brilliant. 'I'm a Believer'. 'Shipbuilding'. You *know* . . . ' Steve shakes his open hand in front of his face. It is red-raw around the knuckles; his cuticles look bloody. 'You know — fell out of a windah . . . '

'Robert Wyatt,' says William neutrally.

'That's the fella. So, Lucy, are you going to ask *him* if he knows Jolyon personally? Are you going to give him the third degree as well? 'Hey, *Rob*-ert, so when did *you* become besty mates with jolly old Jolly . . . ?"

'OK, Steve,' says Lorna, snapping out of unreadable mode, 'I think you've made your point, whatever it is. Back in your box now, there's a good dog. Time for us to be getting along, I think.'

Lucy is already canting herself out of grabbing range. She lets her feet follow.

'Steve,' she says, turning to go. 'Steve, you're a nice guy. Don't be horrible, eh? It doesn't suit you.'

'Don't be a prick, Steve,' says Lorna.

'I am a prick,' says Steve gloomily.

★ ★ ★

Halfway up the staircase Lucy taps Lorna on the shoulder and yells at her to go on and get her a drink. She'll be up in a minute. She goes back down.

She finds Steve back in his seat, rolling another cigarette. He doesn't look up. Lucy pulls up a chair and sits down opposite him.

'Steve, I'm sorry,' she says.

'Yeah, but *are* you?' he says without looking up, his voice thick.

'Yes, I am. In as far as I can be. Genuinely. I thought it might work out between us and it didn't. I thought we might be able to carry on the business and be friends — but we can't. I'm sorry for all of that, I really am . . . '

She pauses, but Steve is now licking his Rizla. She knows she has nothing to say to him really. Nothing that will help anyway.

'Gimme a puff of that, will you? When you're ready . . . No, I won't have a whole one. But look, Steve, what do you want me to do — not go out and see my friends? And avoid public spaces on the off chance that you might be in them? I told you that I'm not seeing anyone, and I'm not. I'm pretty screwed on the income front too, if truth be told. Remember, it wasn't me who couldn't make it work between us — '

'Oh, fuck off, Lucy — I know that. Do you think I don't know that? I might be a prick but I'm not stoopid. Der.' Steve cogitates theatrically for a beat. 'Or maybe I am. Maybe that's it: I'm a prick *and* I'm stupid . . . '

'Steve . . . '

'No, Luce, no. I'm sorry too. It's obvious to

me that I'm a total fucking mess and it's all my fault. I am a total faaaarcking waster. I mean, it's not as if I didn't know how good we could be together. I mean, weren't we, Luce, when it was good? Good, I mean. I'm not wrong, am I? And I tried to change you too much — '

'No, you didn't, Steve. Stop — '

' — although you'd probably say that I didn't try hard enough to change myself — which is certainly true. I didn't — and I dunno . . . Maybe I should. Try to change. What do you think, Lucy? Who knows what might happen? I might be happier and better at business and not so fucking self-pitying all the fucking time.'

'Look . . . '

'You know what, Lucy — I'm sure I could do it. I know I could do it if I had you around, that's for sure. I don't mean 'change' in the Californian wanky sense but in, in . . . well, y'know . . . trying not to be so fucking realistic all the time. Let a bit of light in, maybe. I mean, that's the point, isn't it? Letting light in; brightening things up. Opening the curtains and the windows and that.' It was as if a lamp had suddenly been switched on behind his eyes. 'And that's just it, Luce. You're my light. Lucy Light. In fact — ' Steve puts one finger to his temple and closes his eyes for a moment, as if receiving vital information — 'that's what it means, doesn't it . . . in Latin? Lucy — *light*. You are lucent, my Lucy . . . '

'Probably, Steve. Probably.'

'Or lucid. You're pretty fucking lucid at the best of times. I always knew what you wanted or what you were saying. It was always clear. Even if it wasn't what I wanted. But then I never fucking know what I want — even when I've got it, you know what I mean? That's the other thing, my darling . . . ' And Steve reaches over the table with one hand — not to touch but clearly in the hope that he'll be touched in return. 'That's the other thing . . . uh, what I've got, what I've actually got in my life, it's like, like shit if I haven't got you in it too. You make sense of everything else to me . . . '

'OK, Steve, I'm going to stop you there,' Lucy does not touch the outstretched hand but instead leans back on her chair and holds up her own right hand, flat and perpendicular to the tabletop, like a policeman on point duty. 'Right there. You're pissed and rambling and I think you're about to say something you'll regret tomorrow. You're probably going to tell me any minute now . . . I dunno . . . that I *complete* you or something. And we both know that I don't. And even if you do think that, you're wrong, Steve. Just wrong. People don't complete each other — that is just romantic marketing bullshit perpetuated by Hollywood and pop music and anyone else with a product to sell. And you know that perfectly well, Steve. *Real* Steve knows this. Not-pissed Steve. Boyfriends and girlfriends do not finish the job started by Mummy and Daddy and, before them, the gene pool. It doesn't work like that on the ground for all kinds of reasons, many of them quite good, actually, if you think about it.' This is not where Lucy wants to go with this. But she's started now. 'People just form dependencies, dependencies which they can't shake off — and while I'm perfectly happy for people to experience love as a feeling, I don't buy it as an objective reality. As an organising principle in society. Even an organising principle in people's individual psychology. Never have done, never will do. We are not destined to do anything with our lives, least of all *complete other people*. I'm sorry, I'm sorry. It's all just random shit happening all of the time to everyone and . . . and . . . and, this is what gets me . . . You *know* it, Steve.'

Lucy pushes her chair back, stands up and put her palms down flat on the surface of the table. It is slimy.

'Look, Steve. I like you. I've always liked you. You're a good bloke — great to have a laugh with and do stuff with, and I wish it could be like it was. But you know as well as I do that it can't be like that any more. It just can't. I don't *want* it to be like that . . . '

She pauses to let him speak, but Steve is mute. His lower mandible twitches slightly but not enough to form speech.

'And I think,' she goes on, 'that we should suck up the shittiness of how we're feeling — just *suck it up* — and get on with our lives. That's certainly what I'm going to do right now. I'm going to go back up those stairs, find my friends, have another drink, listen to some more appalling music, then stagger home for some cocoa and a good night's sleep, God and Baby Justin Bieber willing. And I think you should do the same, don't you?'

208

Lucy taps once on the table with one fingertip, fixes Steve with a kind eye, turns and opens the heavy fire door as if it were a fly screen. She is at the top of the stairs before the half a dozen smokers in the smoking area have found it in themselves to recommence their conversations.

'Faaarcking hell,' says Steve.

19

Glitter Ball

I'd forgotten all about Jolly's Robert Wyatt connection — and in truth, I know very little about it. Nobody does.

All I know is that Jolly's tenure in the rehearsal studio with the great man was enjoyable but brief and the results never saw the light of day. It came right at the end of Jolly's time as a working bassie. By then, he was so disillusioned that he'd started to miss sessions and was acquiring a reputation as a flake. I used to get calls on Thursday nights from exasperated producers who seemed to think that I was his dad and would I happen to know of his whereabouts? And would I smack his bottom for him? Actually, to be fair, I think it happened once. But the Wyatt thing was in reality a very good thing and very nearly saved Jolly's career. The sessions were fun and productive and seemed to require a creative input altogether lacking in the other jobs Jolly was getting at the time — but never resulted in anything concrete, either in the way of recordings or performance. And after that, Jolly just walked away. I'm not entirely sure why. Not in detail. But I think he felt it might be better to do the walking off the back of something good, rather than something that made him want to club baby seals.

And here I am, standing not a mile from where I live in a scuffed but still dazzling clone of the set of *Phoenix Nights*, ten feet from Robert Wyatt, thirty feet from Jolly Bizzle, and the space between the three of us yawns not only in physical and experience terms, but in existential ones too. And it's getting bigger with every passing year. Every passing minute. In fifteen minutes or thereabouts, I will clamber up the wooden steps at the front of the stage, plug in my Tele, empty my face, assume the position, concentrate like a mama on doing the basics right, on showing Jolly in the best possible light, on showing a good time to everyone canoodling on the dance floor and, in so doing, attempt somehow to bridge the abyss of years — as if it's actually physically possible to get there, to the other side, where one's youth resides and everybody else's illusions are stored in some big fucking light-industrial storage unit of the soul.

And then it will be over and nothing will have changed. Robert Wyatt will listen politely, no doubt, and clap at the end, whether I balls up the chords or not — but he will no more connect with what is going on inside my body and mind than I will with what's going on inside his. Or even with Jolly's, and Jolly is one of my oldest friends, whom I love dearly. Hear that? That yawning sound? That's the sound of the abyss yawning . . .

The best I can hope for is this: if the playing goes well, then I will be able to accept the plaudits as sincere and not as a kind gesture by people who feel sorry for me. Which is something, I suppose.

Better be good then.

Then there's the other thing. The Lucy thing. Who *am* I kidding? I need to get that thought right out of my head and keep it out, with menaces if necessary. What was I thinking? I wasn't thinking at all, is probably the answer. I was just listening to the noises inside my body and the voices inside my teenage head. Idiot. And who *was* that guy Steve? An ex-boyfriend, pretty clearly, and a fairly unprepossessing one at that, as well as fairly recent. 'Always a fan' indeed. I'd be shocked if I wasn't already chock-a-block with mixed feelings.

Lucy is standing next to me with her friend Lorna. They are showing some sort of interest in what's going on, arms crossed, tapping their fingers in time to the music on the shorts glasses crooked lightly in their elbows, slight movement — a mere shifting — evident beneath the Mason — Dixon line. They look as if they're enjoying it, slightly.

That's probably because the Rudies have gone — hopefully for ever — leaving only a few shudders behind to remember them by. Jolly and Simon are now occupying the stage with Roy Dodds. They've got a woman singer in her thirties I've never heard of doing a Van Morrison song rather nicely, with a piano player I half recognise from somewhere. And a horn section. Trumpet, tenor sax (never heard of either of them either) and Annie Whitehead on trombone. It's got feel. They've obviously rehearsed. They're taking solos. I am up soon.

'Who's the girl?' yells Lucy into my ear.

'Haven't a clue,' I yell back, touching her hair with my mouth.

'*Call me up in dreeeam-land,*' toots the woman onstage, to whoops from all around. Quite a lot of people appear to have heard of her.

Then Lucy is holding my hand. It's not a finger-to-finger thing and no palms are involved. She's not interlocking. She's holding my hand from the side, the fleshy bit, and pulling on it slightly, hooking it like it's a fish. She wants my attention, not my body.

'When are you on?'

I can feel her breath on my cheek and ear, and the breath-like touch of her hair again. She lets go of my hand. I want to grab it back.

'Shortly, I think, Lucy. They're doing a couple, then it's me . . .'

'OK. Are you nervous?'

'Yes.'

She grabs my hand again; again from the side, but taking a little more of it this time. Tugs it.

'You'll be fine,' she says. 'You'll be brilliant.'

I think: I will now.

★   ★   ★

'Ladies and gen-tle-*men*,' announces our MC for the night, a noted digi-DJ who once worked for the *Melody Maker*. 'Our next guest performer . . . is the man who stole the birthday boy from the Rudies and made him into a star . . . himself a shooting star of the London alternative rock scene back when London's

213

alternative rock scene was still interesting — when you, yourselves, were all knee-high to a grasshopper the size of Selfridges. Yes, it's the Telecaster king of N16! The pulsating aorta of VineHeart! The Amazing Mister Please Please Or I'll Fucking Kill You himself! You knew him as Gil but now he's Will . . . Please *wel*-come to the stage . . . Mister WIL-LIAM *CARBER-RRYYYYY*!'

Oh, for God's sake.

Head down. Get moving. Acknowledge cheers and claps with modest wave. Mount stage without tripping over. Clap Jolly on the shoulder as I go, pausing briefly to squeeze his hand and look him in the eye. Shake Simon's hand vigorously and give him my best presidential point-and-grin for the benefit of the assembled whoopers (as if we hadn't already had a touching private reunion this morning at the soundcheck). Wink at Roy Dodds and mouth something respectful but enigmatic in his direction. He's a drummer — it doesn't matter what you say to them. Smile at the horns, especially Annie. Locate guitar on its stand behind the amps. Sling it on, plug it in and have a quick tune. Gaze non-committally out into the audience while Jolly and Simon have yet another committee meeting about something — and then spot . . . Steve. He's down the front, right in front of me — his face is catching the light reflected by the glittery upstage streamers. He's grinning wildly and nodding. Showing all his teeth. He's got his hands on the front edge of the stage. Really gripping.

'. . . Two, three, four!'

And we're off.

Slightly too slowly, which I like. That's why Dodds is so good. He's pulling it back, to force everyone to dig in and lock properly — plus we've got horns and I've never had horns behind me before, humping the upbeat — uh-*hump*! — then spreading out to form a whole new environment, a new weather system on the downbeat side of the bar line. The thing surging but restrained at the same time. Held back, pushing. Push, pull, drag, swing. Lock-tight. Teetering. *Faaaarck*. It's like being on the edge of orgasm — and this is only the intro . . .

I have yet to open my mouth . . .

Then . . .

Uh-*hump* . . .

Out it comes.

'*Mus-tang Sally . . . Huh!*' . . . *Uh-hump . . . 'Guess you better slooow your Mus-taaang down . . . '*

★   ★   ★

We do 'Mustang Sally' and then we do 'Barefootin'', like naked children playing in open fields under sun. It is bordering on the heavenly to do it. Seven or eight or even nine minutes pass, but it might have been a long, beautiful afternoon for all my consciousness of time passing. People dance on the dance floor like sylphs, or so I imagine, a blur of movement beyond the scope of the stage lights and beyond the region of my sight. But I am scarcely touched by their rapture. I am too busy. Too busy being in the moment *I'm* in, which has no time for any other kind of moment. Or anybody else's. 'Mustang Sally' rocks, 'Barefootin'' flies — I get the armpit lift . . .

I enjoy a protracted break from the inertia of things.

And there is actual cheering to go with the clapping at the end. People are standing at the stage front and looking up as they clap, and turning to each other. I can see nods and smiles and the occasional pair of clapping hands raised above heads, votively, that final push into the air being an adrenal push. Unwilled. You know . . . You *know*. I am reeling with pleasure.

But where is Steve?

Then Jolly moves in front of me to the microphone. I step back to give him space.

'Uh, thank you. Thank you very much,' he says, with all the charisma of a bass player. He turns and opens a hand to me. Smiles. I bow graciously. 'William Carberry, ladies and gentlemen. William *Carberry*. Always does the business. But I wonder . . . ' He turns to face me again, his shoulder blades momentarily to the audience. He is now not smiling but grinning slyly. Then back to the microphone. 'I wonder if he remembers how to do *this*?'

Bom-bim. Bom-bim. Bom-bim. He's playing a curt two-note phrase halfway up the neck of his Precision, with a fixed hand position. Facing me now. The rest of him might have bulked out over the years, greyed and settled in transit, but his hands look no different to the way they did in

216

1986, no different at all. They are beautiful, like huge black tarantulas, mobile and animate, *tensile*, alive, even in a fixed position. Then reversing it. Bim-bom. Bim-bom. Bim-bom . . .

Bastard.

Then Simon chimes in. Duddle-uddle-uddle-uddle . . . Duddle-uddle-uddle-uddle . . .

Bastards.

It's our old backwards arrangement of 'Marquee Moon', which we used to do as an encore on good nights, sometimes for ages.

Bastards, bastards, bastards.

I am trapped. I can refuse, I suppose. I can unsling my guitar, wave graciously to my new constituency of swooning fans, blow kisses and walk off, leaving the bastards to it. Then have it out with them later. Yes. I could do that. In fact, yes, that's what I'm going to do . . . Right now. Now, before it's too late . . .

Except that I am not. I am not going to make myself look like a cunt and, furthermore, like a cunt who can't cut the mustard any more — the complete sad-eyed cunthead of the lowlands. I'm not that stupid. I am William, not Guillaume. I can only smile and mouth 'You bastards!' cheerfully, so that everyone in the audience can see. I can feign bemusement and good-natured indignation and panic . . . But I can't flunk out. Not from this position.

Which means that I am obliged to do my own bit of chiming. Right now. Come on, William, do it. Roy can't start, theoretically, until I'm doing my tchanga-tchanga-tchanga part — the easy part — the tiny screw in the works that holds everything together and shows which is front and which is back and which the right way up and the direction we're going in — the part that the original Television version starts with. I have to do it, for everyone's sake.

All right, you fuckers. Here goes . . .

*   *   *

We get there all right, as Jolly knew we would. After a slightly curtailed, decidedly hesitant, unswaggering rendition of 'Marquee Moon', with a beautiful solo from Simon and without a solo from me (I make it clear with my most authoritative glare and head-shake that I won't be delivering), it is over.

'Ladies and gen-tle-*men* . . . VINEHEEE-AAAART!!!' screams our man in the wings with the distorting microphone and — now that I can see him in his little box — the wrong kind of face for his hectoring voice. 'Giiive it up for VINE *HEEEAAAART*!' His features are strangely inert, passive, pudding-like, even as he bellows into the mike. His eyes drift as his mouth works. '*Viiine*Heart! A little taste of what we've lost and maybe didn't deserve in the first place because we were too busy investigating the contents of our own rectal cavities — *VineHeart*, ladies and gentlemen!'

But I am too far gone to make a scene with Jolly and Simon. Too far gone to do anything but get down off the stage and find Lucy; bask in her approval, if that's what she has to offer, or take it on the chin, if diffidence is all she feels. But I

218

have to see her and take what she has, whatever it is. It feels like the only thing to do.

But I can't find her.

I am generously patted from all sides as I make my way down the side of the dance floor, through a surprising number of people who appear to want to study me closely, some of whom I'm sure I'd recognise and say hello to if it weren't quite so gloomy and I had my specs on and I were even bothering to look. But I have no time for that. No time to acknowledge the pats either. Lucy has disappeared. She's actually nowhere to be seen, even after a complete circuit of the dance floor and a purblind squint into the table-lily alcove. Not a sausage.

Nor Lorna.

Nor Steve.

They've done a runner.

Unless . . .

And there I find them, on the other side of the swing doors in the 'foyer', on the large square of red lino at the top of the staircase; Lucy leaning against the wall, her back to me, one arm straight out at ninety degrees from her shoulder, her palm flat against the paintwork, her head hanging, her hair sticking out; next to her and down a bit, what looks like Steve hunched saggily in the seat of the stairlift, which is parked at the top of the staircase. No sign of Lorna . . .

Then, before I have time to address myself masterfully to the situation, *bang!* Lorna emerges noisily from the ladies' toilet on the landing, just behind Lucy, who swings round with her mouth open to face her, sees me, and both say my name in the same instant — which stirs Steve on his stairlift. His head comes up with a delayed jerk to reveal a face that has given way at last to misery, in all its totality. Collapsed in on itself. A punched cushion. It is apparent that he has been crying.

Lorna lays one hand on Lucy's wrist.

'I'll deal with this,' she says. Then to Steve: 'Come on, you.' Then back to Lucy: 'You go back in and have fun. I'll get him home. Come on, you hopeless case, stir yer stumps — I'll walk you home and make you a nice mug of Horlicks, and if you're lucky I might even tuck you into bed. You're in no fit state for human consumption, that's for sure. Furthermore, you have ruined my evening.'

'Lorna, can I help?' I offer, as enthusiastically as I can, stepping lightly in Steve's direction.

But Lorna shakes one finger forcefully. 'No, William — I rather think not.' She turns back to Steve with a motherly inclination of her head and a consequent tumble of her gorgeous hair. 'We're old muckers, aren't we, Steve? And we know what's best for all concerned. Come on, you smelly old git . . . ' And she puts one shoulder under Steve's and literally hefts him off the stairlift and onto the top step, where the broken man steadies himself for a moment against the central banister with one flapping hand and they begin the slow descent together, one step at a time. Lucy and I are waved away silently, without a backward glance.

So Lucy turns to me.

'I'm sorry,' she says, eyes wide and grey as the

220

eastern sky, mouth straight as a ruler. 'I'm really sorry. I only got to see your first song. Well, most of it. And then things got a bit tricky. I'm so sorry. I thought it was really good though, what I saw. The song. You were great.'

She puts out one hand and rests it on my forearm.

20

Electric Darkness

He smiles and looks for a moment as if he is going to say something. He even opens his mouth. But in the end he says nothing. He lays one hand briefly on Lucy's forearm in return, inclines his head and turns away. Lucy follows him back into the hall.

Inside, it is darker than before. No one is dancing and there is much toing and froing on the stage. Heavy things are being lugged around in the gloom. Boxes, wires, stands. Something dubby is playing at comfortable volume over the PA system. Lucy and William sit in the alcove, hemmed in by tabletops and separated by one.

'I thought it was really — ' begins Lucy, but she is silenced by William, who puts one finger to his lips.

'Tell me another time,' he says. He has enough information to be going on with. He has other things on his mind. 'What on earth was that all about?' He twists a thumb back in the direction of the foyer. 'I was a bit worried for a minute there. Is Steve all right? Are you all right?'

'Yes, I'm fine, thanks. Thank you. Yeah. Steve is too, probably. But he doesn't hold alcohol well.' Lucy narrows her eyes. 'One over the statutory three and he falls off a cliff. Splat. He tells himself too much booze makes him into a brawler, to make himself feel better about it — well, more hairy-arsed and manly — but the fact is he gets so drunk so quickly and completely, he's only a danger to himself and the carpet. I've seen more actual fight in an unconscious hamster, to be honest. He's a good guy but he's also an unhappy guy — and he's very unhappy that we split up, as you probably gathered.' She shifts from one buttock to the other, leans forward to place her elbows on the surface of the table and fixes William with a gaze so open and uncomplicated that he catches himself catching his breath. 'It happened ages ago, but he's struggled to get used to the new reality and it's worse than usual at the moment for reasons I won't bore you with. I'm really sorry about the way he spoke to you outside. And so would he be, if he could hear himself.'

'That's all right. I barely noticed . . . '

'And I am really pissed off I missed nearly all of what you did. I'm going to tell you, whether you like it or not, that what I *did* see was really good.' She taps the edge of the table with three fingers, hard enough for the tap to be audible over the music. 'In fact it was because Steve saw me getting into it — looking rapt, no doubt — that he came over and started to pick a fight again. He was jealous, I suppose, and I can understand that. I haven't been as kind to him as maybe I should've and I think the sight of me . . . well . . . the sight of me focusing on the activities of another . . . person . . . I think he couldn't stop himself from disrupting it, that's all. Having a brawl.' She sticks a hand into her thatch and pushes it back from her face. She seems to look down at the table in the gloom. 'Lorna will take care of him and probably give him an almighty bollocking too, which he needs. Just not from me.'

She looks up again. And as she does so the few lights that remain in the building go out completely.

There is sudden, plunging silence and then an almighty crash from the direction of the stage followed by a tidal wave of curses, laughs, doggish howls and whoops from all around. The darkness is total, save for the modest green glow emitted by one emergency exit sign forty feet away, presumably sited over the steps down to the smoking area. Nothing else can be seen.

'Oh,' says William's voice, just about audibly.

'A power cut? In north London? In the twenty-first century?' replies Lucy's. It's a comedy voice she once used routinely with Steve.

And then one voice begins to dominate all others in the blackness, chiefly because it is neither whooping nor cackling but making a stentorian announcement. It sounds Irish. It is certainly female.

'Keep still! Keep STILL, everyone! *EVERY-ONE!* Quiet too, please. I'm very sorry, ladies and gentlemen, but would you please keep still and quiet and we'll have this sorted in no time . . . '

Noise levels drop instantly to virtually nothing, to a level where the clop of furtive movement can be distinguished above the whispering and gig-gling.

'Jesus,' breathes William, 'I can't see a bloody

thing. Shouldn't they have emergency lighting running off an independent circuit or something? More than that exit sign at least. It looks like it's about to die.'

The loud Irish voice again: 'Please don't be alarmed and just stay where you are everyone . . . That way nobody gets hurt.'

'That a promise or a threat?' says a voice, to a chorus of giggles.

'Fookin' hell,' says another. 'My fookin' foot!'

'We're just looking into the problem, and as soon as we have any news, we'll let you know,' continues the Irish voice, apparently unfazed either by the catcalling or by the foot. 'We think it may be a fuse.'

'You know what's going to happen, don't you?' says Lucy's normal voice, quietly. 'The lights will come on again in a minute and Jolly will be revealed spreadeagled on the drum kit in a spotlight with a sharpened mike-stand plunged through his heart. At his fiftieth birthday party. Spreadeagled. Stuck like a butterfly. But what I need to know, William, is whether, in those circumstances, you would fall under suspicion — and for what reason. Just what *is* your history with Jolly?'

William utters one very short, choked syllable — 'Huh!' — more a grunt than a syllable, possibly the beginnings of a laugh — and in the quiet that follows, Lucy extends her arm out into the darkness where she knows William is sitting and finds to her surprise and embarrassment and pleasure that William's hand is coming in the opposite direction. The two hands meet, little finger to little finger in the blackness, bump, withdraw, then meet again, and then manoeuvre laterally until their palms are touching — William's on top, Lucy's below, opening out. Then they hang on, clasping gently, suspended in darkness for four or five seconds before descending jointly to the tabletop with a yielding gentleness that takes away all of Lucy's breath and causes her eyes to close momentarily. Sightless in the black.

Nothing further is said.

And in the blazing instant in which the lights come on again, a short while but a long moment later, both Lucy and William find their eyes locked not onto one another's faces but down at the tabletop, at the suddenly illuminated spectacle of their two hands, moving one on top of the other in furtive, alien embrace, like crabs at the bottom of an ocean trench — both William and Lucy looking down as if the effort of looking up were really too much to contemplate right now, in the circumstances, given the situation . . .

And then they do look up.

'I do apologise, ladies and gentlemen.' It's Mrs O'Shouty again. 'That's all fixed now. Nothing to worry about. All sorted and it won't be happening again. As you were. Please carry on with your evening.'

William and Lucy smile. They smile long enough to allow them to unclasp their hands without either one of them being solely responsible for the unclasping. But they do not lean towards each other or shift in their seats;

226

they just stay in position, smiles twitching at the corners of their mouths, wondering behind their faces whether their hands have ever felt so empty before. William is the first to move.

'Drink,' he says. A statement, not a question.

'Please. Same again. Double,' says Lucy. 'And let me get them.'

'No, no. You got the last round — it's my turn. And besides, I need a walk, even if it's just over there.' He dips his head towards the bar but his eyes do not leave Lucy's. 'Back in a jiffy.' And he leaves the alcove.

Lucy drags her attention away from the white-bright illuminations of the bar to what is unfolding on the section of stage visible from her seat. Activity is redoubling and the house lights have now been illuminated, presumably to hurry things along in greater safety and with greater efficiency, and perhaps to cleanse the collective palate prior to a fresh start. Musicianly people are now filing up the stage-front steps and into position beneath the rectangular proscenium. It's a crowded space. There must be getting on for a dozen up there, plus their horns, drums, guitars, microphones, more percussion. Amps. Jolly . . .

Jolly is looking anxious and a little lost, Lucy decides. But alive at least. In fact everyone on the stage has that wide-eyed thousand-yard stare on, the one you get when the pressure's almighty and nobody's really sure what they're doing — the rictus she remembers freezing her own features when going onstage unsure of her lines.

Where's William?

Jolly appears to be issuing last-minute

instructions and the flop-haired public-school guitarist is amplifying those instructions, or perhaps just making them clearer, while Jolly gracefully cedes authority and returns to fiddling with his settings. And now the horns gather round Flopsy Bunny to squint at a sheet of paper in his hand and point at it, concentration furrowing every brow. Beneath them all, on a patch of dance floor in front of the stage, a new spotlight is brightening a small circle of parquet. Those who are caught by it withdraw in feigned alarm, as if pulling back from an unexpected source of heat. They leave an empty disc of light on the floor, not quite as round as a penny.

William returns with another G and T for Lucy in one hand and what looks like a pint of tap water in the other. He begins to neck it before he's even sat down, and then plonks himself rather clumsily on the chair next to Lucy's. Their table shudders and shifts.

'This looks interesting,' he says, pointing with the little finger on his left hand, which is also the one holding his pint glass, leaving the hand next to Lucy free on his thigh, his elbow touching hers. 'I wonder if — '

Then the house lights go down yet again, leaving only the stage lights and the bar lights at either end of the hall to parenthesise the darkness. There is a hiss-crackle over the PA, which quickly dies.

'And now, ladies and gentlemen,' intones the MC from his position in the wings, as distorted as ever. 'And now, let me reintroduce you to the birthday boy himself, the man we're all here to worship unconditionally and embarrass to hell. Here he is, right here: Mister JOL-LY BI-ZZZLE!'

There are whoops and shrieks and the applause is surprisingly thunderous. William and Lucy emerge from their alcove and join the back of the throng on the dance floor, William standing directly behind Lucy. He is tall enough to see over her head without craning and, without having to lean forward more than an inch, to feel the breath of her hair against the lower slopes of his face.

Jolly ceases to fiddle with his amp and makes his way purposefully to a downstage microphone. He has the sealed face of a man inhabiting his moment with the exercise of maximum effort.

'Uh, thank you,' he says, his voice booming awkwardly. He withdraws an inch or two, with a jerk, as if shocked. 'I'd like to thank everyone for showing up tonight and making this such a great night. Everyone. All of you; all of us.' He waves a hand over the neck of his instrument. 'But especially the musicians who have done this out of affection, I hope, and enthusiasm and passion and love for music, rather than out of any expectation of payment for their hard work. Because they ain't getting any. *Plus ça change*, is the phrase, I believe. Thank you, everyone.

'But — ' he holds up a hand to forestall a matey heckle from the foot of the stage — '*Bu-u-ut* now we'd like to try something that hasn't been done before, not like this.'

Jolly turns his face but not his body to his

small orchestra, twisting to offer them what he must hope looks like a reassuring grin, but in fact resembles a panic-stricken smirk — visible as such even in profile. There is a brief outbreak of hooting from the floor. Jolly returns his mouth to the microphone bulb and empties his features again. One hand is still raised, the other hung like washing over the curvature of his bass. He is going to make a speech.

'Back in the day — twelve years ago to be fairly precise — the last job I did as a professional musician was in Lincolnshire. It was cold and windy and there were loads of cabbages everywhere. It was great. I stopped being a pro after doing that job not because of the cabbages but because I wanted to leave music with a good memory, not a bad one. And this had been one of the best experiences of my whole music life — and I say that with due respect to Simon and William and all the other people I've played with over the years. They know where I'm coming from — don't you, boys?' Jolly gestures vaguely out into space, as if Simon and William and the others are drifting in the air like ghosts above the audience's heads. Behind Jolly, Simon allows a hank of hair to shift affirmatively. Behind Lucy, William ducks his nose into Lucy's cloud. Jolly carries on. 'I went to Lincolnshire to work on a special project which was being put together up there by a great musician. A *great* one. It was great fun. It was so much fun that I couldn't believe it when it never went any further than the R&D stage — you know, half a dozen sessions spread over a long week and into the weekend;

hours and hours doing the kind of playing and thinking and interacting *all* musicians want to do, given the chance and the budget and the time. Proper music.' Jolly drops his shoulders wearily, breathing audibly through his nose, and lifts his draped hand to the microphone shaft. 'And it remains for me one of the best memories of my life, even though nothing ever came of it, you know? Apart from being paid of course. Nothing. Not a thing. No records, no performances, not even any demos. Not that I've ever heard.

'And it was my last thing, ever. So I remembered quite a lot of it, in detail, as you do; partly, I have to say, because it was made of such interesting *parts*; partly because of, well, just the emotional experience, and . . . ' He looks down, through the veil of stage lighting, into the faces of the audience for the first time. 'Well, I was able to put some of the bits back together for tonight, for a one-off performance in front of you lot, because . . . well, because you all deserve it, for being such good friends to me over the years. Probably.'

'Christ,' mutters William into Lucy's hair, 'this is the longest unbroken utterance Jolly's ever made . . . '

'And here's the really great bit,' continues Jolly, brightening into his stride. 'I'm pleased to say that the musician who dragged us through the cabbages to Lincolnshire is here tonight and he's agreed to sing the one song we managed to finish all those years ago — and when I say finish, I mean in the sense that it had a beginning wiggly bit and a middle wiggly bit and a long, unresolved wiggly bit on the end, which is about as concrete as Robert ever gets when it comes to song structure. But then he is a one-off — and I am very grateful and honoured that he's here and agreed to let me do this and then participate himself. This will be some treat for all of us. Ladies and gentlemen, will you welcome to the offstage spotlit area down there — make way for the great, the incandescent, the *bril-li-ant* Mr Robert Wy — '

And before the second syllable of his name can be uttered, a burly, bearded figure shoots his wheelchair out of the crowd and into the spotlit circle in front of the stage, a hearth animal on castors, smiling broadly and performing a brief pantomime of gracious waves and bows in acknowledgement of the hullabaloo all around.

The clapping and whooping are barely diminished by chords from the horns onstage, conducted by Simon; odd, drifting, unresolved harmonies which hint at forward motion but don't actually go anywhere — they just hang and puff a little, like ruminative clouds . . . joined from below by a loping tarantula-fingered rumble from Jolly, who seems to be adopting an entirely different playing posture to his earlier one, no longer anchored on his heels but pressed up on the balls of his feet, chin out, eyes flashing, almost dancing on the spot to the strange metre spelled out by his hands, serpentine but not symmetrical, wiggly but earthed. Then drums and percussion and Flopsy Bunny all join in at once and the horns flare out into shapes almost recognisable as block harmony ... and Lucy feels William's mouth in her hair and then a hand on her hip ... and as the man in the wheelchair brings a microphone up from his lap and opens his mouth to sing, she turns first her head and then her whole body to William's and, pressing in, allows her mouth to catch his and their kiss to unwind into its long, giving length while the man in the wheelchair's voice carries over their heads, shockingly high and thin, like a choirboy's.

PART THREE

21

Egypt

We do a nice Egyptian cotton own-brand at the store. I'm not sure *how* Egyptian it is, but it is certainly 'Egyptian', with a high thread count and a reversion to crispness after washing which ought to be the envy of some much more expensive brands. Our price is keen and it brings all kinds of propositions within reach, theoretically. Imagine — clean sheets every day . . . What would that be like?

It would be like living in a hotel, I suppose, with commensurate laundry bills and the great temptation (always assuming you don't have servants) to leave last night's on for one more night, because let's face it, changing sheets is an enormous fag — I know I'd be as slovenly as the next man. But even so, it does bear thinking about: would the experience of nightly clean sheets for all change the world for the better? I suspect it might.

It has been clean sheets twice a week in my flat over the past three weeks, that's for sure. And in one of those weeks — the first one — it was three times, although that was more out of necessity than luxury. But I can't pretend it hasn't been good to have the excuse to feel like a pharoah at bedtime. I am dizzy with it. Drunk on the crispness, the scent, the cool, dry, cleansing balm of the experience. And that's just the touch of Lucy's skin. The sheets are something else: a sort of lush orchestral accompaniment. So clean. So fresh. Indeed, we pursue our nightly rituals with an enthusiasm that borders on the prayerful. Clean sheets are as healing as steroids and a fraction as bad for you, but also an agent of revelation. As an old smack-addicted chum once confessed, many years ago, he only realised just how much he loved his parents after going to bed every night in their clean sheets throughout his year of recovery. Clean sheets are the sun on your back, the grass between your toes, the love of a sightless God.

We have been fucking each other's brains out.

I worry afterwards of course, when we've finished. I worry about my own flesh and its witheredness. I am fifty-three going on fifty-four, and softening fast; she is thirty-eight and still pretty firm. She acts as if my little belly were invisible and my invisible arse were somehow present. She has thus far made no jokes at the expense of my skinny legs or my bristling ears and nostrils. And, graciously, she has refrained from squeezing the love handles which are comfortably settled like doughballs on the tray of my pelvis. And of course I worry about the fact that I can no longer do it all night, not as I once did; that sometimes, halfway through, I want to stop and fall asleep in her arms because that would, in the moment, result in still-greater accessions of rapture — and not *necessarily* because I have run out of puff. On only one occasion have I been forced to put a sudden stop to our bouncing and that was as a consequence of unwonted head-spinning dizziness of a kind I did not recognise. Most weird. Yet even then, in the throes of my panic-stricken submission to sleep, my face buried in her flank, I was pleased that Lucy whispered 'Poor baby' in the tiniest mocking voice, clearly disappointed at the failure of her baby to act like a spring chicken. Anything is better than 'Poor old fella' spoken kindly.

We make great lovers, I think. We talk incessantly, as all new lovers must. She tells me about her fecklessness and her parents; fantastic stories too about her ridiculous-sounding brother with his job in financial services and his wife in telly ('a future Head of Drama' it is said), which remind me somehow of the Thackeray I couldn't be bothered to read properly when I was an undergraduate. They seem to have married one another as if each were a guarantor of the other's desired lifestyle — as a sort of well-considered consumer/career decision — and then had children on the same basis. Fair enough, I said to Lucy: you wouldn't want them to marry out of their species and start contaminating the field for the rest of us, would you? She did not laugh at this and I choked down a further series of witty observations PDQ.

She also told me about her failure to love Steve and her distaste for children — as if the two failings somehow intersected with each other. She became unusually inarticulate and hesitant while telling me all this stuff and I, in response, found myself tidying her hair frantically with two fingers, and kissing her shoulder.

239

She couldn't hold my gaze at all and there was a moment when she actually turned her head to look away. When she brought her face back to mine, her grey eyes had darkened and filmed over. I did not feel threatened.

She has her questions too. Perhaps not so oddly, she seems much less interested in my tales of sex and drugs and rock 'n' roll than in the 'strangeness' of my life afterwards, my post-accident life in retail — I suppose that stuff would tell her more about the person I am now than the person I once dreamed I might be. By that, I don't mean that she asks penetrating questions about thread count and the procedures of the Crown Prosecution Service, but about the details of my daily routine and what goes on inside my head when walking the floor at the store. She clearly has real trouble computing the fact that I like doing what I do. The second Sunday morning, while we lay in bed — listening in silence to Dylan's 'Blind Willie McTell', for what that's worth — she seized me by the wrist and held on, squeezing a little harder than was comfortable. I asked her what she was doing and she told me that she was 'just holding on'.

'I'm not going anywhere,' I told her resolutely, in best Churchillian style.

'Don't be so sure,' she said. 'We're all going somewhere.' Then she let go. 'But if you're going,' she continued, 'you're going. It's not my job to stop you.'

So I went into the kitchen and made toast.

These momentary enigmas aside, we got on like a house on fire.

She does not share my hybrid post-war/Sixties angst and appears barely to have heard of the Post-War Consensus. Indeed, when I asked her what the Sixties did to/for her, she didn't appear to get what I was talking about at all, and didn't seem all that curious about it either. It's interesting how those old enough to have fancied the forty-year-old David Bowie but too young to remember the 1960s even slightly, seem to register that most vivid of decades not as a passage of history but as an old wives' tale.

'But then I wouldn't have room for real feelings about it anyway,' she explained patiently. 'We had Thatcher and Duran Duran.'

'But,' I spluttered, mock-indignantly to hide my real indignation, 'you couldn't have had Thatcher and Duran without Austerity and the Beatles.'

'Yeah, and we couldn't have had any of it without the Black Death and the Counter-Reformation,' she replied dully, with a sigh, as if any more rehashing of the GCSE history syllabus would result, here and now, in her making a new kind of personal history for the both of us. 'I mean, come on, William: history's just the stories you fancy telling at any given moment, to make a point. No one who has lived through thirty-eight years of my mother's life can be in any doubt about this. History has no special *weight* . . . '

And there we left it because I sensed that further pursuit of the subject would indeed result in flaming persecution and the extirpation from history of William the Conquered. And, besides, I had somehow acquired a new hard-on.

⋆ ⋆ ⋆

And then there was the letter from Bére. A letter, not a phone call. It was written in English, in a variety of pens, and as usual she insisted on addressing me as Guillaume. The letter was long, histrionic and moving. Whether I was moved more by Bére's detailed account of the state of our mother — evidently written over a number of days in journal style — than by the unhappy sound of my sister's voice under psychological stress is impossible to say. Two different kinds of moved, I suppose. Thankfully, the tone of resentment I often detect in our morning phone calls was absent. Maman is on her way out, that's for sure. It is only a matter of time now. It's a matter of timing for me.

I read some of the letter out to Lucy over breakfast this morning. Then wished I hadn't. Not because she responded in any way inappropriately, but because it seemed like too much information in the circumstances. We should be spooning dainty morsels onto each other's morning plate at the moment, not dumping hoppers of shit.

Lucy looked pained and even slightly frightened at the stuff I read out, which was all about the steep decline in Maman's cognitive powers. Bére wrote that confusion was now a starting point in our mum's mind, out of which some

242

kind of sense only emerged accidentally, randomly, as a bonus and against all expectation, like a red bus coming round the corner when you've got used to purple stripy ones and ones made of jelly. For the first time in our mother's life, disorder has taken over the reins. Bére has become accustomed to finding the old lady half naked in the strangest places, trailing her wires. Indeed, that very morning, while Bére had been out shopping in town, five minutes' drive away, Maman had managed to transport herself down to the marshy woodland that borders the eastern edge of the farm and installed herself in the cleft of a divided ash. She had one shoe on and was holding onto each trunk like a lover, caressingly, turning from one to the other to whisper *douceurs* into their barky ears. 'It was as if she had two boyfriends and she couldn't decide which one she preferred,' wrote Bére, in the only sentence in the letter that betrayed anything other than despair.

At this point Lucy asked me to stop reading and I saw that she was close to tears. I told her that I was sorry and explained that I would have to go over to the Haute-Vienne soon. Lucy looked at me levelly.

'Of course,' she said. 'Of course you do. Can you go now? How much notice do you need to give work?'

I explained that compassionate leave from the store tended to be generous and seemed to be offered in the right spirit but there were limits, and that I couldn't afford to flit back and forth, nor would they let me. I'd have to be pretty sure that I was needed in St Mathieu before setting out. And then Lucy went all hedgehoggy, pulling her knees up under her chin on the chair and folding her shoulders and arms over her knees, as if making herself into as small a ball as possible. She even rested her forehead for a moment on top of her crossed arms, her untended hair sticking up and out like soft spines. When she looked up again, the tearfulness had gone from her face. It was replaced by something much less soft. In fact it was the hardest expression I had ever seen on that most expressive of all faces.

'How much do you get paid?' she said.

'I beg your pardon?' I replied, not sure that I'd heard her correctly.

'How much do you get paid? For your job? I've always wondered how much people get paid who work in department stores. I mean, you must be quite far up the career ladder for bedlinen by now — you've been there an awfully long time, haven't you? That's an awful lot of annual pay rises — well, until the last couple of years at least, obviously. I don't mean to be rude, but . . . how much?'

'It *is* rude and I'm not going to tell you.'

'Fair enough.' She shrugged, still looking hard and, all of a sudden, young. 'But I bet they don't pay you enough, given your experience and what you know about sheets and pillows and sleeping and everything.' She sighed. 'I don't mean to be rude. I'm just curious. Sorry.'

'In that case, since you apologise so sincerely, I'll tell you . . . '

And then my mobile rang. It was Bére. She seemed to be experiencing some difficulty in speaking. I told her to take her time and start at the beginning.

'It's not possible to start at the beginning,' she said, with what I can only describe as French *hauteur*. 'There is no beginning any more; it is all about the end. This is our mother . . . '

'In that case,' I said, as gently as I could, 'let's talk about the end. Why not cut to the chase, Bére? Huh? Just tell me what I need to know. How she is. How you are. How soon you need me to be there. That sort of thing . . . '

'Guillaume, please don't be harsh with me.'

'I'm not being harsh,' I said even more gently, 'I'm trying to get a clear picture of what's going on so I can respond appropriately. At the moment I'm not getting anything.'

'You see? You *see*! That's what I mean about harsh. You're thinking only about what *you* need.'

'Bérengère, do you want me to call you back in a while? You sound angry and frightened, and . . . and there's nothing wrong with that — I completely understand: I'd be angry and frightened if I were in your position, miles from anywhere with a dying mum and no help and the nearest surviving relative hundreds of miles away — '

'Oh, shut up, Guillaume. You can be such a prig.' I did not respond this time. 'Look, the doctor has just been — he says it will be days probably, weeks at most. Certainly not more than a couple. It's just a matter of time. She's

245

very heavily medicated and doesn't know what's going on or who she is, and I don't even think she knows who I am any more. Did you get my letter?' I conceded that I had done, yesterday. 'Well, she's already worse than that. She can't get out of bed any more, which is a blessing I suppose. But it also means she needs more help, and there's a special nurse coming twice a day to . . . to help me. It's awful of course, but it's also beyond awful. I think you need to think about coming very soon indeed.'

'OK, Bére. I can do that. How about the weekend? Do you think the weekend would be OK, or too late, do you think? I can probably come tomorrow if you think I should. I'm sure they'd be all right about it at work.'

I have to say that now that we were coming to it — the sharp end, as it were — I felt a jolt, and then a metabolic spasm rushed through my body like some kind of tidal bore in a complicated estuary. It started in the pit of my belly and ripped outwards, concentrically, tearing everything up in its path and scattering my senses for a moment. It took everything, as if carrying away rooted plants and trees and heavy garden furniture and all manner of normally immovable objects. That's how it felt anyway.

Bére said she thought the weekend would be fine. I conceded the dry ground to her and sat down clumsily. 'I'll ring tomorrow,' I said, 'when I know what I'm doing. Bye, love.'

I then hung up.

I looked at Lucy. Lucy looked at me. For several seconds we didn't say anything.

And then we both spoke at once.

'I'm really sorry,' said Lucy, just as I said, 'I'm really sorry.'

She then deferred to me.

'I think I'll go at the weekend,' I said. 'Saturday morning, if I can get a ticket. I'll fly to Limoges and Bére can pick me up. And if she can't leave Mum for a couple of hours — which kind of sounds likely — I'll just hire a car, I suppose. It's too far to St Mathieu for a taxi, really.' I felt a sudden gust of embarrassment. 'Only trouble is, I haven't driven in years. I'm not sure I can any more, and not on the wrong side of the road. Gawd. Maybe a taxi then. Maybe Bére can organise someone to be with Maman while she gets me — we'll have to see what can be done . . . '

'How long does your sister think your mum has left?' asked Lucy quietly.

'A few days. A week or two at most. But probably days.'

'I'm really sorry. I don't know what to say.'

'That's all right, darling.' This was the first time I'd used the word; and I'd only been sleeping with her three weeks. 'There isn't anything you can say or do. Just be nice to me, and maybe allow me to drone on a bit. I've done grief before but I was much younger and my biochemistry has changed a lot since then.' I looked at her and all the hardness had drained from her features. She just looked beautiful. 'What I don't remember from then was this fear.

It's kind of paralysing. It's making me want to fart.'

'Go ahead. Be my guest.'

'Certainly not. I hardly know you.'

'Oh, I think you know me better than you think you do.'

I didn't know what to say to that, so I didn't say anything. I squeezed out what probably looked like a watery smile and Lucy smiled back, got up, walked round the table and enfolded me in her bathrobe, so that my nose pressed against her sternum. The desire to fart was displaced by a desire to cry — or at least to whinny a bit. But I didn't. Instead I turned my head and kissed the underside of her left breast. After a while, she pulled away.

'Come on, William,' she said. 'You need to go to work. And I need to find more work. You have no idea how broke I'm going to be pretty damn soon if I don't. And then you won't want to know me any more.'

'Oh, I doubt that very much.'

'Don't be so sure. Nobody likes a sponger, however much they like them. If you see what I mean.'

By this point she had reached the door and was halfway into the bedroom. She stopped and looked at me.

'I'm going to see Charlotte about the extra shift and the delivery idea — and if she doesn't go for it, I'm going to pull a few other local strings; and if that doesn't work, I'll have to sell my body. Or maybe just my internal organs, the ones I don't need . . . '

'Lucy . . . '

'Oh fuck, William. I'm sorry, that was tasteless.'

'Lucy, I'm not going to tell you how much I earn, but I will tell you this: strange as it may seem, my really quite modest salary is the price I pay for my freedom. It's my new deal. Not that it's a very new deal now, obviously, after nineteen, twenty years — but it is a deal, and it's enough to keep me sane and happy and . . . I don't have to be a person I don't want to be. I am free enough not to do what I don't want to do. I am certainly free from the obligation to activate the psychopath chip we all have in us, probably — the one that makes us competitive and grabby. The one that makes us anxious and want to kill people.'

Lucy twisted her mouth but kept it closed. I carried on blundering.

'Actually, I should only speak for myself. Let me rephrase: I don't have to activate *my* psychopath chip . . . ' I hadn't thought out loud like this for a very long time. Normally, thinking goes on inside my head, not outside it. Weird. A bit like doing music, actually. 'But what I earn is enough to keep you too, if you want . . . until you've got a new deal of your own. It's enough to feed me, warm me, shelter me, clothe me and pay for a flight to Limoges at short notice every now and then. I suppose that's one of the virtues of having no children. And I see no reason why I can't be your safety net-stroke-shelter too, for a while. I'd like it.'

I looked hard at her in an effort to read how

this was going down but, for once, she was totally unreadable. She didn't say anything. She just looked at me with her wide grey eyes, blinked once and closed the bedroom door behind her.

★ ★ ★

I had time to brush my teeth, wash my face, don my crimplene, comb my hair and put on shoes before Lucy uttered another word to me — whether I was in the same room as her or not, and for quite a lot of that time I was. In fact, I was grabbing my keys off the shelf by the kitchen door and slinging on my trench coat quite huffily when she finally emerged from the bedroom and, chin first, addressed me with the kind of cool formality I hadn't seen since she attempted to tick me off in the bedlinen department.

'William,' she said, 'is there anything else you want to say to me?'

'No. Why?'

'Nothing at all?'

'Nope. Was there anything you had in mind?'

'No,' she said, sounding defensive. 'I was just wondering.'

'Oh, come on now, Luce. Don't do this . . .'

'I'm not doing anything. I just thought for a moment that there might have been something you wanted to say to me but weren't able to, for whatever reason. The circumstances, maybe. The fact that you're upset, which is completely understandable . . .'

'I'm sorry, honey. I have to go to work. I don't

know what gave you the impression that I was biting something back, but I wasn't. I don't really feel capable of biting anything at the moment.'

'It really doesn't matter — forget it!' This was said with a curious mixture of belligerence and self-reproach. In fact, Lucy was blushing visibly. And then it dawned that I had been less than verbally generous to her over her kindness and solicitude, and I had been rather clumsy in reading the letter out like that. It had obviously upset her. Perhaps she wanted me to say how much I appreciate her; how much I . . . *love* her.

Oh God, not now.

'Lucy,' I said, 'there are a million things I could say to you right now, nearly all of them good. But now, when I'm rushing out the door a little upset and late for work, is probably not the best time for it. It might not come out right. I might say it clumsily or not sound sincere. Or, perish the thought, not even *be* sincere . . . And that would be awful and I really, really — '

'William, shut up!'

I shut up. She scraped her fist along the line of her mouth, opened her hand in front of her and jabbed it in my direction.

'William, do you want me to come with you? To Limoges. I will if you want . . . '

I opened my mouth and then shut it again. This I had not bargained for. The pause between us grew into a silence. Lucy stood her ground, her hand still out in front of her, open, fingers splayed, supported at the elbow by her other hand, her eyebrows up and her face now puce.

She closed her hand and let it fall to her side.

'I'm sorry,' she said. 'I'm really sorry.' She turned rapidly and went back into the bedroom, pulling the door shut behind her.

I followed her.

'Lucy. Lucy. Lucy-y-y-y,' I said, for want of something better to say.

She said nothing. She was sitting on the bed, staring into the mirror as if into an abyss. I felt a tiny gush of relief that I had not told her the Mireille mirror story.

'William, I am so sorry,' she said, looking at me and then back into the mirror, clearly focused not on her own image but on some other mirror dimension beyond self. 'I don't know what I'm doing, do I? Fucking hell. I don't think I've ever felt so embarrassed in my life. In fact, I'm sure I've not. I feel sick with embarrassment. Literally sick . . . '

I sat down next to her on the bed and looked into the mirror with her. Put my arm around her shoulders. She didn't flinch. We looked crumpled, the pair of us. Crumpled and clueless. She snorted and slumped further, but did not lean in.

'Christ almighty. I am virtually autistic,' she said.

'We all are, love . . . '

'What was I thinking? Have I got any sort of editorial hold on myself at all? I don't think so. It's pathetic. That was without doubt the stupidest thing I have ever said.'

'Come on, Luce. I'm sure that's not true. In fact I am willing to bet you have said several stupider things than that since the weekend . . . '

'Thanks, mate.' Instead of punching me in the biceps, she punched the air in front of her with a short right jab.

'No, I mean it,' I went on. 'I'm being serious. Everyone says stupid things all the time — I know I do: *all* the time — and, as it goes, what you just said wasn't all *that* stupid.'

'It was *fucking* stupid, William. Please don't patronise me.' She shuddered under my arm, as if involuntarily shaking the arm off — but I left it there. 'It was stupid, selfish, deluded and it puts you in an awkward position. And the worst of it is is that I was trying to get *you* to ask *me*, so I wouldn't have to risk the embarrassment of offering and then being turned down. So, cowardly as well. Really, really pathetic. I mean . . . manipulative or what? Eh?'

She slumped almost double on the bed and I pushed her over onto her side, pressing my mouth into her temple, working my front arm under her two arms, which were clamped firmly around her torso as if straitjacketed.

'C'mon, c'mon,' I badgered quietly. 'It's all right. It really is. I'm not offended at all and not hurt and not indignant . . . Just a little surprised. You took me completely by surprise — I really couldn't think in the moment what it was you wanted me to say . . . And I can see why you wanted *me* to say it rather than say it yourself, I really can. It's, it's . . . fine.'

'No, it's not.'

'Would you like to come?'

There was another pause which, again, became a silence. My ear was now pressed against hers, and both our faces, cheek to cheek, were still facing the mirror, although our angle was now too low to create a reflection we might actually see. I could hear her blood hammering — although I suppose it might have been mine.

'It really won't be fun, y'know,' I said. 'In fact there's every chance it will be one of the most unpleasant experiences of your entire life. And I can't guarantee that I'll be available, so to speak, to make things better. In fact, one of the reasons it never crossed my mind to ask you to come in the first place is that it never crossed my mind you'd want to. I mean, it's going to be horrible, Luce . . . '

'Well, that's it. I know. I just want to be useful, William. Do some good. Look . . . just for starters, I can drive you. I don't drive often, but more often than you do by the sound of it — and I've driven a fair bit in France. If it's only forty-five minutes from Limoges, I'm sure I can manage that; and that'll leave you time to concentrate on more important things while I drive. And I have enough money for the plane ticket, easily . . . ' She paused and snuffled through her nostrils, as if considering an itinerary. 'I can run around doing practical things for you and Bérengère while you concentrate on the important stuff. And if push comes to shove and you think your mum would mind me being there, even in the background, then I can stay somewhere else.'

'It's more Bére I'd be worried about,' I said, picturing the expression of disdain — or worse — that can all too easily take up residence on her

254

face. 'She isn't the most accommodating soul, my sis, especially when taken by surprise. I'd have to discuss it with her first and, if she objects, then we'd have to respect that. On the other hand, she may see it as an opportunity to get back to Paris for a few days . . . She's barely seen her kids over the past month and since she can be in St Mathieu in a matter of four or five hours, I imagine she might even see you as an authentic boon to her useless brother . . . '

'Well, then. Can I then?'

Lucy's body was softening underneath me. She made to turn with a heave and I rolled off and sat upright. She pulled herself up too. Her colour had quietened and the pronounced, and very sexy, bags under her eyes were no longer twitching.

'William,' she said, with the utmost care, 'we have to be right about this. I don't want you to say yes just because I made a stupid scene. And I don't want to come to prove a point — I think I may have done enough point-proving in my life already and I'm tired of it. I want to come because I think I can be useful and . . . and I'd like to be with you. I'd like to be there with you when whatever happens or doesn't happen, because . . . well, because I'd like to.'

She studied my face in the same way that she studied my face that first time, in the bedlinen department. She did not blink at all.

'But I want you to be sure.' She blew her hair out of her eyes and followed up the puff of air with a swipe of her hand. 'Really sure, as in super-sure, with no doubts at all, and with an additional dollop of extra-value certainty on the side.'

'Come,' I said. 'Come.'

22

St Mathieu

The sky was a race. Or at least the clouds appeared to be racing each other — 'scudding' as the cliché has it.

Hooey, of course. They were not racing. Presumably the clouds that Lucy could see through the windscreen of the car must all be going at the same speed — the ones that were visible to her, at least; the ones pinging along at the same altitude — so the racing thing was cobblers; one of those illusions created by language. Also, the fact that the car was going along the road must have some impact on how the clouds looked too: general relativity and all that. Movement always looks different — *is* different — when you're moving yourself . . . So why do we instinctually want to say that clouds 'race'? Why not that they are flowing or skulking or wooshing or just jogging along in amiable companionability? Why racing? Why bring competition into it? What *is* 'scudding', anyway, and where does it come from? Sounds kind of domestic and Anglo-Saxon . . .

To Lucy's right, William sat slumped in the passenger seat, one finger hooked into the grab handle above his head. In her peripheral vision she could see him doing it and trying not to be seen to be doing it. He was saying very little, apart from issuing directions and occasionally making observations about the landscape and the 'peasants' which dotted it.

'You don't *really* think of them as peasants, do you? Not in this day and age, surely,' she said. 'You sound like Boris Johnson or someone. Like someone from the Bullingdon Club.'

William said nothing for a moment — sufficient for Lucy to think that he was irritated by the question — and then mumbled something about the French word '*paysan*' not being as pejorative as the English 'peasant', but that they were inextricably linked both in etymology and in his head, and were effectively interchangeable. 'But yes, no — you're right. I don't mean to put anyone down. My mother is a *paysanne*. She is not ashamed of it. I'm not ashamed of it. It's metropolitan English snobbery that says that anyone who lives and works in the countryside who isn't gentry has to be denigrated automatically with 'peasant'. I suppose '*paysan*' and 'peasant' really aren't actually interchangeable at all, semantically . . . '

He didn't sound irritated, just remote and a little *distrait*. Lucy decided not to follow up. She could not begin to imagine what was going on inside his head and she tried not to think about it, for fear of what she might discover. Fear? She wasn't frightened exactly, but she did fear. She feared what might happen. She feared what might happen to him and what might happen to her. Anything could happen. It really could.

They were heading south-west in a tiny rented Citroën that, to Lucy's relief, was extremely easy to drive. It virtually drove itself. The roads were sparsely populated, and because the airport was located on the same side of Limoges as their destination, the small town of St Mathieu, there had been no need for full-on urban driving. After the initial burst of frantic overconcentration on everything — road markings, signs, lights, other road users, even anxiety-inducing pedestrians threatening to cross the road at ambiguous French zebras — Lucy had settled to the task and was now in a position to talk.

It was not clear that William was in a similar position, though. He hung on to the grab handle over his head with grim persistence, while his left hand wandered, confusedly, between the space in front of him and a clenched position in his groin, either flapping in anticipation of terrible events unfolding on the road in front of them — 'God, I'm always freaked out by traffic lights that stay orange' — or grimly retracted into his lap, as a passive expression of inner tension that would be hard to better anthropologically, Lucy thought, in any context. His voice was thinner than usual, higher, his efforts at conversation stilted. He had told Lucy three times between the airport and Aixe-sur-Vienne how relieved he was that she was there with him, taking the helm and providing him with stern moral support.

And now he had fallen silent. Their route had become rather more curly as they negotiated the last ten kilometres or so to St Mathieu; curly, dippy and increasingly forested. The light was bright for the time of year and the sun low. When they weren't shadowed by trees, everything was a dazzle of warmth and brightness, and this included Lucy's own sensibilities. She felt dazzled by providence and by the turns things had taken lately. Almost overwhelmed. Overwhelmed enough to lose her sense of judgement, perhaps . . . What *was* she doing? What had she let herself in for? Where was she headed? She might have been sleeping highly successfully with this guy for the past three weeks, but really, she hardly knew him . . .

How exciting was this?

How potentially fraught too. Lucy had rinsed her conscience over and over again to remove from it the speck of doubt that this expedition might not, on balance, be all to the greater good. She'd entreated William repeatedly to confirm that he did really want her to come with him; she'd thought of dozens of ways in which her presence might be of practical benefit; she'd balanced them rigorously against the potential for disaster, and always the positives had outweighed the negatives by a considerable margin. It made sense, yes it did. Especially now they were in France and the sun was shining and the clouds were jogging along together amiably.

She reached over with her right hand and squeezed William's left, which had been settled in his lap for some minutes now and seemed slightly less clenched than last time.

'How are you doing?' she asked, as kindly as she could manage.

'Oh, I'm all right,' he replied. 'Less nauseous than I was ten minutes ago. God, I feel funny, though — scared and wanting to run away and, at the same time, desperate to get there . . . But absolutely not able to feel or think about anything else. Or distract myself. It's one thing or the other. I'm sorry. I must be being really boring . . . '

'Don't be silly.' She squeezed again and returned her hand to the wheel. 'Tell me the best thing about your mum.'

William laughed tightly. 'You're very sweet,' he said. 'The best thing about my mum? Hmmm . . . ' He fell silent. After a minute or so, Lucy flicked her gaze to her right to make sure he was still with her and found that William was looking at her. She looked again, and he was still doing it, his head turned on his shoulders, a totally unreadable expression shimmering on his face.

'Don't do that,' she said. 'Or at least, if you're going to do that, tell me what you're thinking.'

'I'm trying to think nice thoughts, to distract myself.'

'What, though?'

'I couldn't possibly tell you because I couldn't possibly articulate them. But it's probably true to say that being here in this part of France with you . . . well, it allows me to think quite clearly about the best things about my mum.'

'Please don't tell me that I remind you of your mother . . . '

'No, no, no.' William's laugh was slightly less tight. 'Noooo. Not in the least. Well, not physically, spiritually or in any other way that I can think of. Certainly not temperamentally. Christ, you don't occupy the same temperament universe. But then how could you? Look where she came from — a goose farm in the middle of nowhere in German-occupied France; and look where you come from: Finsbury Park. I suppose the important thing is not where you come from but how you travel to get away from there, but even so . . . ' He fell into silence. Lucy elected to stay shtum.

'Look, my mum is very different to you,' he went on suddenly. 'But that doesn't mean I'm not allowed . . . *feelings*, that — that might connect in me because I know both you and my mum and I'm in France and you're about to meet here, and so on. Oh, fuck it, Lucy — what am I saying? I don't know what I'm saying because I don't know what I'm thinking or feeling. All I can think about is where I'm going and I don't want to go there.'

'Go on,' said Lucy.

'I can't,' William snapped. 'I just can't. And anyway, we're nearly there.'

★ ★ ★

'Actually, we're not,' he said about thirty seconds later. 'Turn right here . . . '

'What, *here*?' said Lucy, standing on the brake before peeling off the road and onto a smaller, much less promising single-tracker through the trees. 'But the sign for St Mathieu said straight on. I'm sure it did. This one goes somewhere else altogether.'

'Les Salles-Lavauguyon.'

'Pardon?'

'Les Salles-Lavauguyon — it's what the sign

262

said. It's where we're going first.'

'William . . . '

'It's not far out of our way. I want to take you there.'

'William, you're not serious — your mother . . . '

'I am serious. I'm . . . ' Williams seemed momentarily unsure how to explain himself. 'We're in very good time for lunch — I told Bére to expect us about an hour from now. And I just don't think . . . I don't want to be early.' He ran his hand up the surface of his face, starting from his chin, scrunching the tip of his nose as he went and then forking his fingers into his hairline. Lucy thought it was about the most neurotic gesture she'd seen William make. She tried not to interpret it — but nevertheless she felt the fine hairs at her napc and on her forearms prickle.

'Look,' he went on, 'I just want to be somewhere calming for a little while before we get there. It's the right thing to do, I promise — and I think you'll like it too. It'll be a little tiny micro-holiday together before the serious stuff starts.' He then used the flat of his hand to bang on the interior roof of the car, as if urging it on. 'C'mon. Let's go. If you let me do this, everything'll be fine. I'll stop being twitchy. Promise.'

Ten minutes later, as they rounded a corner in another barely populated medieval settlement, William said, 'There you go — park over there . . . ' and Lucy pulled the little car into what looked, in the circumstances, like a rather generous car park given the size of the village. There were ducks squatting on the far side of it.

'This,' said William, with gravity, 'is the green church.'

He waved a hand over Lucy's shoulder and she turned in her seat to look back at what she had just driven past blindly while concentrating on the road ahead: fifty yards to their rear, the looming facade of what her mother would have called a 'Romanesque sepulchre'. It was not green.

'It's not very green,' she said.

'No, it isn't now. But it used to be. On the inside. Come on . . . '

As she climbed out of the car, hot, anxious, tired and slightly irritated, Lucy was visited by the memory of childhood summer holidays spent executing this very manoeuvre in gritty parking areas the length and breadth of Europe, her mother resolutely ignoring the resentment of her children, her father compliantly going along with her mother, the four of them barely speaking to one another while trailing in hot sun towards the looming facade of some Romanesque sepulchre and then mutely enduring the lecture that would ensue once Martha had located the informative printed matter stacked in piles on a blackened table at the rear of the church. She would read from it out loud, whether or not the material came with an English translation, and the kids were expected to glean what they could from her reading. 'I want you to listen even if you don't understand a word,' Martha would announce to her downcast offspring. 'That way you'll still be absorbing *something*, if only the music of another language.' In fact, perversely, Lucy and Oliver always preferred it if the text came without an English translation: that way they were able to switch off completely as they were far less likely to be tested in the car afterwards on what they'd learned.

Inside the west door of L'Eglise de Saint-Eutrope in Les Salles-Lavauguyon, William placed his hand in Lucy's, squeezing it gently.

'It's lovely, isn't it?' he said.

Lucy could not disagree. An elegant tiled nave extended in front of them like a road between trees, slightly, weirdly, crooked to the left as it drew closer to its culmination in a chancel of small area proportionate to its towering height. The honey-coloured columns on either side of the nave still bore traces of their original decoration and she could see high on the walls all around the foggy imagery of frescoes painted, by the raw look of them, in the early medieval period. There was very little visible in the building, in fact, that suggested much activity had taken place here since the Middle Ages, save for the obligatory chandelier hanging in the chancel, the stained glass in the east window, and the altarpiece which was clearly a modern pastiche of a dull baroque design. The font was lumpy and barely decorated. Strangest of all, the nave inclined from their feet like a ramp towards the altar, maybe sixty, seventy feet away. To reach the business end of the building you had to walk *uphill*.

William had started speaking again.

'I haven't been here since it stopped being green.'

'It certainly isn't green, you're right. I'd say it was peach in this light. Peach and orange.'

'Yeah, but it was vivid chlorophyll green once, until quite recently in fact, and certainly when I was a kid — and for many years before I was born too, I should imagine. Decades. Maybe even centuries. Green algae and moss creeping down from the tops of the columns, sometimes all the way to the floor. Bright, bright green — luminous slime you could scrape off with your fingernail. The brightness was probably intensified by the whitewash underneath. It was the worst case of damp in Europe. You could taste the moisture on your tongue and in your nose, and you could feel it on your cheeks, sort of clinging — like having ivy on your face. Decay you could ingest . . .'

'So when did they get Dyno-Rod in?'

'We-e-ell, it wasn't just a plumbing issue. As you saw, the church is built on the side of a hill, next to a stream, and I imagine rather too close to the water table.' William rotated on the spot, while continuing to gaze up into the vaults. 'I used to imagine the building was a sort of sponge, an engine for sucking moisture out of the land and then soaking it up and holding it in, like a cistern. Why they didn't cut into the hill to give it a flat floor, I have no idea — they seem to have just followed the slope. But to me it's all part of the magic. I love the way it goes up towards the altar, and not even in a straight line.' He stopped rotating. 'I haven't been here since it was reconsecrated a few years ago. They must have cleaned it up properly after uncovering the frescoes under the whitewash in the Eighties, just about when Maman moved back here . . . ' He scraped at his stubbly chin. 'But I first saw it . . . oh, I don't know . . . probably at the back end of the Sixties, on holiday. It was the local weird wonder. My parents brought me here with some ceremony and . . . I've always felt it meant something special to them. Something secret.' His eyes were now drifting over the pillars and walls, as if caressing them. 'Perhaps they fucked here for the first time, during the war.'

'A hard surface on which to have your first fuck,' said Lucy.

'It still had its earth floor as recently as twenty years ago, I think. I remember it quite vividly. There were some pews in here and it still seemed to function as a working church but maybe not for a parish — just for the priory next door. Who knows. Presumably they tiled the floor for the reconsecration. But I got the impression it was always open. Always.' William started to walk up the nave, knees slightly bent somewhat unnecessarily against the gradient, towing Lucy by the hand. 'It must have been just as green in the 1940s when they first came here, maybe even more so then — and that was long before they uncovered the frescoes: just an utterly decayed vault dripping with slime and mystery . . . '

'Well, I can see why your mum and dad thought it was special . . . '

'That's just it. It was seriously special to them, for reasons I have never understood and don't really expect to understand ever. It's just the way it is, a given.' He frowned and scrubbed at the side of his nose with one finger. 'But because they brought me here so ceremoniously when I was about ten or eleven, as if to show me something important but without ever actually saying *why* it was important, I've loaded up the memory with a kind of weight I can't even begin to measure . . . It's like those small boys who are made to go to the football by their dads, without their dads ever giving them a proper explanation of why they have to do this every other Saturday, or why it has to be this team and not that team . . . just having the experience and not elaborating on the reasons why. I dunno. The not-telling about it seems to be almost the most important aspect of the whole deal. It's just ritual behaviour, isn't it? We all do it.'

'I don't.'

'Of course you do, Lucy. You're just not particularly conscious of your rituals, I imagine, because you don't need to be.' William opened a palm. 'What about going to the bakery?'

'Yeah, yeah, fair enough.' Lucy shrugged. 'Though I don't have anything invested in the bakery itself, either symbolically or mystically. Or financially. And certainly no special memories of childhood associated with anywhere in particular I can think of.'

'I bet you do. I *bet* you do. I bet there are places you like to go for reasons you don't fully understand . . . '

She laughed. 'God, you can be patronising sometimes.'

'No, no, I'm sorry — I don't mean that patronisingly. I'm sorry. All I mean is, there must be places you like to go which give you a particular feeling for reasons that you don't understand, but which keep you coming back; places where you've got it all going on at the unconscious level. Places you liked as a child . . .'

'Churches certainly don't figure in that, I have to tell you.'

'Maybe not. Nor for me, as a rule. But this one does it for me, with knobs on. I feel like a sacrificial lamb here, ready for the chop — comfortable and unknowing and very vulnerable.' He stopped abruptly, leaving a small echo of his footfall in the cool air; he looked at her for the first time since they crossed the threshold. 'But here's what I'm trying to say, I think . . .'

The postern in the west door clanked open, sending reverberations seething up the avenue of pillars. Another couple came in. They were elderly and seemed to have business in the church. They clopped slowly up the north aisle, heads lowered, and then disappeared through a doorway hidden in the side of the chancel.

'What I'm trying to say, I suppose, is that coming here is like going to see my mother but without having to actually see her. You know — we could go back to London now and that would . . . *do*. It'd be OK: part of me would think that I've actually seen my mum.' He smiled doubtfully. 'How weird is that? God knows why it was important to my parents, this joint. They weren't proper churchgoers at all — just Christmas and christenings and weddings. And they certainly weren't married here. But this church was really important to them for some obscure reason. And I've carried the . . . the *wondering* around with me ever since. My unconscious mind is dripping with algae, you know.'

'You should ask her when you see her.'

'Don't worry, I will.' He grinned at Lucy, looking slightly less tense. 'I feel better for having come here.'

And they ambled back down the nave, past a table covered in leaflets, and out into the sunlight. Back in the car, Lucy looked at William and William looked back. His face was at least composed. He looked almost handsome in the morning glow, in a slightly wrecked and toothy way that made her want to eat him up.

'Home, James?' said Lucy.

'Yes, home,' William replied.

* * *

It took a little over twenty minutes to get there. They drove through the small town of St Mathieu, which was very much as Lucy had pictured it ('Look, a *mairie*!'), and out again into the forest beyond. More dark trees turning to brown and orange, more orange cows, more piles of logs.

The farm was located in a tiny, clenched hamlet a quarter of a mile south off the main road out of town. To enter it was to be squeezed back in time. Lucy negotiated the single-track passage between the buildings with some hesitancy and

270

then, at William's instruction, pulled the car onto a small grassed recess between an ancient barn and an equally ancient house, which towered above its half-dozen neighbours with ivy-drenched authority. There was a small Renault already parked at an obliging angle on the grass.

'This is it?' she said, nodding at the tall house.

'Yep,' replied William, his voice tiny. Lucy switched off the engine and turned to look at him. She smiled. He smiled back, but it was not a convincing smile. It slipped onto his face and then off again as if oiled.

'*Courage, mon brave*,' she said.

'Come on,' he replied. 'Let's get in there.'

They had a bag each, which had just about fitted in the boot, and William had brought a pillow from the store for his mother. ('A posh one.' 'What, even posher than my one?' 'Oh yes.' 'Not . . . not *snow goose*?' 'Bloody Nora, not that posh, no.') It had travelled from Limoges on the back seat in its store packaging and, while retrieving it from there, William dropped it on the verge next to the car, where it picked up a light coating of dusty, grassy debris. Cursing feebly, he beat its plastic sheathing with the flat of his hand. Lucy turned to face the sound of scrunched gravel and a woman in denim dungarees opening a low gate next to the house.

'Hello, William, hello. And you must be Lucy. Welcome.'

Lucy put out a hand. 'Hi. Uh . . . *bonjour*, Bérengère.'

'Hi is fine,' said Bérengère, her English touched only by a slight sing-song intonation.

271

Her smile was as sharp and short as William's one in the car had been, her mouth remaining closed. 'I *do* speak English . . . And please call me Bére. Everyone does.'

Lucy wanted to study her face. Bére and William did not look that similar, facially, even if they did share teeth and build. Where William's eyes were mobile, brown and up for it, his sister's were hazel and recessed, pinched in even, as if the flesh and bone supporting them were crowding in to shut out their light. Her mouth was thinner too and her forehead an expanse of furrows beneath a hairline that did not follow the same deep contour as her brother's. Lucy thought it the most strained face she'd ever seen. But she did not get to look for long. Bére and William were suddenly engaging in a clumsy hug which neither of them appeared to want to commit to fully.

'Maman is asleep,' said Bére as they separated. 'But lunch is on the table. Well done for getting here on time.'

★ ★ ★

The kitchen was darkly handsome. Dark floorboards, dark chairs surrounding a huge dark table; blacked ironwork backing the woodburner in a vast old fireplace; dark beams hanging above their heads like the roots of ancient oaks. It was the perfect peasant kitchen, Lucy found herself reflecting ruefully. There was food on the table under beaded muslin and pots and baskets and mighty utensils hung from the beams overhead.

'Sit down, please,' said Bére. 'Just put your bag down where you like and please sit down. It's so nice to meet you.'

Lucy suspected that it was taking something out of Bére to sound so hospitable. She felt bone-sorry for her. Hers must have been an attritional, life-destroying experience lately, to be endured and no more: day after day of repetitious selflessness, gruelling, bitter, remorseless and with no prospect of reward except in the termination of a beloved life. Lucy was unsure whether, when faced with the same situation, she'd be up to the challenge herself. She tried to think about tending to her mother in equivalent circumstances a decade or (hopefully) two down the line and she found that she could make nothing of it. The thought simply did not take, or would not. It seemed to have no purchase in her imagination. The door was shut. So, rather than linger pointlessly outside a closed door, she brought herself back into the kitchen.

Bére and William were already seated, lifting muslin and pouring water from a cracked white jug. They were being practical.

'Have something to eat and I'll keep an eye on Maman,' Bére was saying. 'I am not so hungry . . .'

'Come on, Bére,' said William. 'Eat with us — you won't help anyone by not eating.'

'No. I'm fine, Gui — . . . William. I had a big breakfast and I find that if I eat in the middle of the day I get depressed in the afternoon. Just let me do what I do, and not do what I don't, please. Yes?'

William cocked his head and pursed his lips and looked, for a moment, sceptically French. But Bére was not to be daunted. She punctuated her words with stabs of her opened hand — her hands were like William's at least.

'I'll keep an eye on Maman, and the moment she's awake and seems ready, I'll come and get you. I don't want you to go up now because those stairs creak if you don't know where to put your feet, and what she needs, more than anything else, is sleep. The nurse this morning thought she seemed a little better than yesterday and put that down to better sleep last night — so let's not disturb her until we have to, unh?'

Bére smiled and this time opened her mouth, to reveal her Carberry teeth. The teeth and hands were the only way you'd ever connect the two of them.

'And William, don't be nervous. You look really anxious and there's no need to be. Why don't you and Lucy sort out your arrangements — I've made up a bed in the barn loft — and maybe go for a walk while there's still some warmth in the air?' She turned to face Lucy. 'There are lovely walks round here, Lucy — you may as well make the most of them while you're here . . .'

William cut in. 'What are they saying about . . . about time? What are we looking at, conservatively?'

'If you mean, how long does Maman have, I'm afraid I don't have anything further to tell you. Nothing, no news.' She puffed out her cheeks. 'But what I infer is 'any time'. That's what the doctor implied the day before yesterday and the nurses aren't telling me any different, despite her comfy night. You'll see later that there isn't much of her left at all; she hardly ever comes to the surface now — in fact I fear she may not surface again properly at all. But — ' tears were now rolling down Bérengère's cheeks, despite the persistence of her sing-song, and she sniffed ' — she is . . . she is peaceful and not in pain, as far as I can tell.'

William had started weeping too, completely silently and apparently unselfconsciously. Lucy found herself joining in.

'Oh, but look at us! *Mon Dieu!*' These were the first French words Bére had uttered since Lucy and William's arrival. 'We need to be strong, no? I certainly need you to be strong — because I am starting to worry that I'm running out of strength. I promised Pierre and the children that I would go back to Paris for twenty-four hours tomorrow morning, if you can hold the fort for that long, so it's going to be a bit of a tough experience for you, I'm afraid. A bit shocking. William?'

'Yes, no, that's fine. The least we can do. Well, yes . . . the least — and I have an able assistant in Lucy here.' He rubbed his eyes, sniffed and looked at Lucy for the first time since crossing the threshold. 'We've talked about it in some depth already, haven't we, Luce, and we think we're equal to anything that the old lady might throw at us.'

'We certainly are,' Lucy chipped in and looked at Bére, who returned her gaze steadily. 'We certainly are.'

'Come on, eat,' said Bérengère.

After lunch they walked up the lane for about half a mile to a point where the road forked, and then they walked back. The sun was no longer generating much warmth. Autumn was drawing in. The oaks still clung on to their leaves, but the leaves were turning and the trees did their clinging with an air of resignation. The hedges looked weary.

William and Lucy did not talk at all.

Bére was hanging a sheet out of an upstairs window as they approached the house. She put a finger to her lips and mouthed something, before jerking her thumb over her shoulder. They met her in the kitchen at the foot of the stairs.

'Maman's awake and she knows you're here. Well, I've told her — I don't know how much she understood. Why don't you go up and say hello, William? But, Lucy, you stay here with me — it's best we take things one step at a time. I'm sure she'll be delighted to see you but she is very, very weak and gets easily confused and overwhelmed with more than one person in the room. William, she's awake. But I may as well introduce you to the quiet stairs now . . . You need to use the first step and the third one; then, as you go up, keep your feet as far apart as you can, then miss out the last but one completely . . . Got that?'

William nodded and started up the dark wooden spiral as if stalking an animal.

Lucy sat down at the table in the hope that Bére would do the same, so that they might talk properly and not at this declamatory, almost oratorial pitch. But she would not. Instead, she bustled around the kitchen firing off observations and instructions for Lucy's benefit during the period of Bére's enforced absence — she actually called it 'my enforced absence' — and then disappeared into the *salon* next door, where Lucy could hear her scraping chairs on a tiled floor and beating cushions. She heard the French windows open with a squeak and then silence: Bérengère had temporarily left the building.

Lucy poured herself some water from the white jug and tried to catch any sound that might be drifting down the staircase from the rooms above, where Maman languished and her son paid his respects. But there was none. Lucy looked through the open door at the shadowed afternoon. There were perhaps a couple of hours' proper light left in the day.

She got up and went to stand in the kitchen doorway, at the top of the short flight of stone steps up from the yard, to look out over the gravel below and to the meadow beyond and into the phalanx of trees which apparently marked off the outer limits of the land attached to the house. She stared listlessly, as if at a blank surface, and then began to realise that, contrary to first impressions, the trees did not constitute an impenetrable wall. To the right, away from the great barn and towards the neighbouring plot, the trees appeared to thin a little and the meadow sloped down darkly under their canopy, as if to invite exploration. It was clear that if Lucy were to walk to that point where the meadow began its descent, a new vista might be available, a new perspective —

'Go on, explore!' It was Bére, coming round the end of the barn with a basketful of washing. 'The land doesn't end with the trees — it goes on for a hundred metres or so into the forest, through a small fen. A swamp, really. It's beautiful and quiet and smells lovely when it's cool like this. You'll need boots and you'll have to be a bit careful, because a lot of the mud is hidden by the plants and vegetation, but it's well worth the effort. There are frogs and snakes and all kinds of wildlife there. Hornbeams. Oak. Ash. Explore!'

Lucy smiled. 'Thank you,' she said. 'I will. But not right now.'

Their exchange must have reached the ears of William somewhere in the rooms above. Behind her in the kitchen, Lucy could hear the squeak as his feet descended the staircase. She returned to her seat at the table just as he reached the bottom, forgetting to miss out the last but one step — which duly let out an appalling shriek.

William did not appear to notice. He was ashen. Lucy stood up. She began to open her arms to him but thought twice about it — then did so anyway. He took the necessary three paces to reach her and then, instead of embracing her in return, placed his forehead against the bone of her shoulder, his arms hanging limp by his side. He exhaled noisily.

'Come on,' said Lucy, and he joined his arms in the small of her back. He was absolutely rigid. 'Come on, love. Come on.'

'I don't know where you want me to come to . . . ' he began, just as Bére emerged from the *salon* with an empty wash basket. She stood in the doorway for a moment and said nothing, then crossed the room to the door to the bathroom, where she deposited the wash basket and returned to the kitchen. She filled the kettle.

★　★　★

The loft in the barn was cosy, if minimally appointed. A shaded Velux window in thc roof let a dim rectangular outline of starlight into the room. Lucy stared at it as she listened to William toss and turn. She was not close to sleep herself but did not want to involve William in her sleeplessness. They lay silently encamped next to one another, like opposing armies. And then, at some hopeless point in the very small hours, he got up and creaked down the stairs to the toilet below and then, with the faintest click of a latch, conveyed himself out into the darkness of the yard. His feet were not audible on the gravel, so Lucy presumed that he must be just standing or sitting on the bench on the patch of grass outside the barn postern. She pictured him there, rigid in the darkness, face to the sky.

The world appeared to be holding its breath.

In the hope that such activity might send her to sleep, Lucy tried to remember the lines from *Henry V* the night before Agincourt — the 'secret whispers' of the sentinels, their 'creeping murmur and the poring dark' — but could no more join up the fragments of half-remembered

279

verse than she could piece together solid sleep from the tatters of her wakefulness . . . Something — de-dum de-dah — about 'humming through the foul womb of night'. No, no — that's not right. And anyway, the pair of them were not going into battle in the morning, however worrisome the prospect of Bére's departure. Nothing like. They were going to nurse a dying old lady, and look after each other while they did it — well, Lucy was going to look after William while he did it, and she was going to do whatever she could to lessen his pain. No one was going to be hewn limb from limb. And William, not Lucy, was going to be the child rawly left . . .

An owl hooted close at hand. Just outside the barn. Maybe even under the eaves.

But not inside the room, surely . . .

Lucy switched on the lamp next to the bed and squinted into the webby recesses of the ceiling to satisfy herself that she did not have company. No. Nothing. What now? She berated herself for not bringing a book with her. This really was no good. The owl repeated its rippling call; it was clearly not inside the building but was nevertheless close enough to excite something in Lucy's stomach. This was hopeless — she'd be no use to anyone if she got no sleep, and she was not going to get there by trying to remember quotations from Shakesepeare. She was only going to wind herself up further . . .

She rolled over, sat up and put her feet down on the grainy, splintered surface of the floor, felt for her shoes with her toes, pulled on a sweatshirt and descended the stairs as noisily as William had done twenty or so minutes before. Clearly, quiet was an incidental luxury in the countryside.

A lamp was glaring on an internal wall to one side of the barn door, one of those clip-on agricultural lamps which plug in to a wall socket and then attach to a handy nail or hook or, in this case, an obtruding metal bracket in a moribund goose barn. Lucy shielded her eyes and unlatched the postern, then stepped out into the quadrilateral of light thrown out through the door by the lamp.

'*Luuu*-cy!'

Her name was hissed from close by. William was sitting, as Lucy suspected he might be, just beyond the scope of the lamplight on the bench against the barn wall.

'Lucy, the light of my life — come hither; warm me up!'

'Come back to bed, you idiot: we'll both freeze to death.'

'No, no, no — can't sleep, just for a change. You come here and give me a cuddle. And shhhh . . . '

Lucy thought he sounded slightly drunk. Yet the three of them had only shared a single bottle of wine over dinner, after which William had tipped down a glass of brandy as a nightcap. 'A duller,' as he'd put it. 'A what-er?' 'A duller. It's the opposite of a sharpener.' It hadn't worked. William sounded horribly awake as well as tipsy. And then she saw what sat plumply on his lap: the posh pillow from the store, now birthed from its polyurethane sheath and arching pertly on his knees, soft and lofty, like a jealous pet.

'What are you doing out here? And what are you doing with that thing? Tell me you weren't planning on bedding down out here for the rest of the night. It wouldn't be hygienic for the pillow . . . '

'No, no. I just brought it out to keep my knees warm, while I do some thinking.' William looked down at the bulbous envelope, as if surprised by its subtle infiltration of his personal space. He flipped it over. 'It's bloody freezing out here. I thought we were in the south of France, almost.'

'We're not in the south of France, anything like. And it's September. No, it's not. It's October. You should know what it's like here at this time of year. I mean, how many times have you been here? Twenty, thirty, forty?'

'Good question, Luce. Good question. Now what about my cuddle?'

'I'll give you cuddle if you come back to bed. I'm not standing out here for a minute longer. C'mon.'

* * *

Bérengère departed soon after daybreak. She roused William with a whisper from the foot of the loft steps and then issued final instructions to him in the kitchen, while Lucy slept on. He made groggy notes, cursing the treacherous properties of Armagnac.

'Always used to make me sleep like a log,' he grumbled over breakfast, two hours later. 'Just a sniff used to put me out for hours, like temazepam. Not any more, though. It's one of the curses of middle age, along with afterdrip and lowered tolerance of young people's music . . . '

'Speak for yourself, buster.'

'I am speaking for myself. Besides, you're not middle-aged, so you're not allowed to comment. Listen.' He pushed his plate away and looked Lucy in the eye for the first time that morning. He seemed oddly lively, now, for a body who'd had no sleep. 'The nurse is due at ten. According to Bére, she'll be here for an hour or so, at most, unless anything untoward happens, so why don't you take the opportunity to go out and get some stuff in for the next couple of days? There's a pretty good Intermarché in town — why don't you do a shop and have a cup of coffee in the square while you gaze in rapture at the *mairie* or the *quincaillerie* or whatever it is that thrills you so much, and leave me to deal with Nursey and Maman's tubes — frankly I'd rather you were out of the picture for that: there's no reason for everyone to go through everything.'

'But I — ' Lucy began to protest.

'No,' said William, flattening his hand on the tabletop. 'I really would prefer it if you came back to me afterwards, all fresh and lovely with a bag full of good things and in the mood to distract me, rather than we both get contaminated. Huh? You must be able to see why, Lucy. And when she's freshened up and feeling comfy again, I can introduce you. How does that sound?'

Lucy looked at him.

'OK,' she said slowly, drawing out the second syllable. 'Wanna do me a list? Or do you trust me to do my own thing? I'd really like to cook today.'

'You are in charge of all things culinary,' said William. 'The queen of the kitchen. Remind me to give you some cash.'

★ ★ ★

Lucy departed before the nurse arrived and returned after she'd gone. She found William in the kitchen nursing a bowl of coffee, looking shattered again.

'Successful trip?' he asked half-heartedly.

'Yes, very. I think I could get used to living like this. Had a coffee in the cafe opposite the *mairie*. Laaarvely.'

'Well, don't get too attached. It's phenomenally cold here in the winter and this floor never, ever gets warm — there's an enormous *cave* under here.' He tapped with his feet on the floorboards and Lucy felt rather than heard the resonance of a void beneath them. 'Plus there is higher than average rainfall in this area — because of all the trees, I imagine. But never mind the precipitation, feel the accessibility. You can get here from the Channel in eight hours by road now, so despite the unreliable weather, the English have discovered the Haute-Vienne big time in the past ten years or so.' William seemed to be adopting a jaunty new tone, perhaps to distract himself, perhaps to unveil another

284

as-yet-unrevealed layer of feeling.

'What used to be proper *paysan* country is now a giant holiday camp in the summer, full of little English boys and girls splashing in lakes while their mummies and daddies sit around wishing they could afford to fly to the Mediterranean. Talk about ethnic cleansing. Nowadays, the young locals naff off at the earliest opportunity and the old ones are either selling up or dying off. Another ten years and it'll be like the frigging Costa del Sol here, minus the Sol. And the sea.'

Lucy humped a large bag of provisions onto the tabletop.

'You said I was supposed to distract you with my enthusiasm . . . '

'That's true. I did. I'm sorry. Let me show you where everything goes.'

And so they spent the next few minutes filling the fridge and cupboards, opening their mouths only to issue or reciprocate instructions.

★   ★   ★

'How is she?'

'She's asleep.'

'But how is she when she's awake?'

'Barely . . . '

'Oh shit,' Lucy hissed abruptly, hunching her shoulders. 'Can she hear us?' She pointed one finger straight up and bared her teeth in a rictus of theatrical guilt.

'No, no, it's all right. This'll be a murmur up there, and no more. And besides, even if she could hear every word, I'm not sure how much sense it would make to her anyway — she's pretty out of it. She speaks English, of course, but hasn't had to properly for years and years. The most important thing is that she doesn't appear to be in any great pain. She's pumped full of morphine . . . '

'Have you given her her pillow?'

William looked faintly surprised. 'Oh. No, I haven't. I was going to ask the nurse to help me lift her. Completely forgot. Damn. And I don't know whether I can bear to move her myself — she looks so fragile. Like she might snap. Oh fucking hell.'

Lucy looked at him. She did not know how to interpret his face. But pain is ugly, she thought. Poor guy. Poor, poor guy. His really isn't a pretty face at the best of times and, like most faces, it is best served by happiness — or comfort at least. This was a face losing its cohesion.

'You know what, Lucy?' His cheeks were home to a tiny vibration under his eyes, on both sides. 'You know what? I don't know how to handle this. I managed all right when my dad died, but I was a lot, lot younger then, and my mum was around to suck up a lot of the unpleasantness. It's amazing how resilient you are in your twenties — not yet sensitised, I suppose. Virtually impregnable. It's one of the privileges of being a new-made adult — being able to ride over the rough shit like it's barely even there.' He blew through his nostrils. 'I suppose you're distracted by having to concentrate so hard on staying on the horse. But not now. Look at me.

Fucking hell. I felt awful then of course, but not like this. Not like I'm — '

'Let's go up and see her.'

'What, now? But she's asleep.'

'Introduce me to your mum, William. I want to see her, even if she is asleep. I want to be with you when you see her.'

William's mouth sagged open, but made no sound.

'Go and get the pillow from the barn and let's go up,' Lucy went on. 'If she's awake you can present it to her, and I'll help you move her. If she's not awake, we can leave her to it. But I want to see her with you.'

She put out a hand.

His mouth closed again and, without a word and without touching Lucy's hand, he heaved himself up from the table and disappeared out through the door. She heard his feet scrunch across the gravel and then the barn door bang. She got up and positioned herself in the doorway at the foot of the stairs, and waited. It took several minutes for him to reappear and, when he did, he retraced his steps at funereal pace, as if weighed down by the feathers he carried. He'd put a brand-new case on the pillow. It was so fresh from its packaging it still had a crease in it.

'Come on, love,' she whispered and put out her hand again.

'You'd better do grandmother's footsteps up the stairs behind me,' he breathed, the pillow now in front of him like a tray. 'Put your feet where mine go and miss out the last but one at each end.' He cocked his head. 'Actually, that's not grandmother's footsteps, is it? It's something to do with Jesus . . . '

'No doubt it is something to do with Jesus. But you're not Jesus. Come on.'

She put her hand in the small of his back and gave him a gentle shove.

They reached the top of the half-spiralled stairway after unleashing a fusillade of squeaks and creaks on the way, each one of them a stab to Lucy's nervous system. William did not turn round on the landing. He took three careful steps and pushed with two fingers against an emulsioned door which, to Lucy's abundant gratitude, swung open slowly, smoothly and silently. Now William turned and beckoned her forward.

She found herself in a small, beautiful bedroom painted the colour of duck eggs. There was no dark wood here. No heavy furniture, or beams crowding down. A single large watercolour hung on the wall, of an expressive grouping of trees (one of Bére's?), a pale chest of drawers, a white-curtained recess with the curtain drawn back slightly to reveal the head of a rack of clothes; a full-length mirror, rugs on the foot-polished floorboards and a shuttered window opening, through vine leaves, onto a painterly vision of shimmering birches. The room was bisected by a modest brass-framed double bed of the sort that Lucy had only seen in recent years in the expensive 'vintage' emporia of Upper Street and Holloway Road.

She deliberately kept her eyes from the discordant clinical rig standing next to the bed and merely hoped that she would acclimatise to the sour perfume in the air. She tried to look at the figure lying within the bed, almost lost among folds of white linen. There was very little to be seen, only a tiny sleeping head, the colour of silver-birch bark, drawn tightly to itself, as if the skin were gripped from behind and pulled back. The mouth slightly ajar. A black line in the silvery bark.

Lucy looked at William.

He was standing, expressionless, gazing at his mother.

Lucy returned her gaze to the diminutive occupant of the bed and realised that she did not know her name. Not beyond Madame Carberry. She was unrecognisable from the pictures Lucy had seen in William's flat of a small, intense, slender but sturdily alive-looking woman. They had been washed out and grainy, those snaps, the earliest ones in fading black-and-white. But they had life. This woman did not look alive in any meaningful sense. How must she seem to her son, who loves her? Lucy felt something she did not recognise rise in her throat. She looked again at William.

His mouth was working slightly at the corners. She put out her hand to his and squeezed tightly. He returned her gaze for a moment with a weak smile, his eyes glassy. And it was as if this tiny complex of small, barely audible movements — hands, arms, neck, sleeve, collar, face — fired off a charge at some imperceptible level, a charge to spark life, because it was as William's smile faded and Lucy turned back to look at his mother that Madame Carberry opened her eyes.

At least, her eyelids parted to reveal two dark but perfectly unfocused pupils.

'*Maman*,' whispered William, taking a step towards the bed and laying a hand on the linen directly above where his mother's hand ought to be. '*C'est moi. C'est Guillaume.*' He then added something in a hushed voice too delicate and too French for Lucy to distinguish useful meaning, although she did hear the name 'Lucy' and she did sense from the rise and fall of William's voice that she was being introduced.

The two dark pupils moved minutely, shifting in Lucy's general direction but registering nothing. There was a gulping sound from the clinical contraption next to the bedhead.

'*Bonjour, Madame Carberry*,' said Lucy quietly, finding herself rolling the double R not with a flourish but with great conscience.

'Monique,' said William. 'My mum's name is Monique — isn't it, Maman? She'd like it if you called her Monique.'

'*Bonjour, Monique*,' said Lucy, suddenly engulfed by self-consciousness. '*Comment allez-vous?*' And she really wished she hadn't said *that* — but then there was very little else she could say in French.

Monique Carberry was not in any position to answer, anyway. Her eyes were drifting back towards her son, who had now positioned himself on the end of the bed and was stroking the quilt with long, almost formal passes of his open hand.

'*Maman . . .* '

He talked and talked, quietly and carefully,

like a man in heavy shoes picking his way through a plantation of orchids. Lucy stood and smiled as best she could, although she knew that the old lady had already forgotten her presence. She breathed quietly and listened for clues.

Then William turned to her again.

'I'm going to ask her now,' he said, 'about the green church.'

'Oh,' said Lucy. 'Oh. Right.'

William stopped stroking.

'*Maman, pourquoi tu m'as emmené à l'église verte? Les Salles-Lavauguyon? Qu'est-ce qui s'est passé là-bas?*'

The words were spoken with the utmost tenderness but with a clarity that suggested that this question was in no sense rhetorical; that it required an answer.

They waited. Nothing happened for a few seconds.

And then there was a tiny movement in the folds of Monique's throat and in her eyes, which shifted laterally and then seemed to focus properly for the first time, on William and then, with effort, on Lucy. And then back again on William.

Her mouth began to move. It formed weak, transient shapes, which came and went one after another like bursting bubbles. The shapes might have sounded vowels and consonants, Os and Vs and Ss and long Us, had they any breath behind them. But they had none. No sound came. The face remained expressionless and in due course the word-shapes ceased.

The only sound audible to Lucy, other than

291

the pumping of her own blood, was a choked exhalation which emerged suddenly from the base of William's throat. He stood up and turned to face her, blinking spastically, his features masked with tears. He opened his mouth as if to speak, and then did not. Instead, he picked up the pillow from its place at the foot of the bed and buried his face in it, like a child.

Lucy put a hand to his raised elbow and left it there, with one finger touching, but William did not respond. Then, still holding the pillow at either end, he lowered it from his face to waist level and turned once more to his mother's bed.

'Do you want me to help, darling?' whispered Lucy.

'No, no. No, thank you. I can manage.' William's voice was a husk of sound, no more. 'I think I ought to be on my own with Maman now. Do you mind? I'll be down soon . . . '

Lucy found herself unable to move. She was transfixed by William's grip on the pillow, which seemed raptorial somehow, and by the trembling visible in his hands as his fingers drove into its softness. He saw her looking and relaxed his grip, and then let his arms fall to his side, the pillow going with one of them. But the trembling did not stop. His features looked utterly disassembled. Lucy thought she could see right through him — that she could see his thoughts.

'Are you sure?' she said, her voice sounding thin in her ears. 'Do you want to take a minute or two to think about it? Let me stick around for a minute or two . . . I can help . . . '

'No. Go. Please.' His face was beginning to

set, as if one thought were coalescing in his mind, leaving no room for anything else. It was a terrifying thought.

She ran through her options and realised that she didn't have any. She could not, in decency, stay. How could she? She could not stand there and say to William, 'Actually, I am going to loiter beside your mother's deathbed and defy you, whether it upsets you or not. Why? Because I don't think you should do what I fear you may be about to do. I can tell that you're thinking about it. I can tell that part of you wants to do it, and I understand why and how. I'd want to. I'd be thinking about it myself. I'd want this suffering to end. *I know what you're feeling.*'

But she could not do it. She had to leave them both, and the pillow. She had to trust him.

'OK. I'll . . . I'll be downstairs in the kitchen, if you want me. You just have to tap on the floor and I can be up in three seconds.'

★ ★ ★

Downstairs in the kitchen Lucy discovered that she was shaking too. She gulped water.

What was the proper thing to do here? Leave him to it, as he'd asked? Or stay upstairs, defiantly, as a significant part of her mind had yelled at her to do? Yes, perhaps she should have stayed where she was, vigilant in the blue room, both as witness and deterrent; she should have stood her ground and faced him down — said Sorry, William, I'm not going to leave you here, then gently removed the pillow from his hands and taken him in her arms until the feeling had drained from his body. Of course she should. Of course she should. But other, cooler emotions had been present and they had been strong. They had told her with quiet persistence that the correct thing to do was as she had been asked — to not create a scene and not find a place for herself in this drama and to not interfere, but to leave William and his mother to their agony. Maybe to their peace.

Or was that just the emollient voice of weakness, passivity, cowardice? Come on. Who really needed saving here? William? Monique?

Herself?

Oh, get over yourself, woman.

She tried to put herself in the same position as William, transposing the scene again to her own mother's deathbed at some unforeseeable point in an unimaginable future — a vision that had never occupied her mind before this weekend, not least because her mother was as turbulently immutable as the North Sea. But just suppose . . . What then? What would she feel in that situation, standing over the living remains of a woman she'd loved and felt loved by, even when love was not being shown — and was now close to her end? No longer herself. No longer capable of love. How would she act? She did not know and she could not begin to construct the knowledge, but she could imagine the sick feeling, the desperation for the suffering to end. She could see herself with a pillow in her two hands.

The thought made her queasy.

She gulped more water and then listened for

an indication of what might or might not be going on upstairs, but there was no sound.

She took a deep breath and tried to breathe the trembling out of her system.

Actually, she couldn't imagine William doing it, not really. She could see that he'd *want* to do it. That he might consider it seriously, for a short moment — even a long one . . . She could even see that it might be justified as an act; that it would be an act founded in William's better feelings for his mother and an overwhelming desire for his mother's freedom from suffering. Her right to mercy. But no, she couldn't see him actually doing it: leaning in, pressing down, holding, gritting his teeth while he waited for the sensation of limpness to spread beneath his hands . . .

It wouldn't take much. Hardly any pressure at all.

Lucy put down her glass on the draining board. It sounded like a cannon shot in the morning silence. She had to be up there. It was wrong to be down here. She started for the stairs, the sensation of nausea rising in her throat like smoke. And then . . . *creak!*

He was crossing the landing above and coming down the spiral. He was coming down quickly. She was too late.

Lucy reached the bottom step as he rounded the corner in the staircase, not bothering where he put his feet. He was white. In the gloom of the stairwell he was luminous.

Lucy stood aside from the bottom stair. William did not ignore her. Instead, he smiled briefly, palely, and blinked over the top of his smile.

'Thanks, Luce,' he said as he passed her and went out through the door, his shoulders up, trailing the smell of the room above. He turned at the railing at the top of the steps down to the yard and spoke back through the doorway, haloed by sunlight. 'Thanks. She's comfortable now.'

'William . . .'

'Can I have a few minutes? I just want to be on my own for a few minutes.' He smiled wanly again and pointed towards the marsh in the trees. 'I'm feeling completely shattered and I just want to go and get my head together. Be a bit moody and broody for a while. You understand that, don't you? Won't be long. Promise.'

'William, I . . .'

'Please, Lucy.'

★ ★ ★

Lucy found herself alone in the kitchen again. She felt the silence from the upper rooms pressing down. She moved the fruit bowl on the table a couple of inches, to centre it more perfectly.

She could leave things as they were, couldn't she? Couldn't she? Yes, she could. That would be defensible. She could wait for William to return from his brooding and take it from there. He might go upstairs to see his mum and come down again and reveal or not reveal how things were upstairs, just as he chose; and she, Lucy, would be none the wiser about any of it and guilty of nothing — because she would know nothing. Literally nothing.

On the other hand, he might come down and say that nothing has changed up there and that his mother is hanging on through her pain and suffering and how he wishes it were over, 'because I just can't bear it. Hold me, Lucy.' In that case she would hold him. On yet another hand, if he came down with a shocked look on his face and said, 'Oh my God, my mother's gone,' then she could take him at face value and gather him in her arms in all innocence and offer him comfort from the bottom of her heart. She simply would not know any different. Could not know. Monique might simply have left the building under her own steam in the ten, twenty, thirty minutes since Lucy saw her last . . . Indeed, William might have sensed the moment coming and taken himself out to the marsh to avoid the last agony; or perhaps — in fact more likely — just to prepare himself. No, that didn't make sense — why would he leave her bedside to prepare himself for the event if he was expecting the old lady to expire at any second? For heaven's sake. Still, the permutations were virtually infinite, now she came to think about it — which was a very good reason in itself to just take everything at face value and see what happened. Let it be. Not interfere; not find space for herself in the drama. This was, after all, emphatically not about her.

But she had to know. She had to know because *her* life depended on what was going on upstairs, as well as Monique's and William's. This time she really was in it up to her neck, and not just morally. Everything mattered because everything mattered. There could be no neutrality in this situation. Neutrality would result in the end of everything.

She had to know.

Lucy peered through the doorway. William was already out of sight down the slope beneath the trees. She began to mount the staircase, carefully omitting the second step, feet well separated, legs as bowed as a cartoon cowboy's, one hand on the coarse plaster of the wall for balance; slowly, studiously, not proceeding on tiptoe but laying each foot down flat, gently but firmly, to distribute her weight as evenly as possible, adjusting and stabilising as she went according to the give and groan of each step. At the top she paused, listened. There was no sound. At the door there was no sound. She pushed the door gently and it swung open as smoothly and silently as before. The room was bluer, or so it seemed, but otherwise quite the same. The bed was still occupied but, as before, there was no movement in it.

Lucy whispered, '*Bonjour, Monique. C'est moi, Lucy.*'

There was no response. Something buzzed wearily in the vine outside the window.

'Madame Carberry?'

Nothing.

Lucy approached the bed. It took four steps to get there, supported by a colossal effort of will. One of Monique's arms, its preying canula

298

attached like an insect, now lay on top of the quilt, twig-thin in a half-length cotton sleeve, the hand a mere cluster of tinier twigs, bunched at the wrist and at the fingertips. Lucy forced her gaze to the top of the old woman's body. The tiny head was occupying more or less the same space in the linen that it had occupied before and was as unalive now as it had been then — except that now it rested at a different angle, tipped up in relation to the edge of the quilt, more upright, less recumbent . . . Yes, the new pillow in all its lofty glory was now beneath Monique's head and was propping it forward, chin down, as if to keep her eye fixed on the door. She looked as ordered as a pharaoh's queen. And there were no signs of life. There was no movement in her features, no hint of a breeze disturbing the tissue of skin at her nostrils.

He did it, thought Lucy. *He did it. Jesus. He did it.*

She looks peaceful too.

Lucy's hand went slowly up to her mouth to cover it and then to pinch her upper lip. Oddly, she did not feel panic rising, nor revulsion twisting in her gut. She was not overcome by any sensation at all. Only a question.

What does this *mean*? What does it mean for her, Lucy? William's only witness. His only witness who was not only a witness to what had happened — to what *may* have happened — but was not even sure that that particular something *had* happened . . .

'Monique,' she said again, quite loudly. And Monique opened her eyes.

It was clear that the eyes were not gathering information, merely letting in a little light. Yet after a few seconds, they began to focus, resting first on Lucy and then on some other amorphous thing in the air above Lucy's head as the effort to recognise and decipher and interpret evolved into an effort to think and then withstand the onset of deep, grinding, unscotchable pain. Pain was travelling like a comet in the milky darkness of Monique's eyes. Nothing else moved. Lucy wanted desperately to do so, to move away, but could not remove her own eyes from the old woman's face, its papery skin quivering now, its colour modulating visibly from silver to ash to sulphurous ash; nor from the pathetic, pointless mouthing which had begun again, like bubbles popping from a fissure, soundless words dissolving into puffs and swallowings which, at length, produced some sound from within the cavities of the ruined body, a column of air which began as a distant low flutey whistle, surfaced briefly as an elongated gasp, then disintegrated into gurgles deep in the throat, reaching down and down into inaudibility and extinction — and then the afterquiet.

In the new silence, it dawned quite quickly on Lucy that she was alone in the room.

* * *

The trunks of the trees were black against the green. The green was luminous, the black just black. Sunlight was penetrating the canopy above the marsh in brilliant diagonal shafts, picking out tufts and shrubs and muddy boils in the grass beneath Lucy's feet. She could see William. He was no more than fifty yards away on a small island, balanced in the low cleft of a divided tree with his back to Lucy, his head resting at a comfortable angle against one of the twin trunks, his free arm circling the other, as if it were the shoulders of an old friend. He looked easy in his seat. Easy and distant. There was a small, elongated mere separating the two of them but logs had been laid across its narrowest point to bridge the stagnant shallows. The water was as bloomed and impenetrable as Monique's dying eyes. Lucy remembered the poetic word for it. Glaucous.

She did not call his name. She just squelched up behind him and put a hand on his extended shoulder. He must have heard her coming.

'William, I think — '

'I just saw a snake,' he said. 'Or at least I think I did. Something slithery and fast — disappearing like lightning under that log by the water.' He pointed. Then sighed. 'Oh, Lucy, I love it here. This is the most peaceful place in the whole world, I sometimes think, as if everything good in the world is concentrated in all this mould and decay and stink and slime. It's like this little smelly marsh under the trees is a culture in a dish, making good stuff to cure the world, like penicillin or something — such a shame you couldn't be here in happier circumstances. Such a shame too that she's too far gone to talk; you'd like her, you really would.' He let his tree-hugging hand slide down the angled trunk of the ash and then cross to Lucy's hand, where it hung by her side. He squeezed. 'I really did want to know about the green church . . . '

'William, she's gone.'

' . . . And it would have been rather exciting for me if you'd been there to hear about it too. You could see she was trying to talk about it, couldn't you? It really gripped her mind, the green church — she certainly had plenty to say and was really busting a gut . . . What do you mean, she's gone?'

Suddenly, he was no longer talking to Lucy over his shoulder but was standing up and facing her.

'Darling, I think she's gone,' she said softly. 'It's over. I just went up and . . . and I think she's gone. I felt for a pulse and everything, listened for breath, and there was nothing. I really, really . . . '

'Oh my God. I . . . '

Lucy enveloped him in her arms. He seemed reluctant at first to be enveloped but acceded soon enough after shifting his feet about a bit. Lucy held on, waited for him to speak.

'I . . . I . . . ' he said into her hair.

'What you need to do, my love,' she said, 'is go up there on your own, be with her and make sure I'm right. I am. I know I am. She really has gone. But you need to make sure for yourself — and *be* with her. In the meantime, I will stay here and wait for you. But you take as much time as you like. I'll wait here till it gets dark, if need be. I'm in no hurry. It's lovely here, as you say. And then when you're good and ready, come and find me out here and we'll decide what to do next, yes? Go on, William. Take your time. Go.'

And he went. He went quickly, leaving two muddy impressions in the sodden grass, marking the spot where she'd held him and pressed him hard into the earth. She looked down at them: two holes, nothing more; two dark depressions in sopping grass. And slowly, as Lucy watched, the footprints filled up with water and then melted back into the green.

Acknowledgements

I would like to thank the following for their kindness.

For space: Caroline Stacey, Emma Perry, Dominic Maxwell, Flora Maxwell, Polly Maxwell, Carina Tertsakian, John and Karen Baistow-Clare.

For sound counsel: Jane Acton, Stella Birks, Ian Blackaby, Louise Bowett-Jones, Simon Edwards, Gary Mason, Charles Shaar Murray, Dr Helen Parker.

For research: the Spence bakery in Stoke Newington, London N16.

For being in it: Roy Dodds, Annie Whitehead and Robert Wyatt. I would like to point out that all three gave their permission without insisting on seeing the manuscript first, which was generous in the extreme, so any misrepresentation of them is entirely my failing. I should also point out that, although the three musicians are real enough, the 'Robert Wyatt composition' they play and sing in the story was entirely made up by me for the purposes of this fiction, and that no unreleased Robert Wyatt material of this precise description exists, so far as I know. It's lovely, by the way. One of his best. I wish I knew the title.

For inspiration: Lucy Barnes, who is only to be confused with Lucy Taplow very, very super-ficially.

And of course my abiding thanks go to my

agent Jennifer Hewson at Rogers Coleridge & White and to Dan Franklin, Clare Bullock and Mikaela Pedlow at Cape. Thanks also to Kathy Fry and Peter McAdie for their sterling copy-editing and proofreading.

THE WAY WE WERE

Maeve Haran

Rachel is a promising A-level student — until she falls for sexy, dangerous Marko (Heathcliff with a nose stud). Her mother, Catherine, is trying to be a good parent and work colleague — but wishes the attentions of her attractive boss didn't suddenly seeming so alluring. Grandmother Lavinia is certain of her values, protecting the country village she loves from change — until the return of a long-lost love reminds her that life moves on, for people as well as places. Is it too late for her to embrace change and find happiness? After all these years — and a lifetime divided by convention — could they really throw other people's expectations to the wind and be the way they were?

TRUTH IN ADVERTISING

John Kenney

Finbar Dolan is lost and lonely — except he doesn't know it. Despite escaping his blue-collar upbringing to carve out a mildly successful career at an advertising agency, he's a bit of a mess and closing in on forty. He's recently called off his wedding; and now, a few days before Christmas, he's forced to cancel a vacation in order to write, produce, and edit a Super Bowl commercial for his diaper account in record time. Then he learns that his long-estranged and once-abusive father has fallen ill, and that neither his brothers nor his sister intend to visit. It's a wake-up call for Fin to reevaluate the choices he's made, admit that he's falling for coworker Phoebe, question the importance of diapers in his life, and finally tell the truth about his past . . .

THE HORSEMAN

Tim Pears

1911: In a forgotten valley on the Devon-Somerset border, the seasons unfold, marked only by the rituals of the farming calendar. Twelve-year-old Leopold Sercombe skips school to help his father, a carter. Skinny and pale, with eyes the colour of blackberries, Leo dreams of a job on the master's stud farm. As ploughs furrow the hard January fields, the master's daughter, young Miss Charlotte, shocks the estate's tenants by wielding a gun at the annual shoot. One day Leo is breaking a colt for his father when a boy in breeches and riding boots appears — and peering under the stranger's hat, Leo discovers Charlotte. So a friendship begins, bound by a deep love of horses, but divided by rigid social boundaries — boundaries that become increasingly difficult to navigate as the couple approach adolescence.

THE STRANGER

Saskia Sarginson

We all have our secrets. Eleanor Rathmell has kept one her whole life. But when her husband dies and a stranger arrives at her door, her safe life in the idyllic English village she's chosen as her home begins to topple. Everyone is suspicious of this stranger — except for Eleanor; and her trust in him will put her life in danger. Nothing is as it seems — not her dead husband, the man who claims to love her, or the inscrutable outsider to whom she's opened her home and her heart . . .

LEAVING LUCY PEAR

Anna Solomon

One night in 1917, Beatrice Haven creeps out of her uncle's house on Cape Ann, Massachusetts, and leaves her newborn baby at the foot of a pear tree, then watches as another woman claims the child as her own. The unwed daughter of wealthy Jewish industrialists and a gifted pianist bound for Radcliffe, Bea plans to leave her shameful secret behind and make a fresh start . . . Ten years later, Bea's hopes for her future remain unfulfilled. When she returns to her uncle's house, seeking a refuge from her unhappiness, she discovers far more when the rum-running manager of the local quarry inadvertently unites her with Emma Murphy, the headstrong Irish Catholic woman who has been raising her abandoned child — now a bright, bold, cross-dressing girl named Lucy Pear, with secrets of her own.

THE LUNAR CATS

Lynne Truss

When you are an inoffensive retired librarian with bitter personal experience of evil talking cats (or ETCs, for short), do you rescue a kitten from the cold on a December night? Do you follow up news items about cats digging in graveyards? Do you inquire into long-ago cats who voyaged around the world with Captain Cook? Well, yes. If you are Alec Charlesworth, that is precisely what you do — with unexpected and terrifying consequences . . .

SPECIAL MESSAGE TO READERS

THE ULVERSCROFT FOUNDATION
(registered UK charity number 264873)
was established in 1972 to provide funds for
research, diagnosis and treatment of eye diseases.
Examples of major projects funded by
the Ulverscroft Foundation are:-

- The Children's Eye Unit at Moorfields Eye Hospital, London
- The Ulverscroft Children's Eye Unit at Great Ormond Street Hospital for Sick Children
- Funding research into eye diseases and treatment at the Department of Ophthalmology, University of Leicester
- The Ulverscroft Vision Research Group, Institute of Child Health
- Twin operating theatres at the Western Ophthalmic Hospital, London
- The Chair of Ophthalmology at the Royal Australian College of Ophthalmologists

You can help further the work of the Foundation
by making a donation or leaving a legacy.
Every contribution is gratefully received. If you
would like to help support the Foundation or
require further information, please contact:

THE ULVERSCROFT FOUNDATION
The Green, Bradgate Road, Anstey
Leicester LE7 7FU, England
Tel: (0116) 236 4325

website: www.foundation.ulverscroft.com

Nick Coleman was born in Buckinghamshire in 1960, but grew up in the Fens. Following a brief spell as a stringer at *NME* in the mid-1980s, he was Music Editor of *Time Out* magazine for seven years. This was followed by a dozen years as Arts and Features Editor at the *Independent* and the *Independent on Sunday*. He has also written for *The Times*, the *Guardian*, the *Daily Telegraph*, *New Statesman*, *US Vogue*, *Intelligent Life*, *GQ* and *The Wire* — mostly about music, but also books, sport and travel. Nick lives in Hackney with his wife and two children.